COUNTDOWN TO VENGEANCE

"Ripley," called the unmistakable snarl of Missouri Slim. "If you walk out of there with your hands stuck up, we ain't gunna hurt you. But you stick in there, we're gunna go in and tear you to pieces."

"Boys," said Ripley, "it's a good bluff but it won't work. I put that first charge into the ceiling. The next one is for you. I've got a riot gun, here, and riot guns can see in the dark. I'm going to count to five, slow, and then you can have it."

He shouted in a louder voice: "One — two — three —"

*Books by Max Brand
from Jove*

OUTLAW'S CODE
THE REVENGE OF BROKEN ARROW
MONTANA RIDES
STRANGE COURAGE
MONTANA RIDES AGAIN
THE BORDER BANDIT
SIXGUN LEGACY
SMUGGLER'S TRAIL

MAX BRAND

WRITING AS EVAN EVANS

SMUGGLER'S TRAIL

A JOVE BOOK

This Jove book contains the complete
text of the original hardcover edition.

SMUGGLER'S TRAIL

A Jove Book / published by arrangement with
the author

PRINTING HISTORY
Original edition published 1934
Ace Charter edition / December 1980
Jove edition / October 1986

ISBN: 0-515-08776-9

Jove Books are published by The Berkley Publishing Group,
200 Madison Avenue, New York, N.Y. 10016.
The words "A JOVE BOOK" and the "J" with sunburst
are trademarks belonging to Jove Publications, Inc.

PRINTED IN THE UNITED STATES OF AMERICA

CHAPTER I

The pain in Tom Dallas was both of body
and brain but there was room in his conscious-
ness only for that of the mind. He kept a
photograph on his knee, a round pocket mirror in his hand, and it was his own image in
the glass that gave the marshal such mental
anguish. No lady of fashion could have eyed
herself with more care than Dallas, she in the
privacy of her boudoir and the marshal under
the public eye in his office. He held the mirror
close, boldly facing the truth; then he removed the glass to arm's length and squinted
as though he were trying to soften the colors of
a futurist picture; but, whether from near or
far, he could not help seeing that his face was
too red even for this hot day and too fat even
for his fifty years. The upper eyelid was a
soggy weight. The line down his cheek continued under the chin, now a permanent furrow

in the soft of the flesh.

He jabbed the mirror back into a vest pocket, wiped the sweat from his forehead on the back of his hand, flicked it off the forefinger, and looked at the straight line of black splashed on the floor. Afterward, he stared out the window at the blue sky that trembled with heat and at the hills which sprawled big from the north past Tallyho. What he saw was a time when "Tallyho" had been spelled with a hyphen and punctuated by an exclamation point, usually with a note attached to explain how a fox-hunting Englishman had lodged a bit of his native lore so deep in the American West. He could remember how Indians with rifles balanced across the pommels of their saddles had ridden across those hills, and how gunbelts had hung loose across their bellies.

The telephone began to ring. The Indians and the long years were banished by the time Deputy Dick Ballin got the receiver off the hook. Dick began to say "Yes" at intervals. He hung up and came to the marshal.

"Stillwater," said the deputy.

"A damn mean town," said Dallas. "I remember when Shorty McIntosh and me were—"

The deputy interrupted in haste: "Ripley. They've seen him there in Stillwater."

"I didn't send those men up there to be seeing Ripley. I sent them up there to be grabbing and holding him," shouted the marshal.

"He busted away," said Dick Ballin.

"What happened?"

"He hurt a couple of men. Not very bad. Then he got out a back door."

The marshal looked askance at Ballin, found him an unworthy audience for his thoughts, and leaned forward over a small table on which a map was spread. When Dallas' eyes fell upon it, the flat of the paper sank into valleys, rose to naked mountains immersed in blue. An irregular round of pins had been stuck into one section. Empire, Little Medicine, Rusty Gulch, Westward. In Westward was stuck a taller pin with a tiny red pennant attached. The marshal replaced this with a common pin and searched until he found the word "Stillwater." Into this he thrust the red danger signal.

"They're narrowing him down," said Dallas. "Look here. They're running him round and round and they're narrowing him down like a whirlpool pulling a leaf into its mouth. They're gunna be having Mr. Jack Ripley, before long. When did this Stillwater business happen?"

"Last night."

"And they don't give us a ring till this afternoon?"

Mr. Ballin said: "What I don't understand, with the big job on our hands and the Chinese still leaking in across the border, why should such a gang be sent up there to corral Jack Ripley? What's he done, so much?"

"You don't understand?" asked the marshal.

"What I mean to say, he's only sort of hit

back when somebody took a sock at him first.
He's only been down in these parts about once
a year, just about."

"Like Christmas?" suggested the marshal.
"Yeah, he circulates, Dick. So does a comet."

It was a point upon which Ballin seemed to
feel strongly. "Besides," he argued, "what's he
done—I mean, what's he done that's federal?"

"Shoving the queer, Dick," said the
marshal. "That's federal."

"We've got no proof of that," objected the
deputy.

"Take a look at his mug," said the sheriff,
lifting the photograph that lay on his knee.

Ballin regarded the lean, handsome young
face. He was young, too; that was the reason
for his slight frown.

"He looks like an all right sort of a fellow,"
said Ballin. "Kind of smiling, too."

The marshal took the picture back. He
liked Ballin but his higher expectation was
always disappointed. "He's smiling," declared Dallas, "as though he'd just shot somebody; or as though he was about to shoot."

The jangle of the telephone called Ballin
away.

"That can't be right," he said. "Wait a
minute. Tolman is 'way south. Go hell-bent
after him. Which way would he be heading?
Go that way, then, and burn up the ground."

He hung up.

"There's Ripley again," he reported.
"Broke right through them outside of

Stillwater. He's heading south toward Crystal Springs. He's got his nerve along with him, that Jack Ripley."

"He hasn't got nerve. He's got a gray horse. He's still on that Hickory mare, ain't he?"

"That's what they say. He's still got that jackrabbit—that Hickory Dickory."

"He thinks that she's his luck, but she's going to be his finish," said the marshal. "He wouldn't wear the same coat in every town but he'll ride the same mare, and those that don't know his face, they know Hickory. If a price was put on him, he wouldn't last a month. But just now all folks could get out of him would be glory—and a lot of trouble."

"Yeah, a lot of trouble," agreed Dick Ballin, and his eyes grew far-thoughted. He was a fighting man himself. "Shall I telephone up there to Crystal Springs to have them on the lookout?"

"Hold on a minute. I gotta look." He peered at the map.

"He's heading right south from Stillwater. That would take him to Crystal Springs," observed Ballin.

"Crystal Springs is no good time," answered the marshal. "But over here—it's an extra fifty miles, but there's a lot happening now in old Hooligan Gulch. A regular gold rush has started for there. That's where he'll go."

"Not if he's traveling anywhere," protested Ballin.

"The only place he travels is where he wants to go. Ring Hooligan and tell them to keep their eyes wide open and their guns clean. But don't forget. I want him alive; I don't want him dead."

"Well, it's a funny thing," growled Ballin, going back to the telephone.

The marshal paid no more heed to him because he had located, in that instant, the pain that had been troubling his subconscious mind for a long time. It was in his feet. Dallas looked down over his shabby clothes to the immaculate sheen of his boots. There was sorrow in his heart, for it is sacrilege to alter a bootlast that has served a man for thirty years.

However, this world is more filled with trouble than with joy, and the marshal decided that he would endure. To balance pleasure against grief, he took out a plug of chewing tobacco, shaped to the curve of his hip, and gnawed off a corner. With this old comfort stowed in his cheek, he leaned over the map again and fixed the red flag of danger in the word "Hooligan."

A few minutes later he thrust himself out of his chair with a groan. "Have that damn ding-dong Roman-nosed son of a Gila monster, that Sammy, have him saddled up for me, will you, Dick?" he asked.

"What for Sammy?" said Ballin. "Just his gallop is worse than the bucking of most mustangs."

"He's got a mean gait, but he's never played

out and he's taken me to a lot of luck. I'm going to need all the luck I can find in Hooligan," answered the marshal.

CHAPTER II

A cactus wren was singing somewhere as Jack Ripley rode down into Hooligan Gulch. The wren was singing for Ripley and the gray mare; and the mare knew it, too. For them a sheet of hammered gold had been laid across the rags and tatters of the mountains and the purple dust of evening was pouring through the valley. But the eye pierced this color easily to the town of shacks and tents that lay in the gulch like the drift left by a huge freshet. A pack train was coming down the south trail across the valley, the riders to the rear in the golden haze, those to the fore in the purple, with a little white puff of dust marking every hoofbeat of the horses.

Prospect holes ranged each side of the valley, the deep ones with a gallows-frame above supporting a "whip"; others with a mere windlass for lifting the bucket; and yet more

were merely shallow pits. There were many
noises of creaking from the hoists, the clanging of the single-jacks which worked in the
drills, and now the booming detonation of
blasting at a depth, now the whipcrack reports
of surface shots; but the thin air removed all
sound to a distance and the eye stepped
through a prospect so vast that only the
margin of the great peace was invaded.

Gold that was gained in this way was, to the
eye of Jack Ripley, spoiled by the sweat of the
taking. He preferred an insecure happiness to
one strongly founded on the old maxims and
the hard labor of the hands.

The mare took the zigzag of the descending
trail easily, softening the shock of each downward step with the supple play of fetlock
joints. By the time she had brought Ripley
near the floor of the valley, the upper mountains and the sky were burning. But they were
down in the cool of evening with lights like
gilded stars pasted here and there in the windows of the town. Ripley paused to enjoy that
moment of the day. Twenty-four hours of
hunger had its spur in his side, but he had
learned to take pleasure where he found it. He
drifted the mare quietly into the town.

The telephone was a new luxury in
Hooligan; so was any electricity, but since it
had come it was being used generously. As
Ripley rode down the single street, his shadow
lay before him, behind, and to either side until
the great multiple lights of "Conlin's" put out
all rivals as the moon puts out the stars. The

front of Conlin's was half canvas, half wood, looking as though a mask and a torch were being held before the facade, and Ripley laughed a little softly. He liked the taste of the laughter in his throat and the flow of it as of a clean wind through his soul. How many days was it since he had done more than smile? But this was a night that promised laughter, all the arrears paid at once.

He could ride freely down the center of the street because no one would notice him. Miners and dead-beats and gamblers and thieves flowed up and down and across the street, each man hurrying toward a good time. Here and there girls were moving in couples and the currents split away before them, closing quickly behind. They were never jostled. They walked with an air of command and of wealth, but all that Ripley wanted of them was the lighter music of their voices. Every woman who walked that street should be made to laugh and keep on laughing in order to lend cheerfulness to the roar and growling of the crowd.

He was aware of a greater population than he had expected. There were twenty thousand people in Hooligan. Thirty thousand, perhaps.

He found a stable and turned into it. The stalls were under canvas, in rows. A man sat on a high stool in the middle of the yard with a strong light over his head and a sheaf of money in one hand to make change. It was pay in advance here; five dollars for hay, grain and a stall. Ripley paid and got a ticket for a stall, Number 42. The fat man on the high stool was sweating with prosperity and the heat from his thick cigar.

"That's a mare—that's something worthwhile—that's a regular damn Hickory Dickory!" he called.

That was bad, Ripley realized as he unsaddled the mare in stall 42, and began to rub her down with a wisp of hay. If Hickory had become a proverb, how many people knew the face of her rider in this town? A grain of common sense would take him out of this danger, but he knew that he could not be argued out of his night in Hooligan. He wanted to eat food that other hands had cooked; more than that, he wanted to laugh, quietly, and a lot.

He fumbled the hay and smelled it. It was good. So were the oats that stood in a bin at a corner of the yard with two quart measures at hand and a Negro on guard.

"You the man with the gray, boss?" he asked. "That one can move! Oh, yes, sir, that one can step. When she gallops she cools the eyes, all right. What might her breeding be, boss?"

"Mustang," said Ripley.

"Which? My good Lord! Mustang, eh?" The guardian of the grain put his head back and burst into peals of laughter, an octave above his speaking voice. Ripley gave him a dollar for that laugh and took a measure and a half of oats back to Hickory.

She was almost as drawn with hunger as her master but she had not touched the hay, and she would not touch the oats he poured in the feed box. That was the hardest lesson he had taught her, but a needful one when a single bad ration might make her full for a day. She was tough as hammered iron but the thoroughbred, like her master, had never learned the keen common sense of the range. She whinnied to him now and he loved her with his hand while he gave her the first wisp of hay, the first bit of oats, and felt the velvet of her muzzle gathering them carefully from his palm.

"Mustang, eh?" said Ripley. He chuckled and went out into the street.

Eating came first but it was the least important. He went into the first lunchroom, loosened his belt three notches, and sat on a high stool at the counter. He ate hamburger steak and onions with corn fritters on the side —corn fritters to remind him of flapjacks and let him scorn them the more. He had coffee and a slab of pumpkin pie. When he finished, it seemed to him that he had not begun; but temperance is the only stone which will keep a man sharp as a knife every day and all day. He hated temperance, but he had to be sharp. Physical appetite devoured him, but that was part of the fight.

The cook brought a heap of fresh corn fritters on a pancake turner. They were so fresh from the griddle that butter still bubbled at their edges. "Try these, Mister—" he said.

Ripley looked up. The cook drew back a little. His eyes were guilty.

"Do you know me, brother?" asked Ripley.

"Know you? I sure don't. Have I ever seen you before?" asked the cook.

"I guess not," said Ripley, thoughtfully.

That was the hell of it—to come in off the range and find that even in the thick of towns the guard could never be lowered. The cook, leaning over his hooded stove, began to whistle, but the tune went wrong. Probably he had lied about not knowing Ripley. If so—but a man had to take a chance. For years, Ripley had taken little else. He lighted a cigarette, paid his bill, and went down the street to Conlin's.

There was such an uproar inside that the canvas walls seemed to billow outward. He slid through the four-deep crowd at the bar and bought a beer. He had to move carefully so that the frame of the gun under his left armpit would nudge no one in the ribs. But the sting of the beer was good against his palate. He could feel it in his eyes, too. And he felt safe. The crowd had closed over him, covered him.

A man with black mustaches in the fashion of the eighteen eighties worked his shoulders through the crowd. When he saw Ripley he stopped, blinked, and his mouth dropped open. Then he thrust forward holding out his hand.

"Hey, Jack," he said, "you ain't forgot old Blackie, have you?"

Ripley's visual memory was dim. Somewhere in the past he had seen the shaggy downpouring of those mustaches, but he could not hitch face and place together. But there was honesty in the broken fingernails and labor-hardened palm of the hand. He shook it willingly enough.

"Sure, I remember," said he.

"I'm a lucky hombre to bump into you," said Blackie. "There's three more of us holding down a table, inside; but four-handed poker ain't worth a damn. I'm hunting for the fifth man and I'm collecting you."

"There's too much sitting down in poker," answered Ripley. "Tonight, I'm circulating a little."

"Wait a minute," urged Blackie. There was a greedy intentness in his eye. "The other three all know you. We been talking about you. Come on in and say hello, anyway."

"Sure I'll come," agreed Ripley.

Blackie took his arm and led him sidelong through the crowd into the big gambling room. Many shaded lights hung from the ceiling; cones of white cigarette smoke descended from them upon the flash of cards and dice and reaching hands; and a murmur of many voices went up, speaking hard and short. Over at the roulette wheel one man raised a yell. He leaned across the table, shaking his fist and the croupier. The croupier considered him for a pale instant, drew something from beneath the table, and hit the complainant over the head. He dropped on his face; a bouncer took him by one heel and dragged him across the dirt floor. A trail of small coins and tobacco was left behind.

"Here we are," Blackie was saying. "Sit down a minute and have a drink. You can take the chair against the wall—"

Ripley, smiling, stepped to the designated chair. The three faces lifted to him; the heads jerked back a little; and Ripley's smile almost went out. One of the three was a little man with dust-colored eyebrows. He pulled something from inside his coat and held it in his lap. One was tall and thin, with a blue-flannel shirt three sizes too large at the neck. He reached back to his hip and waited.

"Now—damn you—why don't you sit down?" asked Blackie.

"All right," said Ripley, and slipped into the chair. "I've known all of you fellows, somewhere, but I don't just place you. Except Blackie. Wasn't there a ruction in a saloon up in Montana, and you stuck in the window, trying to get out?"

"You remember now, do you?" asked Blackie. "And what you done to me? But that ain't anything compared to what these fellows want out of you."

"They want my gizzard," said Ripley. He turned to the fourth man, a squat draft horse whose face was blue-black with beard under the skin. His eyes dreamed on Ripley. "You have the biggest grudge. What is it?"

"Tell him, Dutch," said Blackie.

"The way you picked him up and the three

of us waiting," said Dutch. "That's what beats me. But I'll tell you, Ripley. You murdered Tad Sullivan over in Carson City two years back."

"Tad was looking for me and a reputation," said Ripley.

"Yeah?" said Dutch.

"I'm not arguing," remarked Ripley. "It's your turn, Skinny."

"I'm Blondy's partner," said the tall man, and jerked his head toward the one with the dusty eyebrows. The little fellow smiled. He had buck teeth which were only covered when he pursed his lips.

"Jed Morrison only has one leg, now," said he.

"I got him to the doc in time," answered Ripley, "but the doc was a dummy."

"That was too bad for Morrison, and it's gunna be too bad for you," declared Blondy.

Ripley, sitting at ease, nodded toward them all.

"It's a queer chance that all four of you should be sitting in at one table," he observed.

"No chance at all," answered Dutch. "There's a call out for you. It came up today. It's open season on Ripley and the four of us got together because we all know your mug. How come you didn't spot us before you got yourself right into our hands?"

"My private secretary was having a day off," said Ripley.

Dutch said: "Wipe the dirty grin off your face. You're gunna die, kid."

"The four of you will be shooting in self-defense, eh?" asked Ripley.

"We've got in the name of the law behind us," observed Skinny. "Anything we do is hunky dory."

"Tell me how you done it to poor Tad Sullivan," asked Dutch.

"Not without a drink."

"Take mine."

Dutch pushed the filled glass of whisky across the table. When Ripley lifted the drink, he could see a blood-red highlight floating in the liquor.

"Here's to you, boys," he said. He tossed off half the drink and then shuddered as the whisky-horrors gripped his throat. He lighted a cigarette.

"Why not now?" asked Blondy. He was breathing through his open mouth. Now and then he ran the tip of his tongue over his lips.

"Wait a minute," said Dutch. "About Tad Sullivan—"

A red-faced man who walked with a slight limp came through a patch of misty light and into shadow, toward Ripley. Somewhere he had seen that face, but not the red of it. He had seen his picture in a newspaper, or in a magazine.

"There was nobody else in the place when Tad came in," said Ripley. "He walked up behind me and cursed me out. He had a good tongue in his head, if you remember. He told me to fill my hand. Mind you, my back was turned to him but I saw him in the mirror. He was so hot that I could almost feel his breath. I threw my glass over my shoulder and it happened to hit him in the face. Afterward—I filled my hand and turned around."

"You're lying," said Dutch, easily. "There was never a day when you would of looked Tad in the face. There was never a day when any rotten crook like you would look a Sullivan in the face!"

The red-faced man who walked with a limp stepped up to the table and laid the muzzle of a revolver on the edge of the green cloth.

"I'm Marshal Dallas," he said. "Ripley, I arrest you in the name of the law. Stick up your hands and touch the ceiling, Jack."

Ripley's hands rose above his head, slowly, as though through a resisting element. He saw heads turning toward him out of the crowd, but nobody cared. Nobody cared about anything, here in Hooligan. Nobody in Hooligan wanted a thing except gold and ways of spending it, for it is in the spending that gold is sweeter than blood.

"What the hell is this?" asked Blondy, panting like a dying consumptive, flashing his glances between the law and the fugitive.

"It's a lousy frame, is what it is," murmured Dutch. His cheeks pulled back into fat wrinkles; his teeth showed. "He's my meat—"

"Brother," said the marshal, "if you shoot Ripley, I'll most everlastingly let a chunk of lead through your brain."

"It's Tom Dallas, all right. Hold up!" said

Skinny. "It's no frame."

"Gimme those hands," commanded the marshal, pulling out a silver-bright set of handcuffs.

"I never was gladder to give my hands to a girl, even," said Ripley, and he held them out to the marshal in what seemed a gesture of welcome.

CHAPTER III

Before Dallas got Ripley to Tallyho, there were long hours of moonlight, of cold sleeping in the hills, of the dawn when there is too much oxygen in the air, of evening when there is too much dust. And there was golden, scalding heat that fell in a bright mist from the sky and pooled like metal in the hollows. They talked a little about a coyote they saw, and about the sign that crossed the trail or followed it, but most of the way they had the good, strong taste of silence in their throats because Tom Dallas wanted to handle this man with his eyes and weigh and test and probe him, quietly, before he attempted to use him as he never had used a man before. And Dallas had spent such a part of his life in the wilderness that he trusted the evidence of his eyes rather than any of the sounds of falsehood that form in the throats and come

21

past the smiling lips of men.

He paid little attention to Ripley's big, lean body beyond one glance at the thickness through the chest and the narrowness at the hips. He noted more the rifle-straightness of the eyes and their color, which was as if the torrents of the Western sunlight had washed some of the blue away. Close the eyes of a man and he may be sleeping, he may be dead; in them lies the difference of life; and that was why the marshal watched the eyes, and little else. By the time they got to Tallyho he was not sure of his man, but he had a breathless hope that his plan might be a little more than a childish dream.

It was after nightfall when he brought Ripley into his office. By day the room was a place of shelter from the sun, with a mighty picture filling the window; by night it was a ghostly emptiness lighted by one unshaded bulb that hung from the center of the ceiling. Ripley had irons on his hands and on his feet.

"Smoke?" asked the marshal, lifting a sack of Bull Dirham with brown wheat-straw papers.

Ripley kept on smiling. Animosity narrows the eyes of most men but Ripley's gaze remained curiously bright and open.

The marshal rolled his own cigarette with fingers gone suddenly clumsy. "I wanta talk to you," he said. "Not for fun. I wanta do business with you."

"The hell you do," said Ripley.

"You're sour," observed the marshal.

"What's the matter? Can't you take it?"

Ripley continued smiling. He looked away toward the window, a black eye with four glittering facets.

"Do you know what I've got on you?" asked Marshal Dallas.

"Nothing federal," answered Ripley. "And you're a federal agent."

"Pushing the queer. Handling counterfeit is a federal offense. You shoved over some of the queer in Tucson, two years back."

"That's a lie."

"Sure it's a lie. But I can prove that it's true."

"That means about fifteen years, doesn't it?"

"Or twenty."

"All right. I'll talk to you, then. I'll talk business." Ripley added, softly: "Damn you!"

"I'm getting old," said Dallas. "I need young hands and eyes to work for me. You take a badge and go to work for me or else you take fifteen years in the pen."

"Where do I work?"

"Anywhere from El Paso west."

"I've got fifty friends down here and half of them are crooks," said Ripley. "I won't go after them."

"You don't have to go after them. You only have to get one man for me."

"Who's the man?"

"Tell me first if you'll take the job."

"Not if the man's a friend of mine."

"Have you got any friend that's worth fifteen years in the pen to you?"

Ripley again disregarded words and looked
Dallas over with that same impersonal
curiosity. So an unwinking hawk looks at his
prey and at the world beyond it.

"Well," said Dallas, yielding the point,
"here's a picture of him."

The photograph showed a lean face, already
cast for middle age but not yet worn and fur-
rowed. He might be in his early thirties.
Ripley nodded.

"That's all right," he said. "What is he?"

Dallas sighed, in the greatness of his relief.

"Jim Lancaster is one of his names," he
said. "Height six feet one; weight, a hundred
and eighty; walks with a slight limp in the left
leg; distinguishing marks, a small mole on the
right cheek. Are you taking the job, Ripley?"

He could not help leaning forward. A vein
like a big blue earthworm crawled out across
his temple. Ripley watched it.

"I get Lancaster how?"

"Dead or alive," snapped the marshal.

"And then I pass in the badge—and I'm
through?"

"You are."

"What has Lancaster done?"

"You have to spend some time in the jail,
anyway. I'll take you over there and show you
what Lancaster is doing."

Ripley stood up.

"Are we shaking hands on it?" asked Dallas.

"Wait a minute. That Tucson job you hang

on me with a dirty frame-up. You get that fat man with the glass eye to testify against me?"

"It's a frame, all right. And the fat man does the lying for me. Are we shaking hands on the Lancaster deal?"

"I'll get Lancaster or be gotten; but I'm not shaking hands with you."

"I take your naked word, eh?"

"I don't give a damn what you do," said Ripley.

But Dallas persisted: "From now on, I don't have to worry about holding you? You're held to my job till you get Lancaster?"

Ripley took a breath that raised his chest. "That's the way it seems to be," he said.

"Not how it seems to be—what way *is* it?"

"Well, your way—till I've finished Lancaster."

"Good," breathed Dallas.

He went over to the table and unlocked the drawer. A slight shiver ran through him when his back was turned to Ripley, but he took from the drawer a key with which he freed Ripley from the irons on his hands and feet. He threw the manacles into the corner, where they fell with a clanging crash. When he glanced back, Ripley was settling back on his heels. He had been on tiptoe—until he had changed his mind. The first impulse still gleamed in his eyes.

"We'll go on over to the jail," said Dallas, and led the way out onto the street.

Tallyho was quiet, but not still. Bellowing laughter sounded from the saloons, the noise withdrawn behind walls, and out of the Mexican half of the town rose a little pulse of sound, irregularly beating, of the thrumming of many guitars.

It seemed to Dallas that the tall man beside him was touched a little by every noise, as a tree is stirred by wind. There was a pausing quality in his step as though he were prepared to spring in any direction. And he seemed to go a shade more slowly through the shadows of the trees. For the citizens of Tallyho, through a great outburst of public spirit, had planted little trees up and down the main street and the high-riding moon cast inky stains from the tree tops on the white of the street.

Yet all of these hesitations of Ripley were slight, like the stopping and starting of a dog too well-trained ever to let the leash grow taut.

The jail stood off by itself, the most expensive building in the town—square, heavy, dependable. The sheriff took his prisoner into it past the towheaded jailer who stammered: "Hey! I thought—I thought—".

"That's the trouble with you, Bud," said Dallas. "You're always thinking a pile too much. Take us to that Chinese feller—that Wung Su."

They went down a narrow corridor. One light from the ceiling overcast the cells with dark or penciled the interiors with the shadows of the bars that fell across the sleeping inmates—ineradicable stains on some of them. So they passed through a door into a separate group of four cells.

"All tool-proof, in here," said the marshal, and stroked one of the bars fondly. "Hey, Wung! Wung Su! Wake up!"

A little figure leaped from its couch. A pigtail bounced behind its head like a jumping snake. Now he stood barefooted, in flimsy shirt and trousers of cheap cotton, close to the bars. His face was round as a ball of yellow clay, with the features clumsily pinched onto it, or thumbed out. He kept bowing a little up and down with his hands crossed on his breast.

"Wung Su, where from you come?" asked the sheriff. "This number one gentleman. You tell him."

The eyes of Wung Su grew blank with the strain of mental effort.

"I Wung Su, born San Flancisco," he said. His voice had a rippling, mournful intonation that flowed up and down. It was a childish voice that would never grow deeper. His incapable hands made gestures. "Water so—hill so—Mahket Stleet—Gollen Get—Wung Su born here—"

He paused. He came closer to the bars and his eyes entreated tall Jack Ripley who suddenly put a hand through and patted the shoulder of the Chinese boy. The shoulder bone was sharp as a wooden edge.

"Poor little devil—what's he been saying?" asked Ripley. "Born in San Francisco?"

"That's what they all say. The dealers get hold of the boys in China, ship 'em to Mexico, and work 'em over the Rio Grande. On the

way over, in the ship, they all have lessons.
They learn how to say that they were born in
San Francisco—if they're caught by us—and
they prove that they know San Francisco. Understand? Water out here—the hills are back
there—the Golden Gate to the north. Here's
Market Street. And over here is the place
where Wung Su was born. Wung Su came
down here looking for his uncle, but no can
find."

"The Chinese are all right," said Ripley.
"What's the matter with the Chinese?"

"After these boys get inside the States they
go to work in laundries and starve like
mongrel dogs. Anywhere from Chicago to New
Orleans. They work for years paying off the
passage from China and the cost of smuggling
into this country. They're slaves. They die off.
They live on a handful of rice and a beating a
day. The swine that gather 'em in China tell
them they're going to a heaven, and take them
into a hell. This here trade of running Chinese
over the border is the dirtiest business in the
world, Jack. And I'm gunna stop it. Come
over here and I'll show you your quarters for
tonight."

He unlocked the door of the cell opposite
that of the Chinese boy.

They went in and sat side by side on the
hard bunk. The stale sweetness of cookery
could never be cleaned from this air.

"That's what I want you for," said the
marshal. "To break the back of this smuggling
business. Jim Lancaster is the head of it. Get

him for me, and the machine will break. He's the one that put the engine together and keeps the cogs oiled."

"Yeah?" said Ripley.

The marshal looked at him with a side glance of troubled thought.

"What's the matter, Jack?" he asked. "You see what the idea is. If you finish Lancaster, you're doing a good job for everybody—the Chinese and whites."

"Yeah?" said Ripley. "But what about that poor guy across the aisle? Suppose you find out he *is* born in San Francisco—and give him a white man's chance?"

"What you mean, find out he's born in San Francisco? He never saw the place."

"A first-rate federal marshal can find out anything he wants to," declared Ripley.

"Uh huh!" grunted the marshal. "I follow your drift now. Well, I could fix up the poor kid, I suppose."

"Thanks," said Ripley. "Dallas, you're damned white, and that's all there is to it."

"That's all right," declared the marshal. "Take this key. When you think a good time has come, reach through the bars and unlock the door of your cell. The same key will fit that back door at the end of the aisle. And you know where your mare is kept. In the barn behind my office."

"Is there a guard outside the jail?"

"Yes. I've put one on."

"You'd better call him off again."

"If you can't get through one guard, you'll

never get to Jim Lancaster."

"I haven't got a gun."

"You don't use guns any more—except on Lancaster."

Ripley sat up straight and peered.

"The marshal put me under lock and key and set a special guard on the jail. But the fugitive melted through and got away. Is that it?"

"I've got a reputation to protect," answered Dallas.

He waited for no more words but stood up.

"So long," he said. "Maybe I'll be seeing you."

"Yeah. Maybe."

Dallas went out from the cell and clanged the door shut. The bolt hummed a minute in the lock, while Dallas paused across the aisle to speak to Wung Su, jerking his thumb back, several times, towards Ripley.

When the marshal was gone, a voice of joy rose softly from the cell of Wung Su. Two little yellow hands extended through the bars in thrusting gestures that tried to take the place of speech.

Ripley stretched himself on the bunk, turned his back on this gratitude, and was instantly asleep.

CHAPTER IV

In his mind he had set a little alarm clock which would sound after three or four hours. In about that time, Ripley wakened, sat up, and pulled out the key from his pocket.

If he used that key, he was launched on a chase with the law after him and Jim Lancaster ahead of him. He kept weighing the key on the tip of his finger. Against the madness which Dallas demanded of him bulked the certainty of fifteen or twenty years in jail.

He made a cigarette and smoked it out. The white smoke worked through the bars and extended unshapen hands towards the light. At last he stepped his heel on the butt of the cigarette and slid his hand between the bars. The key fitted the lock easily, turned it as though it worked in oil.

He took the first step towards freedom, into the aisle. To a man condemned to fifteen

years of cell-life, even that corridor would
seem an open desert of space.

Someone was snoring. Not the little Chinaman. He was already gone from his cell and
the marshal had kept the first promise. In the
end, if good were poised against evil in items,
there would be no broken promises checked
on the record of Tom Dallas, but that he
should have laid the weight of his trust on
Ripley set the teeth of that young man on
edge. The whole gesture of the marshal had
been big and casual, as though in one day's
ride he had penetrated to the heart of his man
and judged him sufficient. He had not named
Lancaster's probable hangouts, or described
the smuggler's chief cronies. As though he
spoke to a master, he had named a subject to
be dealt with and thus closed the matter.

Ripley tried the rear door. It opened easily
until, through a narrow crack, he looked at a
world of white moonlight, more garish than
the sun. A thin current of the outer air, the
sweet night air, set him breathing more deeply. Then he closed the door to a hair's breadth
of light for he heard sand swishing around
footfalls; and now he had a dim glimpse of a
rider who went by on a down-headed mustang
with a sawed-off shotgun balanced on the
pommel of the saddle. The sight of that gun
was a physical pain to Ripley. At short range,
it needed no more aiming than the spray of a
garden hose.

The horse turned the corner from view.

Ripley was instantly through the door. He grudged the second needed to close it; then his boots were in the soft white of the sand. Someone began to laugh, with a brawling, drunken persistence. And yonder was a clump of high shrubbery.

He made for it at full speed. The sand yielded, watery, under the drive of his boots. Each forward stride cast a sheen of fine spray before him.

"Hai!" yelled a voice from the rear. "Hai—come back! Halt, there—"

A double-barreled shotgun needs no more aiming than a garden hose, he remembered; and he doubled his work. The gun spoke. It had a sharp, short bark without the deadly resonance of a rifle. Behind him, the bullets splattered on the ground. Then he dived into the shadows of the brush like a fish into the divine dark of water.

The guard was still yelling. He had never stopped. The mindless persistence of that voice enraged Ripley, but he had worked through the brush to the farther edge and had to lie still with the hoofbeats, sodden in the loose soil, hurrying towards him; beyond, lay a brief open stretch, then a scrub of small trees. Other voices had wakened. A door banged with heavy weight and with a clangor as of metal on metal. That was the door of the jail, perhaps.

What had Dallas wanted? Legal murder instead of a prison term? To bait his captive and then watch him die? To see how a mature man could be led with hope thinner than a ray of spider's silk?

The mustang came crackling through the brush. Ripley looked up and saw the horse striding short, the rider bumping heavily in the saddle. The brim of his sombrero flopped, too. The revolver in his hand waved up and down as he turned the bronco through a circle to scan the shadows of the brush, and then darted it away for the scrub of trees.

Ripley got out of the bushes on the run, heading for a house on the left.

"Hey! Lookat!" shrilled a boy's voice.

He saw the white figure of the lad in a night-gown at an open window and then heard the comforting boom of a man who was saying: "Shut up and leave him be. Leave him have his chance, if he's won it."

So Ripley got past the corner of the house, dodged through more brush, and cut down his pace to an easy stride. Voices kept pealing. A troop of riders made rapid thunder down the main street. And here he was behind the marshal's office at the door of the barn.

He shouldered the sliding door back with care, damning the rusted wheels which screamed at speed and groaned at slowness. Inside, he saw the gray mare like a ghost, a mist. The second saddle he hefted was his own, with ten vital pounds of weight saved in its making, since it would never have to withstand the shocks and jars of roping cattle. The good mare turned her head as though she

would help him. Two jerks drew the cinches
tight. He dragged on the bridle and mounted.
Then he was in the deadly flood of moonlight,
jogging Hickory Dickory toward the hills.
There was no use burning up her strength until she was sighted and then—let them catch
her if they could!

He went up a slope with the noise of the
town collecting beneath him. He could see
light after light appear in windows, and the
lank old hills shouldered toward him like
friends.

Dallas had been right: a man who could not
pass through such a danger as this would never deal with Jim Lancaster.

As the hills flowed away behind him, he
knew where he would go, the one place. He
had plenty of friends, but who save Jose Oñate
would be glad to see him now? The thought
startled him. If he sifted life, there remained
to him the gray mare and that greasy-faced
Oñate. Other men who remain in one place
strike down longer roots and more adheres to
them; to him, who had been so long in action,
there was left little except the swiftness of the
years. The thought troubled him until he
lifted his face to the bare sky and breathed
liberty so deep that he was happy again.

The hills parted. He had a view of the Rio
Grande in shadow and moonlight, black glass
and white. On the bend of the river stood the
town of Los Altos. The distance made it no
larger than a full-page illustration; from the
height he could see the streets, the loom of the

old Spanish church, the double row of trees
dotted regularly around the plaza. Men prefer
to spend their small lives on a tiny stage. Jack
Ripley came down out of boundless space into
the little town like a hawk from the sky to a
perch in a tree, with a muttering of hoofs instead of the whirring of wings. He went
through Los Altos with the liquid dust spilling
black or white from the feet of his horse.

Beyond the verge of the town he came to a
small adobe house set close to the bank of the
river. The air was suddenly cool and humid,
for the moon, as it hung in the west with dis-
tended cheeks, showed Ripley fields of green
vegetables. And yonder, with its shafts pointing down into the ground, was the cart with
which Oñate peddled his crops through the
streets of Los Altos.

He dismounted and pushed the door ajar.
Soft snoring made the darkness tremble.

"Jose!" he called gently. "Are you there,
Jose?"

The snoring stopped.

"Mother of heaven!" said a groaning voice.

"Are you there?" repeated Ripley.

"My señor!" cried Jose Oñate. "Maria! Do
you hear? It is his voice. Anna, Juan! Up! The
señor!"

He came stumbling, half-dressed, through
the doorway, holding up his hands. His teeth
flashed, his face was seamed with laughter in
the moonlight.

"Quickly, Juan. It is he—and the mare is
still with him. Kind God, what a happiness to

send us by night. I was dreaming of good, strong new wine, and roast kid. But this is what I find!"

Little Juan put the mare away in the shed. He went to her without fear and she warded him off till she remembered him. Afterward the fire was kindled, the lamp lighted, the iron pot of frijoles thrust into the blaze on the hearth. A chicken squawked once in the darkness after moondown and squawked no more. It was scalded and plucked. Little Anna and Juan tried to get the feathers off, but all their wits were in the shining of their eyes as they watched the stranger, and Maria had to take over the work. The fat of her brown arm trembled as with vigorous strokes she stripped away the feathers. In no time at all the chicken was frying, the frijoles were bubbling like soft chuckles, the tortillas were ready, the brown-red of the wine was staining the glasses.

Oñate himself had been walking around the room opening his arms and striking his breast in joy. Now he rolled some frijoles in a tortilla which he had torn in half, stuffed his mouth with the food, and washed it clean with a great draught of the red wine. After that, while the guest was eating, Jose Oñate picked up Anna and showed Ripley to her.

"There is the man!" said Oñate. "My friend of the world! Do you see him? They had the rope around my neck, and he paid for the horse they said I had stolen. From his own pocket—and he never had laid eyes on me

before. Use *your* eyes—wide—wide—so that
they can swallow a man. You were a baby
when you saw him before; now you are a big
girl to remember. Mother of heaven, his glass
is empty! Maria! The wine!"

CHAPTER V

Ripley lay at his ease in the heat of the afternoon on a pair of goatskins that softened the rounds of a willow Indian-bed. His head was raised far enough for him to look through the doorway at the willows along the riverbank and at the unending plain that stretched beyond, shimmering with heat waves. Maria, on the threshold, half in sunlight and half in shadow, scrubbed out wet cornmeal for tortillas. The meal glistened on her knuckles; on the back of her hand some of it had dried to white. She sang at her work very softly for fear she might disturb Ripley's thoughts, and now and again she flashed her smile at him. She had a mole on her fat chin and it seemed to move with a volition of her own when she was singing.

That was when the voice of a man sounded outside the house. Young Juan made answer.

"Amigo," insisted the stranger. "You go tell him—I'm an amigo."

"Nobody here!" shrilled Juan. "I tell you, nobody here! Nobody—not one! My father is in Los Altos—"

"Amigo!" insisted the man's voice. "You tell the big man that I'm a friend."

Ripley took out the old-fashioned Colt which Oñate had given him. It was ancient, but he had proved that it shot true that morning. Maria got up from her work. "Go back into the corner, señor!" she pleaded. "I'll keep him away!"

He looked about him at the homemade broom, the irons by the hearth, the peppers red and green and golden and brown that hung in long strips across the ceiling. It seemed to him that the house of Oñate contained happiness enough for the entire world, and that wise men would give up dangerous chance in order to till the ground and water it, and make the green things grow. But since he had chosen the other way, already they were on his trail.

Maria began to gesticulate. A sombreroed shadow appeared, nodding at Maria's feet. Then a man who looked bowlegged in his leather chaps stepped into Ripley's line of vision. The man's face was crooked, but not so crooked as his smile. A scar made a white zigzag from the temple to the jaw.

"Hello, Warren. How are you, Chuck?" said Ripley. "Come right in."

Chuck Warren dodged almost out of sight, the impact of the voice struck him so much by surprise. Then he mastered himself and came in. His smile defaced him more than ever, but Ripley shook the extended hand. Not even money, not even a published reward would ever win Chuck to the side of the law.

"It's a long time," said Chuck.

"What brought you here?" asked Ripley. "The garlic?"

"You bust clean from the jail in Tallyho. You head this way. And Jose Oñate's your friend," said Warren, briefly.

"Yeah. That's easy," agreed Ripley.

"I'm bringing you news," said Warren.

"About what?"

"About a way out. Old Dallas is hot after you, ain't he? I'm showing you a way out. There's somebody up high that could use you, kid."

"Who?"

"You'll know him when you see him, I guess. The biggest man on the border, and it means money. I'm sliding out of here. Be back after sunset. Then I'll take you into Los Altos. Will you be waiting here? I've got to go."

"Sit down and have a drink of this Mexican red."

"If I hang around here, somebody'll see me and wonder why. Think fast, kid."

"I'll be waiting here after dark."

"That's great. So long." He went to the door and turned. "Call off the dogs when I come back, will you?" he asked. He hooked a thumb at Maria and disappeared beyond the doorway.

In the dusk he came again, and called from a distance. Little Anna held Ripley's hands when he stood up.

"If you go, you won't come back," she said.

"This is home for me, Anna," he told her. "Of course I'll come back."

She shook her head. Her face went ugly and puffed with restrained emotion.

"One time a big brown dog came off the road and stayed with us one night and a day. He had a sore foot that he kept licking. But in the dark he began to whine. We opened the door and he went away. He never came back! He never came back!"

Jose Oñate snapped his fingers and gestured. Maria took the girl away and Ripley went out into the night. All the time he was saddling Hickory, he could hear the little girl sobbing. Her voice began to make a sing-song in his thoughts. He would never come back. He would never come back!

When he got up to the road, Chuck Warren was waiting. All the way to town he kept confidentially close, leaning his head toward Ripley.

"The best break you ever had in your life," he declared. "The biggest thing that ever happened to you."

"And you picked me out for it? I'm going to owe you something, Chuck," said Ripley.

"Don't laugh," said Warren. "No matter
what this is, don't laugh!"

They got through the town. There was no
wind. The heat lay thick across the streets until they came to a short row of houses on the
very bank of the river. They could smell the
Rio Grande and the wet cool of it was in the
air.

The buildings were adobe, low, white-
washed, with narrow windows cut through the
thick of the walls. The men stopped under a
wooden sign. A glint of light from a neighbor-
ing window enabled Ripley to spell ou: SAM LI,
SILKS AND TEA.

The proximity of some great thing made
Warren's voice soft as they dismounted, and
he said to Ripley: "I dunno why he wants to
see you here. Take it easy with him. The
chief's straight, but he's damned hard and
short."

He tapped at the door. Echoes of the knock-
ing reverberated softly inside the house. Then
the light of a carried lamp wavered across a
window, staining the lips of the casement with
yellow. The door pulled open and a girl stood
back from the entrance to let them in. She was
dressed in a tunic and trousers of black silk
with a rich gleam of embroidery on it. With a
raised hand she shielded her eyes from the
glow of the lamp but the light struck the hand
to translucence and oiled to sleekness the hair
which was drawn flat back from her forehead.
She was not young, thought Ripley, but newly
made of an ancient ivory.

"Hello, Ching," said Warren. "Here's Jack Ripley. The chief wants him, and you're to take him in."

She made a curtsey in which only the knees moved, a flexion so easy with grace that the flame hardly stirred in the throat of the lamp she held.

"Very good to see you," said the girl. The "R" went a little wrong on her tongue but the English was clear enough. He could look straight into her face, because her eyes were not raised above the third button of his shirt. He would have liked to look a long time. For the first time he could see why many people love Chinese art.

"So long and good luck," said Warren, and closed the door.

The girl led the way across the shoproom, folds and gleams of colored silk appearing on the shelves, and brushed through a hanging into an inner hall. The light flowed back over her shoulders; the end of her braided hair flipped up and down a trifle; her slippers whispered on the floor.

She stopped at another hanging and pulled it back. Ripley passed into a little room where he faced a huge squatting idol with a face of smooth, hard, yellow stone, and a body of black. The idol came to life by lifting its downcast eyes. It rose and became a man as huge as any that Ripley had ever seen, smiling over a double flow of chin, extending a vast, yellow hand.

"I am Sam Li," said the Chinaman. "I am

happy to see you, Mr. Ripley. My friend who wishes to see you will be here very soon. Please sit down."

He offered, with a wave, a low couch, and Ripley sat down. A sing-song phrase of Chinese bubbled from the fat lips of Sam Li. The girl let the hanging fall and disappeared.

"We'll have tea in a moment," said Sam Li. "My friend should be here quickly to see you. I'm sorry."

"Not a bit. Hope I'm not keeping you up," answered Ripley.

"Happiness is better than sleep," said Sam Li, "and Ching and I are happy to serve our friend. Even by lamplight." He laughed a little, shaking his shoulders as he sat down again, and his fat face was shaking, except for the great forehead of hard, yellow stone. If brains filled the enormous dome of that skull, they could not be the brains of ordinary men. "Kind hearts," said Sam Li, "waken more easily than singing birds. And now—see!"

There was almost nothing in the room except a tall cabinet against one wall and a large bell-shaped object covered with black silk. Sam Li, pulling back the cloth, opened a door, and at once a dozen canaries streamed out of the cage. They whirled around Sam Li's head, their wings a shining yellow mist through which he kept on laughing until Ripley began to feel that Old King Cole must have lived in Asia.

Sam Li whistled. At once the canaries lighted like jewels of gold on his arms and shoulders except one that tried vainly to perch on a button of his coat and kept whirring its wings to make up for a lost balance, and one that perched on the bald top of his brow.

Sam Li pursed his thick lips. Out of an absurdly small, round hole a whistle fluted and instantly a dozen canaries were answering in a musical jargon, ruffling their feathers and quivering their tongues with the might of their song.

Ching came, bringing a tray of tea. She almost kneeled, putting it on the floor before Sam Li, and at once the golden cloud of canaries left the man for the girl. One of them perched on her ear and took hold on a beakful of hair to steady itself. And they all kept on singing until the room was filled with a delightful clamoring.

"See, Mr. Ripley," said Sam Li, "that music leaves the old and goes to the young. But hush them, Ching, or we can hardly talk."

She went to the cage and took the little birds from her arms and shoulders to pass them through the door into the shrouded cage. Last of all, she held up a finger and the bird from her ear dropped onto it. The canary seemed in a great rage, steadying himself with beating wings while it pecked at the finger. But this one, too, was put with the others and the silk veil dropped over musical little complaints.

The girl looked down at the finger which had been attacked. She pressed it against her chin for comfort and then laughed.

"That one!" she said. "What an eagle in his heart!"

Sam Li extended to her the cup which he had filled with tea. It was jade green, delicate as an eggshell; but it was safe in Ripley's hand, for who can learn to pick locks unless there are brains in the tips of his fingers?

He looked openly at the girl because he wanted her to laugh again; her laughter had filled his heart as water brims a well with brightness that overflows. Even laughter was different in her from big-throated American mirth; for her head had tilted somewhat to the side and a little down, almost as though she were ashamed.

"Now they are quiet inside the cage," said Sam Li. "The silk surrounds them. To them it is a mystery as dark and great as our night. Perhaps there is something over us, Mr. Ripley, that draws the blackness around us and then holds up the sun like a lantern and laughs when all the little people run out into the morning."

A bell tinkled, far away, and sent the girl towards the door until a second distant jangling stopped her. Sam Li rose with a hushing rustle of silks.

"I must go, but I come again, soon," he said, and he flowed from the room, bending his head as he passed through the door.

The girl stood by the wall with her hands crossed over her breast and her eyes lowered to the floor so that her face had almost the blind look of a statue. Ripley could not tell whether she were sun-browned or the Mongolian yellow. Feeble lamplight was hardly enough to let him distinguish the difference.

He swallowed more tea and, as he looked up, she was crouching to fill the cup again. She leaned into his mind. The nearness of her face confused him and he could only look down at the delicacy of her hands.

"Have some tea for yourself, Ching," he suggested.

At this, she stood suddenly back against the wall again. Her eyes went up and down. So did her hands in deprecation.

"How should a woman taste such tea?" she asked. "It was picked leaf by leaf. It was dried with sun and prayers!"

She showed how it had been picked and the loose sleeve, flowing back from her arm, showed a bracelet which, like a golden snake, clasped her above the wrist.

"If it only grew a leaf to a bush, and the bushes only grew on a south bank of the emperor's garden, it wouldn't be too good for you, Ching," said Ripley.

"Ah, all of you talk to make Ching so happy that she will laugh," said the girl, and she began to laugh a little at the same time.

Ripley looked away as he listened to that quiet music, for there were strings in his heart that responded with a faint echoing. He wanted to have her close again. This time he would watch how she stooped from ankles and knees and waist, a flowing movement.

"I'm through with the tea," he said.

She came and leaned over to pick up the small tray and, instead of watching all of her, he could only study the hands again. That was why he saw the golden snake slip a little on her arm; and the skin it exposed was clearest white!

For a moment he could not move. She was in her place again, looking down at the floor, before he swayed to his feet, exclaiming: "Ching, you're not the daughter of Sam Li."

"I belong to Sam Li," she said.

He thrust forward his hand. It was sun-blackened and therefore he pulled it back again.

"You're whiter than I am, Ching," said Ripley.

"I belong to Sam Li," the girl repeated.

"Belong? How can you belong to a Chinaman? They have slaves on the other side of the water, but they can't have 'em here. One breath of America makes you free!"

"Are you angry?" asked Ching, in alarm at his emotion. "Listen to a thing that will make you happy again."

She held up a frail hand and whistled; instantly a canary thrilled back a note from the cage.

"Ah, do you hear?" asked Ching. "That is the strong one who picked at my finger. He is so brave that he will even answer me from the dark."

Ripley began to smile, and at that she whistled again, and a whole phrase of ecstasy came fluting from the cage.

She would not talk willingly of herself but he knew that in time he would be able to lay hands on whatever mystery closed her in this house with Sam Li. An anguish of unspoken questions tormented him, and yet it was better to leave her for a little while like this rather than to rush her out at once into that brazen light which squinted the eyes of those free women of whom he had been speaking.

Sam Li came back. The gross fatness of his cheeks wabbled with his steps.

"He is here, Ching," said the Chinaman. "Take Mr. Ripley to him."

He added, to Ripley: "So you have come to the golden gate of fortune. Peace and happiness go with you!"

CHAPTER VI

She took a lamp and led Ripley out of the room. Sam Li was bowing with ponderous ceremony. "Another time I shall see you, Mr. Ripley," he was saying in his perfect English. "Make me happy by coming here, one day. Those for business go to the front door but those who want a welcome come to the back of the house."

Ripley followed the girl down the hall again to a room at the rear of the place. The rushing sound of the river and the damp of its breath came through the window.

A man wonderfully narrow, wonderfully tall, stood in the farthest corner, motionless, like a guard. A heavy cartridge belt sloped down to the revolver on his thigh. Another figure leaned above the lamp on the table, puffing at his cigarette until the end of it glowed and a curling cloud of white mist enveloped the lamp. As he straightened, Ripley saw the lean, hard face of that Jim Lancaster whose capture would mean for him peace with the law, freedom, and hands cleansed forever from his past. This was indeed the golden gate of fortune and fate by some miracle of kindness was filling his hands with opportunity.

If only that figure with the face of idiotic length had not been stationed there in the background, at watch!

"Any cool beer?" asked Lancaster, paying no heed to Ripley.

"At once," said the girl. Her slippers whispered away down the hall, while Lancaster turned his attention to Ripley.

"You're young—damned young for what I want of you," he said. "Sit down."

Ripley remained standing, with one hand resting on the edge of the little deal table that stood in the center of the room. Out of the corner of his eye he could see a flat shallow at the bend of the river with small eyes of starlight looking up from it.

"Sometimes the older they are the harder they fall," said he. "Who are you?"

At this, Lancaster's thoughtful glance went over him again.

"You're one of these tough kids," said Lancaster. "I've seen them before. But when they break, they break through the bone. What have you done? Tell me about yourself."

"I've cut a lot of wise hombres down to my own size," said Ripley.

"Meaning what by that?"

Ripley smiled at him, the same faint smile which had sent a journeying chill through Dallas' blood.

"Don't be a damn fool with your pride," snapped Lancaster. "This is business. Can I use you or can't I?"

"Probably not," said Ripley.

He felt an almost dizzy sense of coincidence but, after all, if a fellow like Warren could trace him to his hide-out, a mind like Lancaster's would be able to find a use for him. Lancaster's grim eyes showed him his past in a clearer light. He had felt that he was simply drifting through early, irresponsible years enjoying life as it came to him. To others, to Lancaster, he must seem to have preferred crime calmly and coldly until he had become a tool for evil, hardened, tempered, fitted by experience to Lancaster's hand.

"You're the kind," said Lancaster. "I can use your kind. I can use them as long as they know I'm a shade harder and meaner still. Do you think you could understand that?"

Ripley smiled again.

"I'm not going to waste a lot of time," said Lancaster. "We do business or we don't. It doesn't depend on you. It depends on me. That's why I say: Tell me something about yourself."

There was a silence. The girl came in with bottles of beer on a tray. Lancaster put his arm around her. "How's everything, Ching?" he asked.

At this, she lifted her head, slowly, and let

Lancaster look right down into her smiling eyes. Like wheels over the hollow arch of a wooden bridge, Ripley's heart bumped twice, and was still.

"I am happy!" she said.

"Are you?" asked Lancaster. "Think I could make you any happier, one of these days?"

"Ah, yes," said the girl.

"I'm going to find the scarface for you. You can tie to that. Now run along."

She went quickly toward the door. She was like ivory, with peach bloom transfusing it. Her slippers went softly down the hall.

"Beauty, eh?" said Lancaster. "Damn her, but she's a pretty thing."

He made two paces across the floor, snapped his cigarette out the window, and returned to his theme.

"If I take you, it's something big," he said. "You know me?"

"I don't know you."

"I'm Jim Lancaster." He waited. Ripley was stone.

He relented to say: "You run Chinese over the border?"

"So they say. What about it?"

"The Chinese are all right," said Ripley, cautiously.

"I want a man I can trust," said Lancaster. "The law wants you and that will keep you straight with me. Warren and the rest say you're honest—for a crook. You seem made to my hand. And this job would mean a lot to you. Say—a hundred a week. No, make it a hundred and fifty. Think fast, Ripley."

Think fast? He was thinking in terms of miles and hours that shot up like star dust through his brain. Not very many hours before he would have his chance at Lancaster if luck held for him. And in the meantime there was Sam Li to investigate and that mysterious leash in which he held Ching. There was Ching herself. He held the thought of her as she had held the lamp; it poured a radiance over his mind.

"Think fast?" said Ripley. "Wages like that do the thinking for me. A hundred and fifty a week? That'll suit me."

"You don't care what sort of work it is?"

"I care. We'll take one job at a time."

"One job at a time? You mean that you'll be free to step out from under any time you don't like my ideas?"

"And you can fire me with a wave of the hand any time I'm on your nerves, Lancaster."

"You could quit me in the middle of a trail?"

"That's my idea."

Lancaster said: "Missouri, what you think of this hombre?"

"He's too damn pretty to suit me," said the tall shadow with the idiotic length of face.

Lancaster grinned. "He won't have a pretty job, though." He nodded at Ripley. "I'm going to take you on, kid."

"When?"

"Now. You start now. If I could leave the border, I'd do this myself. You can do it for me. There's a new shipment of Chinese landed in Mexico, bound for the U.S.A. Coupla hundred of them coming overland now through the Sierra Blanca. You know those mountains?"

"They're a lot to know," commented Ripley.

"They'll likely take the north pass. You find 'em."

"All right."

"I'll give you a note to Dan Tolliver, riding herd on them. It'll tell him to turn over a scarfaced Chinese to you. You won't mistake him. Somebody widened his mouth for him with a knife, once, and they say his grin goes to his ears. You take that Chinaman and bring him up here. Bring him to me. No, bring him right into this house."

Ripley nodded.

"Treat him like he was gold and don't let him wear out on the way. The biggest thing in the world hangs on it for me. A hundred and fifty a week? If you come through with that Chinaman I'll give you a bonus that'll put a permanent bulge in you."

He went to the door and called: "Ching! Oh, Ching!"

A door opened. "I come!" cried the voice, the last note wavering out as she started running. She was breathless as she reached the threshold of the room where the three tall men looked down at her.

"This fellow Ripley is going to get your scarface and bring him up to you," said Lancaster. "Think he can do it?"

She looked at Ripley's feet and slowly upwards, her glance stopping short of his face. In her expression, all emotions except happiness were obscure and dim, and yet it seemed to Ripley that he saw a little hardening of disdain about her mouth.

"He will go as you send him and come as you call him," she said.

Missouri burst into a noisy guffaw.

"Shut up, Slim," commanded Lancaster, chuckling a little.

"May I go now?" asked the girl.

"Go along," grinned Lancaster. "I guess we know what you mean."

He was still broadly amused when the girl had left them again.

"Her and me, we figger the same way on this one," said Missouri Slim.

"You haven't the brains to figure," snapped Lancaster. He explained to Ripley: "I wanted the girl to have a flash at you because the scarface is a big thing in her life. If she didn't like you, forget it."

"Sure," said Ripley. "That's easy."

It was one of the hardest tasks of his life, but he managed to smile straight at Lancaster and keep the bulldog out of his eyes.

CHAPTER VII

In the middle of the night, Ripley crossed the river with Hickory Dickory and went south. Every mile of the dark way, doubt turned his head to the north, for what would Tom Dallas have to say to this journey and how could even a gambler like the marshal understand that his emissary was working for the good cause, though in ways most round-about? But above all the mystery of Ching followed at Ripley's very shoulder. It was for her sake, apparently, that Lancaster wanted the scarfaced Chinaman brought north in haste. It was for her sake that Ripley was hating Lancaster with a deep-seated loathing. It was for her, again, that he looked upon huge Sam Li with a sick suspicion. She belonged to Sam Li, she had said. But her blood was that of a white and she could not be his child; surely she was not his slave; and she must not be his wife. It was the last thought that made Ripley breathe suddenly in through his teeth, in horror. And then, remembering how coldly she had disdained him in the end, he gathered in himself that pride which is the fiercest strength of a young man; but that pride turned presently into sighing and sullenness. He felt that he had been divided and that one part of him remained back there in the house of Sam Li, a ghost that watched the girl from corners. He had been entire and complete, before. To watch the journeying head of Hickory through the mountains or the desert had given him a sufficient sense of companionship, but now a beauty and a glory had departed from the gray mare. Ching, like a subtle little thief, had stolen from horse and rider.

He tried to add her up and find the sum total merely a reasonable thing that could be discarded without pain. She was very pretty, but he had seen girls far more lovely. She had permitted Lancaster's arm to embrace her. And she lived with a Chinaman! But when Ripley had used memory and logic there still remained in him a sensation that was like fear and homesickness combined. More like homesickness, because, although he was miserable, the last thing he wished to discard was the cause of his trouble.

Twice in the night Ripley passed a thin scattering of lights to one side or to the other. He came no nearer to either village than the straight line of his course brought him for he had no desire to appear in Mexican crowds, great or small. It was not the first time he had been south of the border and the freedom of his actions to the north had been nothing compared to the frolics of Jack Ripley on the sunny side of the Rio Grande. He loved the ways of the sleepy republic, but he was more than reasonably sure that the sleepy republic did not love him, and certain memories of contorted brown faces and the rasp and ring of excited voices made him want to glance back over his shoulder more than once. But he kept on traveling steadily, due south.

In the dawn, he found a water-hole and let the mare drink. As he started on, a rabbit jumped from nowhere and scudded towards the horizon. He stopped it with a rifle bullet and toasted the meat over a little fire of mesquite wood. Then he struck a good bit of sun-cured bunchgrass and let the mare graze. The taste of the unsalted meat made him sure that he was out in the open again; the sight of the mare grazing assured him of protection against surprise; so he put his head on the saddle, laid his sombrero on the flat of his face, and went to sleep.

Twice the mare came to him and roused him by touching his sunshade with her nose, but he could not find inside the round of the horizon the cause of her fear, so he slept again. When he wakened, the sun was not very far up the sky but he and Hickory were both refreshed. At his call, she came to be saddled; they struck south again toward mountains gilded with morning and painted blue on their

western slopes and in their ravines. There was
a siesta halt in the afternoon. By evening they
were voyaging through the foothills. In the
middle of the next day they were camped on
the ridge of a long spine that extended to the
east from the Sierra Blanca. It was the one
spot from which he could command a view of
the mouths of both the north pass and the
south. A miserable alkali trickle of a spring
gave them water; there was a sufficient growth
of the bunchgrass; and against the strength of
the noontide a great leaning rock gave him
shelter.

There he waited for three long days until he
knew all about the dotting of cactus in the valley north and the valley south. When a coyote
came and sat down securely on the southern
slope, he spotted the new shape at once and
laughed down the barrel of his rifle at the yellow thief, instead of shooting it. For in the wilderness his rule was absolute that he killed for
food and not for pleasure.

Time lengthened about him, but he had
learned the patience that keeps the body of a
starving cat still for hours while its eyes remain tensely living. There was no monotony.
At night, the shifting of the slow wheel of the
stars made changes in heaven. In the day, between the two glorious fires of dawn and sunset, he could watch the shifting of the colors,
the blazing and the dimming of rocks in the
sun, above all in the swinging shadows of the
ravines, from which new eyes continually

looked out at him. Besides, after weeks of continual action he had now the sense of prolonged rest during which his body was rebuilding. He would come to the end of this pause so repaired in spirit, he was sure, that even the wound in his mind would close and he would be healed of all thought of Ching.

In the meantime, there was food to watch for without ever leaving his place of outlook, and he subsisted on nothing but rabbit meat. The big jacks were lean and tough as wolves, with their hides fitted loosely over the muscles. But all carnivorous life depends on the rabbit as a base in the West; and nearly all that could feed a wolf or a bear could feed Ripley, also. He had learned not to regard monotony but to prize the mere juice of life.

Twice he thought that dust clouds rolling out from the passes might mean the coming of the people he wanted, but one cloud sped outward like a small cyclone and he knew it was a herd of wild horse. That was from the southern pass. From the north another cloud issued the next day in the mid afternoon and at the proper walking gait, but the strong glass with which Lancaster had equipped him resolved the mist and showed him a string of pack-animals. Mules, perhaps.

It was on the evening of the third day that, as the dust of the twilight thickened, he saw the gleam of two fires a mile or so beyond the lip of the northern pass. Those who built the blazes had reached the place under cover of

the shadowy close of day. Ripley was instantly
in the saddle and skimming away to look over
this situation. From a low hill at the verge of
the pass he was able before long to study the
picture in the hollow at his feet.

The two fires were built under big cooking
pots which had been unlimbered from a pair
of heavy wagons; two cooks superintended the
making of supper; four or five men walked up
and down a plot of ground which had been
roped in to make the sort of corral in which
horses may be held precariously, but these
were not horses which were now being bedded
down in rows. They were human beings—
more than a hundred of them raising a chattering sing-song that sounded like a natural
music of complaint. Two guards rode herd
around the entire camp.

It was hard for Ripley to understand the vital nausea that he felt as he listened to the
mournful chatter of the Chinese. Sheep might
crowd and bleat like this; the white men were
the dogs, barking orders. Something went
wrong inside the rope corral. He heard, clearly,
the smack of a fist against flesh; and then he
saw a scattering of the Chinamen from one
spot, like the widening rim of smoke around
an explosion. In the center was a sombreroed
guard. Ripley could trace his nausea to a
source, now. He was taking Lancaster's pay;
and Lancaster was turning this beastly human traffic into gold. That was the reason for
the deep disgust he had seen in honest Tom

Dallas' face. He thought of little Wung Su. There were others like him in this batch of merchandise, frail-handed children.

He himself was unclean in spirit simply because his eyes had witnessed the picture of that rope corral. But in it was the scarface, no doubt, the man wanted by Ching, the man Lancaster was willing to give thousands for; and the mystery drew at Ripley's soul. He would have persisted in his work in spite of the reek of death, as yonder was the reek of slavery.

One of the outriders came past his hill and he called down. The man jerked his horse around.

"Dan Tolliver with you hombres?" Ripley sang out.

"Who wants to know?"

"Friend of Lancaster."

"Come along, waddy," said the other. "I'll lead you to Dan."

So Ripley rode down from the rocks and into the hollow. The night masked the face of his companion, but the first weak rays of firelight showed a week's beard and a bandana in which the wrinkles were hardened by a cement of dust and sweat.

"There's Dan," said the guard, and pointed to a chunk of a man who sat by the fire using its light to read a battered magazine. His head was bent low, a forefinger spotted the words on the page one by one. His face could not be seen but there was character in the red scruff of his neck and in the two big columns of muscle that sprang up his back. He looked up as Ripley dismounted. "Don't kick that damn dust all over me!" he shouted. "Who are you?"

A set of gold front teeth showed as he squinted up at Ripley, who handed him the letter from Lancaster in silence.

It was an open letter and Ripley knew the contents.

DEAR DAN,

The bearer of this is Jack Ripley, that you've heard about. He's on the right side of the fence now and all that. Dallas climbed his frame and chucked him in jail; he chucked himself out again by picking a lot of locks.

Give him the best of everything and let him have the scarfaced Chinese to take along with him. Give the Chinese a good horse. Come to think of it, you'd better give them a relay of horses because they'll be burning up the trail.

Don't rush the rest of your outfit. There were a hell of a lot of sore feet in the last batch.

Sincerely yours,
JIM LANCASTER.

Dan Tolliver pointed out these words one by one with a forefinger. Having finally reached the end, he went over the letter again in the same careful detail. Then he balled up the paper and tossed it into the fire.

"Roll down your blankets wherever you like," he said. "You can have the scarface in the morning."

CHAPTER VIII

It was too easy, thought Ripley. A man with all the mysterious importance that attached to the Chinaman should not be handed over as easily as this. That was why he pressed for a quick start.

"My mare is fresh," he told Tolliver. "I'll take the Chinaman and go along in the cool of the night."

"Your horse is fresh, but the Chinaman ain't fresh. He's been hoofing it all day," said Tolliver.

"He'll be able to sit a saddle for a good few miles," answered Ripley, "and I'm in a hurry."

Tolliver stood up. He was not tall, but there was plenty of him.

"What mixed you and Dallas in one bowl?" he asked.

"Dallas just needed something to do."

"You're the Ripley that did in Tad Sullivan in Carson City?"

"I met Tad once or twice," said Ripley.

"He was a rat," declared Tolliver. "I wish I'd got to him before you did. You owe me something for that."

"Take it out of this," suggested Ripley, and held out the bare flat of his hand.

Tolliver peered at him.

"Yeah, I've heard about you," he said. "But lookat, kid—when I want change, I get it. Leavin' that aside—this damn wall-eyed Chinaman with the hand-carved mug—what's the matter with him?"

Ripley shrugged his shoulders.

"Where's the silver lining in that yaller cloud, eh?" demanded Tolliver. "What sort of juice are they gunna squeeze out of that poor Chinaman once they get hold of him?"

"Tomato," said Ripley.

"What?"

"How do I know what they want with him?"

"Quit being so hard," suggested Tolliver. "Or along will come a cold snap and you might break. All the rawhide wasn't used to make you. What I wanta know—the poor scarface looks like all the rest, only worse. Has he got something inside his head that Lancaster wants to take out?"

"All I got were marching orders," answered Ripley. "I'll take the Chinaman now and start moving, Tolliver."

Tolliver scanned him from head to foot.

"It's after business hours with me, kid," he

answered. "Sit down and cool yourself off by the fire. Is that the mare I've heard about? Is that Dickory Dock, or some damn fool name like that? Why d'you call her that?"

"Because she answers to it," said Ripley.

"What's the price you hang on her?"

"The same that's on my skin."

"I wouldn't give fifty bucks for that mare with you in the saddle," said Tolliver, and turned his back.

Ripley, looking after him, gradually relaxed and found that his jaws were aching; but good advice should be taken from no matter what source, so he unsaddled Hickory and turned her adrift. She would take care of herself, and she would never go far. So Ripley sat down to "cool" himself by the fire and made a cigarette.

Buckets of boiled rice were carried to the Chinese; the yammering from the rope corral died out suddenly; and still three black silhouettes of horsemen circled round and round the enclosure. Nine other men came into the verge of light from the second fire and sat down with deep tins of stew and chunks of hardtack and coffee cups that continually needed filling. A little crooked man who groaned when he sat down took a place near Ripley, on his right. The cook brought provisions to the guest.

"Horse-wrangler?" asked Ripley of the little man.

"Every time I see a bronco hump his back my teeth start aching," said the other. "Yeah,

I put in some time on horses. First time I was pitched it must of knocked all the brains out of my head, because I came back for more. Finally Lancaster kicked me into this job and I've been resting up ever since."

"How does it go?"

"It ain't bad. But there sure is a gang of Chinese."

"I didn't know they were hiked in, like this."

"It's Jim Lancaster's idea. It's slow, but it's sure. We used to get a cargo of Chinamen and some of them would sure die before they'd been carted far into the hills. But this way, they walk themselves hard and healthy. It only takes a week or so to get up near the border. Then Lancaster loads 'em into wagons and takes 'em where Dallas won't be looking. It's a surprising thing how healthy walking makes a Chinaman and riding makes a white man. That's just one of the differences."

"Are they happy?" asked Ripley.

"Why not? They been loaded with promises like dope. Hear that racket?"

A chorus of high-pitched squealing noises mixed with a tin-pan banging came from the camp of the Chinese.

"Fight?" asked Ripley.

"Nope. That's music. If you don't know that's music, I'm telling you. If you listen a while, you start holding your breath. You think you got the beat of the thing—God knows there ain't any tune—and just when you begin to woggle your foot in time with the beat, the Chinese go all wrong."

A single voice howled, the rest being stilled. Dull looks of suffering came over the faces of the men around the fire.

"Chief," said one, "I don't want no pay for this trip. I just wanta go and cut the throat of that howlin' coyote, yonder."

"He's their end man," answered Tolliver, grinning. "They wouldn't know how to make no noise, if they didn't have him to lead off."

"What makes them holler like that? Belly-aches?" asked another.

The "end man" having finished, a yowling chorus took up the good work.

"You'd yell louder than that if you didn't have nothing but rice for your supper," observed Tolliver.

The horse-wrangler confided deeply and seriously to Ripley: "Don't let them kid you. They ain't in pain. They ain't complaining, neither. What I told you first is right. They're singing."

"If you fed them meat, boss," asked the solemn cook, "would they stop their damned racket?"

"If you fed them meat, they'd have to dance, too," answered Tolliver. "They only got fifteen minutes more before they're shut up. Leave them be."

"I heard a guy say what one of their songs meant," said the horse-wrangler to Ripley.

"One of the Chinamen tell you?"

"A bozo that had been out in China. He was an educated bum. He'd gone and killed his

wife or something. That's what education does
to a gent. Makes them cock-eyed. This hombre could talk French and everything, and he
could play a ukulele like nobody's business.
But he'd gone and bumped off his wife. When
a gent gets to thinking too much, you never
know where he's gunna wind up."

"What did he say about the song of the Chinese?"

"It was all about the green land by the river
and the water lilies and the rice fields and the
ducks in the water and the fat pigs in the
mud."

"What else was the song about?"

"Just that sort of tripe. A lot about the great
river that makes slow steps but makes them
forever, and always coming back to the green
land and the water lilies."

"A hell of a lot of water lilies they'll see in
the Rio Grande," said Ripley.

"That's what cooks them," agreed the
horse-wrangler. "When they see the measly
yaller face of the Rio Grande, they sort of
sicken. The fattest faces in the lot all wrinkle
up and turn old. It'll make you laugh when
you see them come to the old Rio. They look at
the river and then they look into the Promised
Land and they see those sandy levels and they
see those mountains with the scalps and the
skins all off of them, and they're fair cooked,
brother."

He laughed a good deal at this repeated
memory.

Then he went back to the sore point.

"It ain't such a bad job. You get a change of scene. You get good pay, and time off."

A gun banged near the corral. All the singing went out as though blanketed. At that, a low groan of relief breathed from the throats of the men about the fire.

"It's over!" said one.

But a single whining voice continued for a few moments.

"That's the end man," observed the horse-wrangler. "He's got all wound up and it takes him a while to wind himself down again."

There was little talk after that. Silence rolled visibly out from the hills and the men felt its presence. Those who spoke did so in murmuring monotones. Tolliver walked about to post a picket over the horses; already snores came from blanketed figures.

Ripley, who had withdrawn with his blanket to the farther edge of the crowd, sat for a time with a cigarette. The mare, busily grazing, was stamping and grinding close to him. The red eye of the fire looked back at him, staring deep into his mind.

It was a bad business, a rotten business. And to fight against it there was a mere scattering of men along the vast frontier with old Tom Dallas working as their brain. How could the law hold? The net it used was woven with meshes far too large and the fish slipped through—and the Chinese. And there was this advantage on the side of the criminal, that he chose his time like a red Indian to strike when the enemy's back was turned.

The mare came to him, picked the hat from his head, let it drop. Then she lay down not a yard away and Ripley, as though he had received a signal which must not be disobeyed, wrapped himself in his blanket and stretched out on the flat of his back. The ground was hard and there was not enough weariness to soften it. Therefore he remained awake for a time with his eyes and his thoughts entangled among the stars before the darkness came over his spirit, and he slept.

CHAPTER IX

A soft whickering—the whisper of a horse—
wakened him. The gray mare had lifted her
head and Ripley sat up.

The night was very black. Clouds had covered the stars and the darkness stifled the face
of the earth. The fire was dead; not an eye of
light looked from that direction. He could not
detect a sound of breathing from the sleepers;
they lay like grave-mounds, irregularly scattered. But following the turn of the mare's
head, Ripley saw a figure moving at the edge
of the camp; it turned at once into the
silhouettes of three men merging into the
darkness as into a fog.

They could not be guards. An unreasonable
sense of strangeness raised him to his feet.
With a gesture he prevented the mare from
rising to follow him as he stepped after the
disappearing group. He had barely paused to

pull on his boots and pick up a gun but in the thick of the night the men were already lost. He followed hastily, stepping long and soft, and presently the same images were wavering before him once more, entering the throat of the pass.

They turned from this, at once, into a little gulley, ragged with outcroppings of rocks. He could see his way better, now, but the closeness of the night still made him keep fending hands before him as he walked through the gulch.

"This will do, Bob," he heard the voice of Tolliver saying.

The three halted; before Ripley could check himself he was almost on them and he held his breath as he slunk in behind a boulder. Leaning on the great stone, he trusted that the outline of his body would melt into the shadow of the rock.

"It's too close," said the voice of the horse-wrangler.

"They'll never hear a gun from here," answered Tolliver. "Do your stuff and we'll go back. You can be riding herd again before nobody knows that you were ever gone from the camp."

"*What* stuff?" asked Bob.

"Steady! Steady!" urged Tolliver. "I drew the first ace, and this is your job."

"Does he know what we're gunna do to him?" asked Bob.

"How would he know?"

"We tied his hands and he might know by that," said Bob.

"Going to hell at a step ain't so bad," remarked Tolliver. "Otherwise he'd have a few years to get to the same place."

"He's the end man, ain't he?" asked Bob. "The one that sings the solos for those hombres?"

"Yeah, he's the one. He's the tin whistle that leads them."

"The nights would be tolerable peaceful without him around."

"Go on and do your stuff. Feel for his backbone and put the gun right under your fingers. It's a sure way."

There was a moment of pause. Ripley grew dizzy. It seemed to him that he was breathing blackness, not air.

"Wait a minute," said Bob. "I'll take a look at him first."

"What's the matter with you?"

"Yeah. Never mind. Leave me have a look at him before I bump him off."

"Well, if you're gunna be a damn fool, here you are."

A match scratched. Ripley shrank farther back around the rock and raised his gun uncertainly. It would be murder to kill a Chinaman. The hand of duty, cold and heavy as stone, lay on his heart. He told himself that he would do something—at the last moment.

The flame of the match spurted from blue to yellow and the trembling light ran with ten-

tative fingers over the weathered faces of the
rocks. It shone into the Chinaman's eyes. He
seemed to be grinning to the ears, for a gleaming white scar ran back from the corner of the
mouth to the ear. He had shoulders humped
thickly forward, as though for the cushioning
of burdens.

There was a gun in the hand of the horse-
wrangler, and the scarface must have known
what was to happen. But he was in fact smiling. The scar so drew and distorted the lower
part of his features that mirth could not appear there; but the smile was in the slight
puckering beneath the eyes—the black, filmy,
patient eyes. The hands tied behind his back
and the stoop of his shoulders made him seem
to be bowing to his fate, helplessly, and the
smile had in it no bravado, but a pitiful helplessness. He looked straight at his executioner;
he seemed in his silence to be saying: "You
and I—we understand!"

And a horror of compassion got hold of
Ripley by the throat. It was a slave facing
death, trying to understand the reason for his
destruction, and smiling because he could not
understand—smiling as beaten men smile
when they reel punch-drunk in the ring.

Why, to shield that poor fellow the lives of a
thousand brave men—who understood—
should be ventured gladly.

"Go on!" said Tolliver.

The match burned to his fingers. It
dropped, a streak of thin red, to the ground,
and shattered into sparks. Tolliver cursed.

"You might of had the light to see by," he said. "Now go on and get it through with, will you? You ain't gunna be yaller, are you, Bob?"

"Wait a minute," panted the horse-wrangler.

He took a turn up and down. "I'm gunna be all right in a minute," he said.

"Sure you are," said Tolliver. "The man in the whole outfit that I'd depend on to use his hands and forget today for tomorrow—you're the only man in the whole damn outfit that I'm sure of, and you wouldn't lie down on the job now. Not after you lost at the cards, fair and square."

"I wouldn't lie down on the job," said the horse-wrangler, with resolution.

"Sure you wouldn't, old timer," said Tolliver, tenderly.

"Only why would the damn fool keep on smiling?" asked Bob with much bitterness.

"Him? Aw, he don't know nothing," declared Tolliver.

"He seen the gun, all right. He ain't as dumb as all of that, is he?"

"Look here, we can't stay here all night, can we? Suppose somebody sees there ain't any night-guard riding—and then the scarface is missed tomorrow morning out of the corral? Wouldn't it look like you done something with him? Hurry it up, will you, Bob?"

"Why would they wanta sock this poor Chinese feller? What's he done?" asked Bob.

"You ain't gunna go into all that, are you?"

said Tolliver in a grieved tone. "If I could of
fetched him away without you seeing, I would
of polished him off and that would of been
that. But you would of seen, so I put all the
cards before you. We played the game and
you lost. You ain't gunna go clear back to rea-
sons, are you?"

"But Lancaster wants this guy, personal.
He'll raise holy howlin' hell if he don't get
him."

"Ain't I told you that I got orders from
somebody a whole mountain higher than Lancaster?"

"Lancaster is the big boss, on this job.
Who's higher than he is?"

"Bob," said Tolliver solemnly, "I'd tell you
if I could. I want to tell you. But I can't. I'd be
a dead man if I talked. Only, you and me
being friends, you take my word that there's
somebody higher than Lancaster and somebody that knows more about the Chinese.
Leave it at that."

"All right," muttered Bob, and stopped his
pacing.

"We've talked it all out," persuaded
Tolliver. "It's nothing but pulling a trigger.
The feller's better dead. If he could know
what's ahead for him, he'd thank you. You
know that, Bob. You ain't such a fool. Just
polish him off. We can roll him into this crack
in the rocks and push a coupla stones over
him. Come on, cowboy!"

"Dan," said the horse-wrangler, "I'm

yaller. Doggone me but I'm ashamed. But I'm yaller. I can't do it."

"You mean that?" snarled Tolliver. "You— you—" For lack of proper words, which would not come to him, he stuttered forth a groan.

"I'm gunna get back to riding guard," said Bob, in haste. "It's easy, Dan. You bump him off. I'll be riding guard. In the morning, we don't know nothing. The Chinaman just must of sneaked away in the night. That's all."

"Sneaked away? Why you—"

But Bob was already on the way back. He began to run, the small stones rattling behind his heels.

After a time, Tolliver said: "Come here." He took the Chinaman by the shoulder and gesticulated with his gun as he talked.

"Bob done me dirt. It's his job," argued Tolliver. "What does bumping off mean to you, anyway? A coupla sacks of rice you don't have to digest, that's all. A coupla years of hell that you'll miss. Mind you, I ain't got a thing agin you. I pretty near like you. You ain't a bad feller. You're just out of luck. That's why you gotta take it like this—"

Ripley came out from behind the rock in three steps.

A gun-butt is apt to crush a skull. Ripley struck with the barrel a little to the side of Tolliver's hat so that the top of the sombrero, folding under the blow, might not offer too thick a cushion to its weight. The blow rang almost like metal on metal. The gun was still shivering in Ripley's grip as Tolliver fell.

A marvel of fighting instinct made him turn as he dropped. He gripped at Ripley's knees with loose, nerveless arms and slid down till his face bumped on the ground.

Ripley cut the ropes that tied the wrists of the scarface and gripped his arm. It was padded deep with thick, rubbery muscles.

"This way—come on—and come fast—pronto—savvy? Quick! Quick!" urged Ripley.

The Chinaman struck into a shambling dog-trot.

"Faster! Faster!" groaned Ripley, and pulled at the scarface's sleeve. But that one gait was the only run which the feet of the Mongolian seemed to understand. At the measured, slow trot he went on with swinging shoulders.

They left the ravine, they cleared the pass, and now as they neared the camp Ripley brought down their gait to a walk. On the verge of the circle of the sleepers, he roused the gray mare with a wave of his arm. She rose and came to him quietly as a ghost. Then, out of the distance, its rhythm broken by the effort of running, Ripley heard a cry advancing.

CHAPTER X

It was the pause, the moment of poise before a blow is struck. Ripley's hands were desperately engaged in the saddling of the gray mare, while the Chinaman moved here and there like a tardy shadow, anxious to help; but Ripley's eyes were seeing the camp where the men lay under the folds of their blankets like the mounds of a graveyard. Off toward the rope corral was silence, but he could see the gradual loom of, and retreat of, a single horseman riding guard—Bob, the horse-wrangler, who had gone back to his post. Then something stirred near the wagons; a man coughed with a groaning sound. That was the cook stirring about at his work, of course, hoping that he could "accidentally" rouse some of the others and gain partners in his misery. To Ripley, as to most cowpunchers, the nature of the camp cook or "doctor" remained

a thing of mysterious evil, a great, dark, inex-
plicable force which caused wretchedness or
content at will. The noise the cook made in his
first stirrings told that the dawn was at hand,
the day's work would soon begin, and his
flight could not but be a futile gesture.

He finished the saddling of Hickory
Dickory and forced the Chinaman up into the
saddle. There Scarface crouched low, in fear,
gripping the reins with one hand, the pommel
with the other; and miserable despair poured
over Ripley's soul. Had he not heard of Mon-
golians who live in the saddle like Arabs? But
this was a useless lump on the back of the
mare, a thing to fall off like rotten fruit from
a tree struck by the wind. Yet the hulk might
be able to cling to the smooth-flowing gallop of
Hickory.

He caught up the first saddle and bridle, re-
maining bent as he stared at the hobbled
horses which were already up and at their
grazing. He would have given much to have
known them by reputation or to have a single
glimpse of them even by moonlight. Instead,
he had to scan them at a glance and try to find
the most important word on the page. He saw
one long-bodied animal, very deep in the
girth, with the outline that promised enduring
strength. He made for that.

As he hurried, Hickory pursued him closely; with the tail of his eye he was aware of the
jouncing of Scarface on her back. And then he
saw that the head of his own proposed mount
was a horrible Roman-nosed caricature set at

the end of a ewe-neck. His heart failed him, but he knew better than to attempt to make a new choice. For behind him, far closer to the camp, Dan Tolliver's wild yell broke out again.

The sleepers had to hear him, now; that voice had to reach them or their dreams.

Out of the darkness before him, like unexpected thought in the emptiness of the mind, a horseman appeared, vaguely seen.

"What's up? Who's hollering back there?" he called to Ripley.

"Ride like hell for it!" said Ripley. "One of the Chinese got away, I think—"

"Away? Tolliver'll raise hell—" said the other, and shot his mustang off at full gallop. He was the picket posted to guard the grazing horses, of course; and, like a lackwit, Ripley had forgotten all about him.

He reached the Roman-nosed grotesque. The beast waited till the last minute to turn and drive at his head with both heels. Ripley side-stepped like a dancer, caught him around the neck with the flying noose of the bridle-reins. At that he stood still, prancing without lifting his hoofs from the ground, swaying like a drafthorse. The saddle clapped on his back; the cinch was caught up and jerked tight, the bit jarred home between unwilling teeth. On the wave of his own frightened impatience, Ripley swung into the saddle.

As he hit the leather he saw the entire camp pitching to its feet; he heard Tolliver's breathless cursing and commands; and then

the Roman-nosed brute that carried him
gripped the bit in its teeth and bolted!

For his own safety, that was well enough,
but what about the helpless human lump that
was on Hickory's back? For certainly she
would outfoot the wind to keep up with her
master. Here she came now. He was half-blind
with the effort of sawing at the iron mouth of
the gelding as the mare strode up beside him
with her reins flying, unhandled, above her
mane and the stirrups leaping at her sides.
Scarface, abandoning all hope except that
which lived in the strength of his hands, clung
with a double grip to the horn of the saddle.
The back of the mare was a mountain of glass
to him, and as fast as he scrambled up one
side to the top he fell off in the opposite direction. Yet he made no outcry. If there were
light enough to see his face, perhaps he would
be found with that battered smile.

Farther back, the camp was a weaving
jumble of dim silhouettes that faded out.
Then the rumbling of hoofs began through the
night.

He tried to quiet the mare, calling to her,
but her only sin was the springing bigness of
her stride. He tried to hearten the Chinaman
but he couldn't make him understand. Then
the gelding blotted his consideration from the
rest of the world. Running was not enough for
him. He started to buck, not steadily, but
throwing in a plunge every fourth or fifth
stride, humping his back into a perfect round,
poking his nose down to the sand.

The easy level going fell away in a steep drop. That would be the end. Even he would have to pull leather to get down that pitch, perhaps, and what would happen to Scarface?

The Roman-nose stuck out his head as though he loved the sharp descent—as though he had wings. He left the brink with a bound, crashed his hoofs into sliding pebbles, and hit the bottom of the draw as a fist hits mud.

The mare was down as soon, her saddle empty, something wheeling obscurely before her—Scarface, of course.

There was one grace—that the impact had knocked rebellion out of the big mustang. He stood puffing while Ripley swung out of the saddle and ran to the end of the reins, leaning over the fallen man. Hickory came with him, sniffing at the prone, living thing.

By the nape of the neck, Ripley caught hold of him. A loose and senseless weight was what he lifted; and behind him came the pouring of hoofs like the rolling of many battle drums. Fear gave them greater speed in Ripley's mind.

He had only to slip onto Hickory's back and peril was ended; he would be away like a leaf in the wind; but he kept remembering that mindless, slavish smile with which the Chinaman had faced death and he could not abandon the poor fellow.

He shook the bulk that his hand was gripping. It stirred suddenly to life. It rose, gasping, with hands extended to feel a way through confusion.

If he were mounted, he would never sit the saddle any more than a sack of bran; at the end of every breath he made little whispering noises; his head swayed senselessly. And that helplessness, for the second time, took overmastering hold on Ripley.

He could not leave the poor devil. And the best he could do was to drag him into the mouth of a shallow gulley that branched away from the main course of the draw. It was one of those meager gulches which the rare rains of an arid country will tear out of the soil. The surface flesh of the earth was gone; only the broken bones beneath remained. Among them Ripley paused and let Scarface drop to one knee while the uproar of the pursuit reached the edge of the draw.

The sharp yelling of the men outlined the danger as white foam outlines the loom of a great wave. Rocks began crashing; each lunging mustang hit the bottom with a thud; and all was so near that Ripley could hear the grunting of the horses as half the wind was knocked out of them. He heard some of the riders snarling at the danger like angry cats; he heard the squeaking of the leathers and Dan Tolliver's wildly cursing voice as he led his host away—straight up the length of the winding draw, and away from his quarry!

The dawn was beginning; the light showed a thin edge, exquisitely curved, with all that spirited grace of distance which painters can never represent. The noise of hoofs grew vague and small.

The Chinaman fell on his face and threw his arms around Ripley's feet.

"Quit it, will you?" said Ripley. "Don't do that, Scarface. You're all right. You're an all right sort of a fellow, and I like you fine. Don't be a damn slave. Quit it, will you?"

He found that he was speaking hardly above a whisper in an involuntary admission that not a word he said could be understood. So he leaned and patted the shoulder of Scarface and the flesh of the Chinaman trembled under his touch.

Something plucked at Ripley's shoulder. It was Hickory, with her ears pricking and the gleam of the dawn in her eyes.

CHAPTER XI

They walked the horses or cantered, because the Chinaman could never sit out a trot. The growing light showed Ripley that he had caught a roan; he should have guessed the color of the mustang by the nature of the beast. It had the trot of a carthorse and a sharp jolt in its gallop, but it traveled with endless heart and courage. And so the sun drifted higher, the heat began to beat up at them from the ground almost as fiercely as it flamed from above on their shoulders.

There were rents in Scarface's clothes. No doubt there were deep bruises under the tears. But he made no complaints. It came upon Ripley with a dreadful certainty that in all Scarface's life he had uttered no laments, and even in infancy, slavery and the dread of the master must have stopped his mouth. Now he

submitted himself blindly to the guidance of
the stranger.

By gestures and signs, Ripley tried to show
him a better way of riding. It was in vain. Val-
iantly Scarface strove to imitate the white
man, but in the first absent-minded moment,
or whenever a canter began or ended, he
dropped the reins and gripped the pommel
with both hands. That had been his first lesson, and he would never learn another proper-
ly. Ripley gave up the effort to teach.

He wanted to be an instructor less than to
be a student of the Chinese man. For he felt
that, since fear disappears with knowledge,
pity should also be banished by the same
thing. He wanted to know Scarface so well
that the pain which continually lay about his
heart when he looked at him might disappear,
might turn into amusement, contempt, scorn.
Anything was better than that aching of the
heart as if for a child that wastes silently, con-
sumed by a fatal disease and so accustomed to
pain that it appears in the face never as a distortion but only as a deepening and a melancholy of the eyes.

Since he could not talk to Scarface with
words, gestures would have to do, and gestures
were not so easy to use on horseback. Therefore he waited until they should make a halt.

Three times in the morning he climbed the
highest hill and used his glasses patiently until they penetrated the heat-waves and proved
that the movements near the horizon were
merely illusions. Nothing stirred. There was

no sign of the hunt that must somewhere be surging behind them.

That trouble, however, was postponed rather than avoided. He was sure of it. The life of the scarface was too important to Dan Tolliver and that other man who, he had said, was above even Jim Lancaster; and the trail could not be abandoned. Far above that would be the agony of rage with which Tolliver must learn that the messenger from Lancaster had been the man who tapped him over the head and then made off with the Chinaman. Such a cause would keep Tolliver's golden teeth locked together in an endless determination. But now there was a vital handicap of time and distance in favor of the fugitives. For Tolliver with his men, having run to the end of one useless trail, would have to return down the draw and cast about until they found at last the sign of the two. And with weary horses they would have to begin the trail. That was why a degree of peace remained with Ripley when he made the noon halt.

He had picked off two rabbits just before. When they found a patch of mesquite and a muddy hatful of water in the midst of the plain, they dismounted and unsaddled. Scarface at once took the rabbits with eager hands, with gestures which showed that he knew all about the preparation of them. And it was he who cleaned the jacks and kindled the small fire whose smoke rose only a step into the air before it dissolved in the wavering heat radiations. Ripley hobbled the roan and

the horses grazèd while he looked over the
land.

The foothills crouched back from the
desert; the blue mountains peered over them;
and not a single dust cloud made its slow
chalkmark across the scene.

He sat down crosslegged to eat rabbit
roasted on little twigs and offered to him with
mournful sounds by the Chinaman. Those
gestures of Scarface indicated sauces heaped
over the meat and delicacies to accompany it,
while the air with which he offered each
brown-roasted tidbit gave it a special flavor. It
was vain for Ripley to thrust the meat back at
Scarface, to indicate that he should eat also. It
was only when Ripley had finished that the
Chinaman would take his turn.

After, he accepted in both hands the
cigarette which was offered to him and the
match with which Ripley lighted it. Scarface
smoked, holding the cigarette between thumb
and forefinger, the palm of his hands turned
out, and he dragged each breath so far down
into his lungs and held it so long that his respi-
ration carried only the thinnest mist. After
that, he seemed to beg permission of the white
man with a two-handed gesture and then
began to sing.

His chin went down, his head to the side,
ripples of exquisite agony appeared in his
forehead and closed his eyes, while he patted
out the time with the flat of his hand on the
ground. Sometimes it was like the howling of a
wolf, followed by the excited yelling of

coyotes; or it was the growling of bigger animals; or it was the drone of a melancholy ghost; but to Ripley there was never anything human in the sounds. He felt a strain in his ears, a pull in his brain which was his vain effort to join a meaning to the jargon.

When the singing ended, the Chinaman remained for some time with the pain of inspiration in his face, swaying his body slowly from side to side. This echo of his delight passed in its turn, and he was able to open his eyes and looked forth, smiling, on Ripley.

"You know one girl want to see you," said Ripley. "That girl—up north—" he thrust a finger in the direction—"Ching!"

"Hai!" cried Scarface, and was still. His frightful mouth gaped, little wrinkles pulling across his cheeks from the white of the scars. Then he jumped to his feet. He uttered a sound from which Ripley could discern a faint resemblance to the name, "Ching," and the whole body of Scarface represented a question. An agony of eagerness froze him as he waited for further information.

"Yes," nodded Ripley. "There—up north—waiting for you—wanting to see you—Ching! Ching!"

And with reverent hands he modeled in the air the face and the body of the small woman.

Over those gestures the Chinaman pored with an utter delight. He cranked his neck to peer around the invisible image and see the front of it. He seemed to recognize the features. He beat his hands together and shouted out a sing-song of strange words.

"Ching?" he kept asking, begging. "Ching?" And he jabbed a finger towards the north.

"Yes," agreed the white man. "Girl waiting for you—nice girl—wants to see you, and her name is Ching. Away up there—Ching!"

He began to laugh with pleasure as he saw the excitement of Scarface, but when the idea had become rooted in the brain of the Chinaman, he grew absent-minded and kept his face turned continually in that happy direction.

They remained in that place long enough for the horses to have revived their strength by resting and grazing; then they mounted and went into the north of their mutual desire. And all through the miles, Scarface was singing. Sometimes the music vibrated so intensely through his spirit that his eyes were shut by the sweet pain of it; but the sounds he made were stifled to the smallness of a fly's song on a blowing wind. Plainly he kept high converse with his soul, and Ripley was silent, observing, smiling a little from time to time. It seemed to him that an innocence more pure than that of childhood was in the spirit of this middle-aged man. And suddenly he wanted to be a householder and have beneath him servants attached to his fortune by something greater than cash on the first of the month.

They halted twice through the heat of the afternoon. Toward the golden time of the afternoon Ripley had grown careless in the visual security which surrounded him and it was Scarface who twisted about in the saddle and made an outcry.

Then Ripley saw the thing streaming straight down on them, and not far away, a cloud of dust whose upper surface rippled swiftly back and away, with small dark forms tossing up and down in the shadow of the mist.

He did not need to use the strong field glass to know that horsemen were driving toward them; but he put his heels in the ribs of the roan and the strong horse swept away at a racing gallop. Beside the gelding, flaunting lightly over the ground, looking about her, ran the gray mare, as ready to dart away with her speed as any sailing hawk is ready to beat its pinions and shoot after an easy quarry.

CHAPTER XII

Their speed was limited to that of the roan; their endurance was his; and he had not enough of either. In five miles this was clear. The sun was near setting and threw more color than light across the world, but the pursuit was not so much closer that the riders had emerged from their dust cloud.

The Chinaman, looking back, saw and understood. He made a gesture to Ripley which plainly abandoned the mare to him. His own life he indicated by clutching at his breast, and this life he threw away with a gesture, as a thing of no importance. After that he loosed both hands from the pommel of the saddle, closed his eyes, and waited for fate, in the form of Hickory's long striding, to jounce him out of his place.

He was already leaning to the side for the fall, a foolish object like a stuffed dummy,

with flopping legs, when Ripley closed the
roan on the mare and grabbed Scarface by the
nape of the neck. His shouted anger made the
Chinaman grab the pommel again and duck
his head in greater fear of the white man's
wrath than of the death that followed them.

The sun was down when Ripley saw, buried
in the smoking fires of the west, a glimmering
like that of eyes, and then made out the growing lines of a little white village. They must
have been climbing an imperceptible rise;
now from the low crest they saw the town entire, with lamplight beginning in it as the sky
darkened; and Ripley turned for it with a
shout. Out of the dusk behind him, he heard a
distant yammering like the barking of coyotes
and the cracking of guns, but still Tolliver's
men were so far away that their yelling and
their guns were pygmy things on a little stage,
a picture rather than a living danger.

The head of the roan was bobbing with ex-
haustion like a cork on running water when
they hit the village street. Through the thick
of the dust the roan kept striking down to the
ruts and chuckholes which were worn in the
winter mud and only dusted over by the summer traffic. The gelding reeled and tossed, but
the gray mare ran as smoothly as a flung stone
into the little plaza which lay before the village church.

Rumor, with a soundless voice, seemed to
have reached every ear in the place by this
time, for men and children were hurrying out

from lighted doorways to see a Chinaman and a gringo who rode for their lives. Bare-headed for the cool of the evening, their smiles and their eyes were flashing; a little musical murmur of pleasure sounded out of many throats as it sounds so often in the crowd about the bull ring. The only loud noises came from the chickens and dogs that scattered with an outcry from the plunging hoofs of the horses. And then Ripley saw what he wanted —a good, tough, shaggy mustang with a gay vaquero gathering the reins and about to mount.

He pitched from his own saddle and reached the Mexican on the run, stuffing good American money into the brown hand. "A hundred and fifty dollars—count them, friend!—and the roan horse along with the cash—"

The vaquero waved his hand, the paper money fluttering in it.

"Ride, brother!" he called. "God and the saints are on the side of a fresh horse and a good rider!"

So Ripley went on across the plaza hitched to a piece of four-legged dynamite that exploded at every jump. He was in the dusty throat of the street beyond before he got his right foot jammed into the stirrup; he was through the whole stratum of kitchen odors and squawking chickens and out on the measureless breast of the desert again before he had the fierce little mustang under control.

The gray mare ran softly beside him, watching the bronco with all the beauty of a high disdain.

Behind them they heard Dan Tolliver's men hit the town as clearly as one hears a train strike the roaring echoes of a ravine, and looking back, Ripley saw the pursuit rush forward onto the open plain.

But that was the last gesture. With increasing distance as well as with the darkening of the day, the riders became obscure, and as the stars came down through the shadows of the sky, the two were alone once more.

The horses were brought to a walk. Safety widened away from them in quiet waves to the horizon.

Ripley found Scarface's hand and gripped it hard.

"Ching," he said.

"Ah-hai!" cried Scarface, and began to laugh happily, like a child.

It was dusk of the next day before they climbed out of the yellow shallows of the Rio Grande above Los Altos where the river spread out in a fordable flat; it was dark when they came to the short row of houses against the river. It seemed to Ripley that through the town there was an extra beauty in the light that streamed from windows and doors, and extra kindness in the voices. For danger was behind him; it was fenced away; and he was coming home.

He took the horses and Scarface to the rear of Sam Li's house, for that was the appointed place at which he must deliver the Chinaman. Even the voice of the river had a welcoming sound and the stars that lay in the still water beneath the bend looked at him with gentle eyes. Somewhere in the back of his mind was the uneasy memory of Tom Dallas, but duty and that promise would have to wait a little. At present he wanted to relax.

When he knocked at the locked door, a light came wavering down the hall.

"Who's there?" asked Chuck Warren's voice.

"Ripley," he answered.

The door opened at once. "That was a damn fast trip," said Warren. "You got him, did you?" He lifted the lamp and stared at the Chinaman. "He ain't any beauty, Jack," commented Warren, "and kind of looks like he'd been rolled in the briar patch. Come on in. I'll tell Sam Li. Come on in this way."

He led the way, shouting: "Hey, Li! Sam Li! Here's Ripley back with the scarface!" And Ripley found himself again in the little room where the shrouded birdcage hung like a black lamp from the ceiling. Chuck Warren said: "The chief'll want to know about this. I'll have him here before long. You're gunna be ace-high with him for this job, old timer."

Warren disappeared, and Ripley turned to find Scarface entranced before the birdcage. He had half extended his hands as though he wanted to catch the cloth from the wires; instead, he held up a finger at Ripley and whistled.

A single inquiring note trilled in answer. Scarface embraced himself with both arms to contain the greatness of his delight and repeated his call; and this time a whole flood of shrill melody answered him.

The huge presence of Sam Li came bulging into the room a moment later. He took Ripley's hand in the big, cool softness of his clasp.

"This is a happiness," he said. "A friend is more than a fountain of gold. Be welcome. Sit down."

He turned to the scarface, who began to bow almost to the floor. Guttural, gentle phrases came out of the fat throat of Sam Li. Whining responses, as though in sorrow, rattled back from the scarface until a door opened and a Chinaman with the look of a yellow bulldog appeared on the threshold. Sam Li waved to him, and the scarface ran to the door. There he paused and turned to Ripley with an eager rush of words."

"He says," interpreted Sam Li, "that you are his master, because you have given him his life, drawing it back like water restored from the desert sand. But he begs you to let him go to speak to Ching."

"Tell him to go," smiled Ripley. And the hump-shouldered Chinaman was instantly gone.

"It was hard to bring him, then?" asked
Sam Li.

"There were a couple of bumps in the road.
that's all," answered Ripley.

"How easily kindness flows from a good
heart!" said Sam Li. "But he will never forget.
Kindness from a stranger is sweeter than a
high post in the court. Shall I have tea brought
to you? Wait for me one moment!"

He was gone again with big, slow, waddling
strides, bowing his enormous head to pass
through the doorway.

And Ripley relaxed on the low couch, his
shoulders against the wall, his legs thrusting
out straight before him. He made a cigarette.

Scarface would be on his knees, now, chattering to Ching. And she would be smiling
above him, making gestures with her delicate
hands.

Lancaster—Ching—the scarface—Sam Li
—well, if he let himself dwell on the mystery,
all peace would leave him. In the meantime, it
was better to rest in body and brain and soul.
Afterward—well, afterward Ching would
come to thank him. There would rise into her
clear face a transient color of shame, remembering how she had last spoken of him with
disdain. She would look up to him and, if her
eyes were wide enough, something from him
would enter them before they were lowered
again.

Above all, he wanted to hear her laughter
again for somewhere in his mind a special

chamber of audience remained open and waiting for that sound.

A door banged at the rear of the house. He
heard Lancaster's voice, saying: "Where? In
here?"

Then the jingling of spurs, the sounding of
many footfalls, and Lancaster came in, followed by that lean giant with the witless
length of face: Missouri Slim.

Ripley eased to his feet to greet them, and
waved. Lancaster shook him firmly by the
hand.

"What's the matter with you, Missouri?" he
demanded of his bodyguard. "Haven't you got
a word for a friend?"

"Friend?" echoed Missouri with his drawl.
"If I took the scalp off that friend I could col-
lect a bounty from the ranchers."

"You're talking like a fool," said Lancaster
in anger.

"Well, I ain't got much of a brain, but that's
God's fault, not mine," answered Missouri.
"I'd rather feed my hand to a wildcat than to
this here."

"He's only about half here," Lancaster
apologized to Ripley. "But it's his guns that I
use, not his brains. Sit down. Where's the
scarface?"

"With Ching," said Ripley.

"Ay, that's where he belongs," said Lancaster, and he sighed from a great depth of
content.

CHAPTER XIII

It came over Ripley then with a perfect knowledge—that he should give Lancaster one word of warning, then whip out a gun and drive a bullet through the wise, restless brain; because he somehow knew, out of the mere nothingness that Lancaster had just spoken, how complete and profound was the evil in him. Why should that knowledge have come to Ripley? He could not have said, but he also knew that the only reason he did not go for a gun was because witless Missouri Slim remained there in the corner, watching everything with little bright, black eyes. The eyes should not have been black. Not in the pallor of that face, or to match that sleek, sandy hair.

"You had to wait for 'em?" asked Lancaster.

"Three days. Then I got a flying start."

"Flying?"

"Tolliver gave me the start."

"He knew I was in a hurry to get the scarface up here," agreed Lancaster. "Tolliver's a tough hombre, but he's useful."

"He was tough enough to take the Chinaman out of the gang the night I arrived and try to kill him."

"Ah?" murmured Lancaster.

"Listen to this snake, and you'll hear a lot more funny things," commented Missouri.

"Send that long streak of nothing away and I'll tell you a few things," said Ripley.

Lancaster shook his head absently: "He stays with me all the time. Don't mind him any more than a parrot. He only has a few words and he has to keep using them. But what you mean about Tolliver—trying to kill the Chinaman? Your Chinaman?"

"I met them in the evening, when they came out of the North Pass. I wanted to take the scarface and start north in the cool of the night. Tolliver shut me up and said the Chinaman was too tired to travel. I woke up before morning. To cut it short, I saw Tolliver taking the Chinaman away from the camp into a gulch beside the pass. Bob, the horse-wrangler, was with him. They were going to shoot the scarface."

"I don't understand. They were dead drunk, maybe?"

"Somebody higher than you had sent Tolliver orders that the scarface was not to come north."

"Higher than me?"

"That's what Tolliver told Bob. I heard him."

"Higher than me—in this racket—that's what you mean? Higher than Jim Lancaster?"

"That's what I heard him say."

"All right," said Lancaster, breathing out the word from a pent store. "I'm listening, all right. Higher than me, eh? Any name given?"

"No."

"Let it—slide," murmured Lancaster. "When I get at Tolliver—well, let it slide. He was going to kill Ching's scarface, was he, after all these months? Well—let it go. You stopped him?"

"I tapped him over the head and got the Chinaman away. They gave us a run that night and the next evening, but we came clear."

"You tapped him over the head? You tapped him *through* the head, you mean! You shot the dog and kicked his face in when he dropped. That's what you done," declared Lancaster.

"Tolliver ain't as much crooked as this hombre," commented Missouri Slim. "Because there ain't as much Tolliver to be crooked. Ripley's lying."

Lancaster turned and glared. "Sometime you're gunna make me do something," he remarked.

"Yeah," agreed Missouri. "You'll be the finish of me, one day. I've always knowed that. But don't you listen to this skunk."

Lancaster turned back to Ripley. "Tolliver tried to bump off the Chinese feller. Then he chased you after you got away. My God, how I wanta see Tolliver! But—I won't forget what you've done, partner. If I'd missed the scarface—if he'd disappeared off the earth— I'd of lost something that means more to me than all the hard cash in the world."

He got out his wallet as though to emphasize the remark. But he added, after a glance at the sheaf of bills it contained: "I haven't got enough here to be worth while—but I'll be seeing you in the morning, Jack."

Sam Li came in, bearing a tray of tea in his fat hands, smiling like a Buddha. He flowed in black immensity across the floor and put down the tray.

"Where's Ching?" asked Lancaster.

"Talking to her man," answered Sam Li. "Happy, too, I suppose. If we listen hard, we ought to hear her voice laughing like a set of small bells. Do you hear them?"

He held up a vast hand to command attention. The straining ears of Ripley could hear, far beyond the house, the thin trembling of a mandolin. That was all.

"Call her down here," directed Lancaster. "I've got to be leaving. So call her down here and let me see her before I go."

Sam Li went into the hall and clapped his hands together and called.

"You can back out of here, now," said Lancaster to the others.

"Not me," answered Missouri. "I don't go

alone with that hombre. Not while he's walking and talking. I ain't that much of a fool."

"Fool?" exclaimed Lancaster. "You're the biggest fool in the world."

Ching came suddenly into the room. She saw Lancaster at once and gave him a smile and a quick little bow of welcome.

"I've got to move along, Ching,"said Lancaster. "I'm saying good-by for a coupla days. I just wanted to know if you'd thanked Jack Ripley for going through hell to bring your scarface up north."

"He? Is he here? Have you brought him? Where, where is he?" cried the girl.

"Where is he? Why, up in your room—talking to you—he's been up in your room talking to you. What's the matter, Ching? What—"

But Lancaster was stopped by the blank face of the girl in which the first smile of happiness was dying to leave an utter blank of bewilderment.

"What's the main idea, Sam Li?" asked Lancaster.

The big Chinaman went to Ching and put his hand across her back and leaned down over her.

"Are you making a little joke on old Sam Li?" he asked. "Little children laugh at old fathers. But don't laugh at me, Ching. This is our good friend, Jim Lancaster, who sent Jack Ripley to get your man. This is Jack Ripley who almost died to bring your man. Why do you laugh at us, Ching?"

"But I'm not laughing," she cried out at

them. "Do you mean that he's here? But I haven't seen him! I haven't had a word with him! Jim—what are you doing to me?"

Ripley drew back to have the entire group under his eyes; but as he happened to near the door the high-pitched voice of Missouri warned him: "Don't try to slide out, Ripley. I'm watchin'!"

He was, with a naked gun in his claw of a hand.

"We'll start understanding this, Sam," said Lancaster. "Damn you if you've let anything slip! I say, if you've let anything go wrong after he was brought up here—"

"Good friend Jim," said Sam Li, "I see what it is. I gave my servant the man to take to Ching. My servant has been stealing a little time to talk about old China before taking him to Ching—but you know that the best servant is always the best thief. I shall punish him, now."

He stepped to the door and smote the flat of his hands together once more.

"Now we shall have a frightened, poor little man," said Sam Li, and turned the immense blandness of his smile back on the waiting group.

The girl ran to the side of the giant and caught his arm.

"I'll see him—I'll see him—I'll see him!" Ripley heard her murmur. "Sam Li, tell me when I can open my eyes and see him—"

But no one came.

And Sam Li seemed to realize that there

was something wrong as suddenly as a horse realizes the spur that drives into its flesh. He sprang through the doorway into the hall and his voice rose to a shout as huge as his body, the sing-song thrilling and chilling through Ripley's brain.

The shout died. The quick echo ghosted away, too. Sam Li came back into the dark of the doorway and his face was pale jade that glowed.

"They are not here!" he said. "My servant is a thief indeed—he has stolen the scarface away—"

"No!" screamed Ching. "He hasn't come to my hand and been lost away! You haven't let them steal him away from me—Sam Li, Sam Li!"

"Take the front way, Lancaster!" exclaimed Ripley. "And I'll take the riverbank. We'll have a chance to—"

Lancaster stopped all talk by lifting his hand. "It's no good trying to overtake him," he declared. "We'd be chasing a dead man, most likely. A two-minute start is a mile. And them that want him, they'll give him wings."

He began to curse in a whisper. The girl, twisted over in an agony as though a bullet had torn through her body, began to sob. The sound was very small and there was a shudder in it that ran through Ripley's heart too. Lancaster went across the room and tapped her sharply on the shoulder.

"Quit it, Ching!" he commanded. "The damn scarface is gone and you'll never see

him again. I done my best and it wasn't good
enough. Sam Li let them get him when I
wasn't looking. But you—you straighten up
and quit crying, will you?"

"Yes," she whispered, straightening.

Lancaster took her by the shoulders. Her
head rose, but it fell over to the side. Ripley
saw the white of her face and he looked quietly down to the floor to keep from seeing it
again.

"You'll never see him again," repeated
Lancaster. "Now that they've got him, they'll
kill him. You'll never see him again—and
where does that leave me?"

She said nothing. Ripley had to look up
again and he saw that her eyes were closed. In
his arms and against his breast he was aware
of an emptiness.

"But I've got to learn about me," said Lancaster. "He's gone. And are you throwing me
over the shoulder to fall on my face? I've got
no hold on you, now—and where do I slip to?"

"Hush, hush, my friend," said Sam Li.
"Let me take her away. When the wine cup is
snatched from the lips, the spirit faints. Come
with me, my child. Quietly—so—so!"

His great arm supported her. Her head fell
over against his shoulder as he drew Ching
from the room.

CHAPTER XIV

Lancaster was striding up and down, stopped now and again, abruptly, by his thoughts.

Ripley said: "How about a little information, Jim? You're on the inside. Let me know what it all means—what hitched the scarface to the girl?"

"Who told you I was on the inside?" demanded Lancaster. "The inside be damned—and I'm damned, too—and so are you. And the whole game is a fool's game, and I'm the biggest fool."

Sam Li came back into the room, the floor muttering a little under the gigantic weight of his step.

"Come here!" commanded Lancaster.

Sam Li went to him. "I am unhappy for you, my friend," he said.

"Leave it off, will you?" shouted Lancaster.

Rage choked his voice off thin. "Have to keep on the damn gibberish even with me? Tell me the straight of this. What happened? What did your flatfaced Chinaman do with the girl's man? You know, and you'll tell me, by God!"

Missouri Slim moved from his corner with a long and noiseless step that carried him sidelong until he was behind Sam Li. There he paused. A smile kept flashing on his face, crookedly twisting it, going out, appearing on the other side again.

But Sam Li was apparently unconscious of danger. He merely said: "At a time like this, when there is grief and trouble between friends, silence is best. Let us be silent until we have thought about a new thing to do."

Lancaster said through his grinding teeth: "I've got the idea now. It's a flat double-cross. You've got Ching, and that means you've got me. If the scarface comes to Ching and talks five minutes to her, she's through with you. She's finished with you. And that means as soon as she goes that *I'll* be finished with you, too. So what do you do? When the scarface comes here, you put him out of the way. You wipe him out—and then the game is to start all over again—the scarface on the loose somewhere—and Lancaster working like a dog on his trail—and the girl still here—damn your rotten heart, I see the game clear through! And I'll—"

Ripley slid his hand inside his coat to the butt of his gun. He saw Missouri lean a little forward to have perfect balance for the shot he was to fire into Sam Li.

The Chinaman said in his soft, deep voice which filled his words with a sort of super meaning: "When I was a young man, such talk would have made me very angry. Now I am not angry. I am too old."

"D'you know where you stand? D'you know where you are?" snarled Lancaster, chewing up his words.

"When I was young," said Sam Li, "I went to war. There is one grief to me now—that I must die with a bullet through my back."

The thing struck Ripley heavily. It struck Lancaster, too, and made him jerk up his head. And suddenly Ripley felt that he was under control again, just as a bolting horse is under control when its head comes up.

"I'm being a fool," said Lancaster. "If I believe in you now, I'm the biggest fool in the world. God, if you're crooking me, Sam Li—if you're crooking me—"

Sam Li said nothing, and his silence was a greater burden than the rage of Lancaster could support. It diminished suddenly. And he said: "Ripley, I'll be seeing you. Stay here, if you want—or up there in the Mexican's house. There's plenty more to do. Wait a minute—I've lost my head a little and started yelling around. But I'm not forgetting what you've done. You caught the fish. Somebody else chucked it back in the water."

He turned on his heel and went through the door. Missouri Slim followed him, his eyes always on Ripley so that he sidled through the doorway in order to keep his glance on the enemy to the last instant.

There was left Sam Li, vast, still, impassive.

"It is our friends who empty our hearts," he said gently, after a moment, "because only they possess the key."

He turned more directly to Ripley.

"Will you come to see Ching?" he asked. "Because now she hungers for good words as the summer earth hungers for the rain."

"Yes," said Ripley. "There's nothing that I'd rather do than see her, if she's not ill."

"Her heart is empty; if it is filled a little she will be well again," said Sam Li. He led the way out of the room with his slow, monstrous strides. And he continued as they went up a stairway: "Who can have much happiness? All that we ask is enough to fill the hand, enough to play with. Though her poor man is gone, give her a few thoughts of him and he will begin to live again in her mind. Hope will not die easily. It may be struck through the heart, but still it has wings that will keep on flying."

He came to a door which he pressed open and drew Ripley with him into a fragrant little room. The hanging light showed on the window sill a blue bowl filled with sunny yellow flowers, and a screen on which birds of green and scarlet and blue flew through marvelous foliage.

The girl lay flat on a bed whose cover spilled toward the floor; she had a pillow hugged against her face.

"Ching," said Sam Li, "I have brought you the man who can give you comfort. He will tell you about the man we have lost. But if we have lost him, we shall find him again."

"No," mourned the girl, "he is lost—he is lost—I shall never see him again!"

"Think," said Sam Li, "that a thing worth stealing is worth keeping. And so they will keep him."

"Do you believe so?" cried Ching, lifting herself suddenly, sitting on the edge of the bed.

Sam Li drew out a silken handkerchief and dried her face. Ripley watched the closing and the opening of her eyes as she submitted to that care. He could have done better than Sam Li, he felt.

"This is our friend," said Sam Li. "This is *your* friend, Ching. Must he remain standing?"

She got up and offered a place to Ripley on a couch that was a mere pile of cushions against the corner of the wall. But he remained standing.

"I just wanted to tell you about him, what a good fellow he is," said Ripley.

"He is so good that no one is like him," said Ching. "Did you notice that?"

"Yes," said Ripley.

"And his poor, dreadful face!"

"Yes," said Ripley.

"Could you see the kindness in it, after all?"

"I did see it."

Sam Li drew back to the corner. He stood there immobile. "This is much better," he said. "When words begin, peace will follow. Tell Ching how you found him, and how you were hunted!"

"Hunted?" said the girl.

"I'll tell you this," said Ripley. He wanted to come closer to her. He felt that if he were nearer she could see his thoughts more clearly. "When we were pretty hard pressed and they were closing on us, the horse I was riding got pretty tired. And he wanted to give me his horse. He wanted to throw himself away. He would have dropped out of his saddle to let me take his place. I had to grab him by the back of the neck."

He laughed a little.

"Did he do that?" repeated the girl. "Did poor old Dong do that? Did he want to give you his horse?"

"What horse was it?" asked Sam Li.

"It was fresher than mine," said Ripley, hastily.

"But how could he ever sit in a saddle at all?" asked Ching.

"He let the reins go and held onto the pommel."

"With both hands?"

"Yes."

She began to laugh. He wanted the sound to go on and on. It was filling that empty chamber in his mind.

"We tried to talk," said Ripley, when the

laughter fell away, "but there was only one word that we both could understand."

"He could say two or three words of English in the old days," said the girl.

"The only one we could both understand was Ching."

"Do you hear?" said Sam Li. "People who love the same thing must love one another."

"Hush, Sam Li," said the girl, and lifted a hand.

"Why are you so ashamed?" asked Sam Li. "Why else do you think he went for Dong?"

"He was sent," said the girl. "Jim Lancaster sent him for Dong."

"Was that why he was ready to die for Dong?" asked Sam Li.

"Hush, hush!" pleaded the girl, and she added: "I'm sorry. Chinese people have different ways. Forgive Sam Li, but tell me how Dong could have vanished out of his house. They will kill him! And poor Dong—he will smile while they *murder* him!"

Now, for an instant of pity, Ripley almost forgot her, remembering Dong's battered smile as he faced the gun. He said: "They won't kill him. Remember what Sam Li says. A thing that's worth stealing is worth keeping. And there's something else—that I'll follow him till I find him for you."

"For you," said the booming, gong-like voice of Sam Li. "Do you hear, Ching? For *you* he will find him."

She made a gesture of infinite gratitude to Ripley; and because of Sam Li's big, blundering speech, wrinkles of pain came into the smooth of her forehead above the smile. But Sam Li came closer so that, as the girl rose, he stretched out his enormous arms and half surrounded them both.

"If there were only one day or one year for our lives, how much happier every moment would be!" said the Chinaman. "Hold out your hand, my good friend."

Ripley held out his hand.

"Look into his hand," said Sam Li. "Now, looking closely, do you see the life he has offered for you? When they rode after him and their yelling came in his ears, it was for you that he kept Dong in the saddle. That was the life—see it in his hand!—that he was offering to you. How shall you thank him, Ching?"

"With all my gratitude, all my days!" said the girl.

"Ha!" said Sam Li. "Is he offering money for pigs and chickens? Is he asking for words and smiles? When a man holds his life in his hand, he is trying to buy love, Ching. How much will you give him?"

Ripley tried to protest but the words swelled in his throat and would not come out. He found himself staring with great eyes, afraid; and the girl was staring in the same fear. She was still looking at him when she cried out: "Sam Li, Sam Li, what do you mean? What is it?"

He answered in Chinese. The smooth, deep rumble of his voice played through the intonations and the pitches of that speech as a river lightens and darkens and swells over the boulders that lie unseen in its channel. He had been speaking of love like a grandfather to children but now a larger theme seemed to possess his voice and, by the inward intentness of her eye, Ripley knew that the girl no longer was seeing him. Perhaps the whole majesty of the timeless Orient was speaking now from the tongue of Sam Li; and what did Ripley comprehend except horses, beef on the hoof, ropes, and saddles and guns? He was present here like a non-believer at a temple of mysteries. That was why he shrank slowly back from the girl and found the door, and at last he was outside it and going down the narrow flight of steps into the lower hall.

He passed the open door of the room in which the shrouded birdcage hung.

How much that was true and beautiful was shadowed forever from his eyes?

He got out of the house, quickly, and to the side of Hickory Dickory. Why had he given her such a foolish name? She was worthy of something better. Ching or Sam Li—they would not have given even a canary such a nonsensical title. They would rather have picked out a name from among the stars and given it to one of the gleaming little beauties.

He walked up the bank of the river. He was glad that there was a bit of distance between him and the house of Oñate, because he could use all the steps to help himself back to a proper self-respect. The mare, as her habit was, walked a little before him as soon as she

had made sure of the direction; but now and
then she paused for him to catch up with her
and run his hand over her shoulder and neck.
He did this absently. His mind was so filled
that it seemed only a moment before he saw
the loom of the squat little house where Oñate
lived.

CHAPTER XV

Out of the gray of the morning, at the open door of the house of Oñate, a voice growled quietly: "Ripley—Jack Ripley!"

Ripley, brought quickly out of a deep sleep, sat up from the blankets. The house was as dark as a wolf's throat. Beyond the glimmer of the doorway he saw the black trunk of the tree that gave summer shade to the threshold. Then a silhouette, half crouching, stole between him and the entrance.

"Never mind, Jose," said Ripley.

Jose Oñate checked himself with difficulty. His muttering voice sounded from a false distance. "No one comes for good before sunup," he declared.

Ripley was dressing rapidly. Something whispered over the floor beside him—the bare

feet of young Juan Oñate. The eyes of a boy
are as bright as those of a cat, even in
darkness.

"Let me go first, to see," said Juan.

"I'll call if I need you," said Ripley, without a chuckle. He stepped to the door, and
looked guardedly out. "Is that you, Tolliver?"
he asked.

"Here I am, Jack," said Tolliver, stepping
into full view.

His hands were empty. He was so narrow in
the hips and so big above that he looked like
two wrong halves fitted together.

"How are things?" asked Ripley.

"You could make them better, kid."

"You make me feel pretty good," answered
Ripley. "Maria, light a lamp."

More feet made hushing noises on the floor.
A match scratched; it threw small blue and
yellow lightnings through the room. The lamp
chimney screeched against its guards, the
flame ran across the wick, the chimney settled
back in place, and a mist disappeared at once
from the heated glass. The four Mexicans
stood gazing. Jose Oñate had his right hand
behind his back and his eyes never left the
form of Tolliver. Little Anna slipped up to
Ripley and caught his hand.

"Away from him—little fool—to touch his
right hand!" breathed her mother; and the
child fled into a corner.

"Come in, Dan," invited Ripley.

"I'd as soon walk into a den of snakes,"

answered Tolliver.

"They'll never touch you, and they only talk three words of English. Come in. We'll have some breakfast. Maria, fire up that stove."

The woman was busy at once, always glancing over her shoulder every moment toward the stranger. Anna helped her. Young Juan stood by his father in an attitude of one ready to deliver the attack.

Tolliver made grudging steps into the house. He snuffed the air.

"Beans and garlic and peppers. I've smelled this before. Kind of thick to sleep in, ain't it?" he asked.

"I've got a good conscience and that makes me sleep easy," said Ripley.

"Whatcha ever do for the Mexicans, here?" asked Tolliver.

"Just a little thing a long time ago. Sit down, Dan."

Tolliver took off his hat—with his left hand. He kept the right close to the butt of the gun on his thigh. Now that the hat was off, the gold showed in his grin. Even by lamplight, his face was burnished red.

But most noticeable of all was the heavy bandage that encircled his head. It covered his forehead almost down to the eyes. He took a three-legged stool, moved it back against the wall, and sat down.

"Sorry about that," said Ripley, nodding.

"About what? The crack over the head?

That's nothing. Gave me a hell of a headache, is all. I was gonna peg you out for it, if I caught you."

"Peg me out?"

"Old time Comanche taught me that. You peg a man out on the flat of his back and leave him there. The sun fair burns the lids off of his eyes. His face boils up in blisters. His lips crack open. There ain't no shade. A gent that's pegged out, he comes to realize how damn useful a hat is. Understand?"

"You were going to peg me out?" said Ripley.

"It only takes a coupla days," said Tolliver. He laughed a little. His golden teeth flashed. So did his eyes. "You give your man water and everything, but it only takes a coupla days."

"Ever try it?"

"Yeah. Maybe. What's this slop?"

Maria was offering a cup of red wine, to the stranger. "Vino," explained Ripley. "They'll pass a lot of stuff down your throat till I tell them to cut it."

Tolliver took the wine. He massaged his bullneck tenderly.

"You're quite a guy," he said to Ripley. "By God, there's something about you that kind of tickles me. You got a sense of humor, is what you got." He laughed, to prove it. Then he took a swallow of the wine. "Lousy stuff," he said. He drank the rest of it and held out his cup for more. "If we hadn't got the Chinaman back, I'd be kind of sore at you," he said.

"You got him back, did you?" said Ripley.

"Yeah, whatcha think?" asked Tolliver. "Which brings me down to why I'm here. But these bozos—they don't savvy English, eh?"

"No."

"They don't look it. You know what I think?"

"What do you think?"

"It's the swell thing about our country, the education. When you think what schools do. It's a kind of a wonderful thing. The way it limbers up the brains of a lot of these dumb clucks."

"Is that why you came here—to put me in school?" asked Ripley.

"That's good, too. I could laugh at that, another time of day," said Tolliver. "But getting down to business, I'm going to let you in on something. I'm going to let you right in at the top. You're a lucky hombre, and I'm gonna let you in."

"Who told you to?"

"The chief—the big chief—the top chief of this whole Chinese job."

"I thought that Lancaster was the top."

"Him? He thinks he is. He don't know enough to know no better. But the chief wants you; that's the good news that I come to bring you, kid."

"He wants me for what?"

"To take Lancaster's place; and think of

that! You only show your mug down here on the border, and everything starts to come your way. Lucky ain't any name for it."

"How much, brother?"

"How much? How would I know? If Jim Lancaster don't make twenty grand, I'm a liar. Twenty grand every year! And you step right in at the top of everything—understand? You're the top—under the big chief."

"Who is that?"

"You'll find out, after you sign up."

"How do I sign up?" asked Ripley.

"That's easy, too. You're trusted, Jack. All you have to do is to give me your word of honor that you'll be with us for one solid year, no questions asked. One year for twenty grand!"

He sighed and shook his head.

"The job is running Chinese over the border, eh?"

"Sure. That's the main part. There's a few other little things."

"I don't want it," said Ripley.

Tolliver rose to his feet. His face lengthened with bewilderment.

"Say it again, slow," he begged.

"Tell your chief that I don't want any part of his job. I've seen enough of it. And to hell with it."

"Well—" began Tolliver. He studied Ripley. "I see," he said. "I seen from the first that you were kind of queer. Now I see *how* queer. Cockeyed, is what you are."

"Suppose you breeze along," suggested Ripley.

"Asking me to go? Well, what would I want to stay for, in a dive like this? You're turning the chief down?"

"Flat."

"Plain nutty!" decided Tolliver. "But let it go at that! So long, kid. I thought that I was comin' with the band; but I wasn't even out of school. So long. I hope to God you get better brains before long."

He went back to the door.

"You ain't turning this down because you think it's phony, are you?" he asked.

"I know it's straight," answered Ripley.

"And still you—oh, well, there's gotta be damn fools in the world, I suppose."

He turned his back, with this farewell, and walked into the growing light of the dawn, which began to rival the strength of the lamp inside the room. The four Mexicans remained staring at Ripley until Juan slid noiselessly out to take observations of the enemy in his retreat.

CHAPTER XVI

The slow dawn had reached the stage of rose and gold when a second messenger stood in the doorway of the Oñate house. It was Missouri Slim, bending to look inside. "You!" he said, pointing a lengthy forefinger at Ripley.

"What about?" asked Ripley.

"The boss wants you. Come along."

Ripley went along.

Jose Oñate insisted on currying and brushing the gray mare, though she winced under his vigorous touch. The other three Oñates grouped about to watch their hero. Juan held his stirrup. Anna had scrubbed her face to rosiness and lifted it for a kiss. Maria puffed and smiled in the background.

But before Ripley mounted, Jose had a chance to say at his ear: "That man has much devil. Do you know him, señor?"

"I know there's a devil in him. It's all right,

Jose," said Ripley. He added, softly: "You
travel all over this part of the country, Jose.
And when you're traveling around, if you see
a Chinaman with scars that run from his
mouth back to his ears, remember where you
saw him and which way he was going. And if
you hear a Chinaman sing like a brake squealing and a rooster crowing, remember where
you heard it, will you?"

"I shall listen and watch," agreed Oñate.
And Ripley swung up into the saddle.

He was far from sure that it was all right.
His position with Lancaster, at the moment,
seemed strong, but one whisper of the arrangement between Dallas and his deputy
would be enough to end Ripley's days if it
came to the ears of the smuggler.

Missouri Slim, who kept his horse reined
half a length to the rear, merely said: "There's
a job up the line."

And they took a trail through the hills, with
the sun rising behind them and striking
warmth against their shoulders.

"Look here, Missouri," said Ripley, "what
made you start hating my gizzard the first
time you laid eyes on me?"

"It's a kind of funny thing, about that,"
said Missouri, half lost in contemplation. "It's
dead easy for me to hate. When I was a kid,
we used to move around a lot and I was always
going to new schools. Well, the minute I got
into a new schoolyard, I could take a look
around and pick out everybody that I was
gunna hate."

"How could you tell 'em?"

"It's dead easy if you got a talent for it," answered Missouri. "Sometimes it's a little gent with a quick looking sort of a face; and sometimes it's a chunky hombre with a grin on his mug and the look of a chew of tobacco in each cheek; sometimes it's an old goat with a beard, and his chin pulled way in. Some-tines it's just a plain handsome, easy-looking hombre like you; but the minute I look, I can tell the gent that I've got to hate."

"How does it turn out, usually?" asked Ripley.

"Mostly I'm right. Mostly always right. There's some of them have tried to open me up with knives, and some have tried guns on me."

"But they never got you?"

"They whittled a lot of nicks in me, though, and they shot some chunks out of me, too. But I was always watching, just the way I'll always be watching you."

"If you were Jim, what would you do with me?"

"Tie a rock to your feet and drop you in the river," answered Missouri, cheerfully.

"It does me a lot of good to hear how you stand," remarked Ripley. "What tied you to Lancaster, in the first place?"

"He licked me," declared Missouri. "I ain't very strong, but I'm fast, and nobody never licked me till I run into Jim. He licked me good. It was a hell of a licking." He shook his head and sighed. His smile was that of one who remembers a thing of beauty. "And I been working for him ever since, waiting for the day when I'll have the nerve to tackle him again. Two or three times I've woke up in the morning and figgered that I was ready to tackle him, but when the time comes, the courage all sort of oozes right out of me, and my stomach feels holler."

"How long you been with him?"

"I've done enough talkin'," said Missouri. "Even if I liked you, I wouldn't like talking this much. Shinny on your own side for a while, will you?"

So they kept on the trail in a long silence, while the sun rose higher and the strength of it drenched the sky and set the heat waves dancing high over rocks and low over the pale, burned grass. At such times, the head of a man is apt to fall. He counts the cracks in the ground and listens to the squeaking of the saddle leather and notices the way the sweat starts in small runlets down the neck and shoulders of the horse, drying to salt before they have gone very far.

They climbed to the top of a low divide. Alkali flats spread out from the base of the hills, dappled spots of blinding white. There was not much wind but it carried an acrid, invisible dust that made the throat instantly dry and sore. A town appeared, the white of its walls softened by one blue layer of distance. It was Dalton, Ripley remembered.

At that moment a rider came around the edge of some tall boulders. It was Jim Lancaster, riding a silken brown gelding with the shuffling feet and the reaching, thin neck of a thoroughbred.

"That's a good one," commented Ripley, as he greeted Lancaster.

"What happened with Sam Li and Ching?" demanded Lancaster.

"A lot of Chinese talk. I didn't understand it," said Ripley.

"How did it sound?"

"Like running water."

"I've heard 'em go along like that," agreed Lancaster. "A girl like Ching, would you think that she'd put up with him? Here's something for you, kid."

He took a flat fold of bills out of his coat pocket and passed it to Ripley. "Thanks," said Ripley, and put it into his own coat.

"That's what comes of gambling," commented Missouri. "You can't please a gambler. No matter how much you give him, he remembers where he's lost more than that, before."

"Will you listen to me, Missouri?" asked Lancaster.

"Sure. Why not?"

"I ain't up out of bed long enough to be really awake. So shut up, will you?"

"Sure I'll shut up. Why not?" answered Missouri, pleasantly.

And he was silent as the three went on. "We've got a little job up the line," continued Lancaster. "Nothing very important, but I want you to get your eye lined up."

"Is that a clean-bred one?" asked Ripley.

"As far as I know. I never sat on one that could move like this gelding, Jack. He cost something, but he's worth it. You take a mare like Hickory, there. She's pretty. She's like a picture. But there ain't the whalebone and the muscle in her."

"I'll beat you to the three rocks, yonder in the flat," suggested Ripley.

"How much will you beat me for?" asked Lancaster.

"A hundred bucks."

"I wouldn't mind taking the coin. Where do we start?"

"From here!"

"Let her go!" cried Lancaster, and sank the lash of his quirt in the tender flank of the gelding.

There was a furlong of slope to cover before the flat and the incline so lengthened the stride of the brown's long legs that it was a half a dozen lengths in the lead before the two straightened out. Then Hickory Dickory laid her ears back and went to work, with Ripley slanting his weight forward and giving the mare just enough of a pull to balance her.

A dry ditch cut the flat unexpectedly. The loose-legged brown flung high across it; Hickory clove the air low and long and landed with her nose at the tail of the gelding. The race was in Ripley's hand. He saw Lancaster throw one glance behind, with fear in his face; then, to the rear the sound of a fall made him glance back in turn.

Missouri's horse was down, scrambling to its feet in haste, and Missouri himself lay flat on his back with his arms flung wide and the wind lifting a cloud of alkali dust from about him. Chance, at last, had stripped Lancaster of his all-watchful bodyguard.

Half a dozen strides brought Hickory beside the gelding, and Ripley tapped Lancaster between the shoulders with the muzzle of his revolver.

"Slow it up a little, Jim," he suggested.

Lancaster, over his shoulder, looked at the gun and then at Ripley. Automatic muscles pulled his mouth into something like a grin. Then he reined in the gelding.

"Unbuckle your gunbelt," directed Ripley. "Take it by the buckle end and pass it across to me. That's the trick," he nodded, as he was obeyed.

They were at a canter, now.

"If it's a play for loose cash," said Lancaster, "I've got about five grand on me."

"It's not a play for loose cash," answered Ripley, hooking the gunbelt over the pommel of his saddle. "It's a play for you, Jim. I've got a steel badge somewhere on me."

"Dallas?" asked Lancaster.

"That's right."

The town of Dalton was near. The three rocks for which they had raced flashed past them, well on the right. Lancaster was perfectly unmoved in voice and expression; there was only an extra squinting of the eyes as though he were peering at small objects lost in the horizon mist.

"Away back there in the beginning, I had an idea," said Lancaster. "About Dallas turning you loose. That jail-break was a little too slick and easy."

"Maybe it was," admitted Ripley. "I just played the hand that was dealt out to me."

"The thing that beat me was your reputation," confided Lancaster. "You had a pretty clean name. Didn't think you were the kind for a dirty job like this."

"I've been packing that badge all the time. Suppose that you or one of your gang had spotted that badge? I was playing a stake, too, Jim."

"Yeah, you were playing a stake," said Lancaster. He nodded. "It's all right. I ain't hollering. Not me—"

He looked back.

"It'll be a spell before Missouri gets on his horse again," he remarked. "All kind of worked out for you at once, didn't it?"

"I started hoping when the horses started running," answered Ripley.

"Old Dallas!" murmured Lancaster. "What did he have on you?"

"A frame that was worth about fifteen years."

"You don't say! Old Dallas using the bean like this—it's sure a happy surprise! What else do you get out of the job?"

"Just the clean slate."

"Wait a minute, kid. You don't want a clean slate. You want a checking account."

"I'm settling down," answered Ripley.

"To what? A house and a job, somewhere?"

"That's the main idea."

"Found the girl, have you?"

"I have."

"Has she found you?"

"I wouldn't be too sure about that," said Ripley.

Lancaster, throwing back his head, laughed heartily.

"That's what beats me," he said, when he could speak. "Jim Lancaster as a wedding present! Can you come anything over that?"

He began to laugh again, putting his hands well back on his hips, so that it was only chance that enabled Ripley to see a lean finger hook down inside the rim of the trousers. A shadowy lump moved up in answer beneath the cloth. "Don't do it, Jim," cautioned Ripley.

Slowly, as though there were reluctance in the fingers themselves, Lancaster's hand dropped away. "All right," he said. "All right. It was a rotten chance, anyway. Just a little two-barreled, old-fashioned pistol in there, but it's played some nice tricks for me when the boys weren't looking. And here we are, old timer. That's Cracken's saloon, where Bozeman killed Little Minnie. There's the blacksmith shop where that road-agent, Duf-

fy, was caught. If I've got to go to jail, it's better to go where I've got such a lot of old memories all around me."

They had entered the main street of the
town. A whirlpool of dust formed before them
and raced away, gathering size. That was
when Ripley remembered that smuggling was
only the smallest of the crimes for which Lancaster was wanted. The dust-cloud struck a
building; the head of it sailed for an instant
longer and then dissolved in the bright air.
And all the courage, the keen cruelty, the craft
of Lancaster would vanish like that. They
would choke it out of him like a wolf at the
end of a dragging rope.

CHAPTER XVII

The jail in Dalton was an old house with some cages of steel bars erected in a few of the rooms; Ripley housed Lancaster in one of those cages and sent the Negro who was cook and man of all work around the jail to wire the following telegram to Marshal Tom Dallas: HAVE LANCASTER JAILED IN DALTON STOP TOWN FULL OF HIS FRIENDS STOP URGE YOU COME WITH STRONG ESCORT TO REMOVE HIM FROM JAIL THAT WILL HARDLY HOLD A RABBIT.

Then he sat down to wait. The deputy sheriff gave him a double-barreled, sawed-off shotgun, some ammunition, and some weighty advice. "There's a whisper around town," said the deputy, "that Lancaster will pay several thousand bucks to any party that'll pry him out of this jail. If I was you, I'd make up my mind quick, whether I was going to fight a mob or not."

"I've made up my mind," answered Ripley. "Start a whisper around the town for me, will you? Tell the boys that I've loaded both barrels with buckshot."

The deputy sheriff was an albino blond with gray eyes. The yellow of his teeth when he smiled gave his face its most characteristic strength. He smiled now as he looked Ripley over. "I'll tell 'em something else," he said. "I'll tell 'em that you like it!"

In the narrow corridor in front of Lancaster's cell, Ripley made down a roll of blankets for the night and put a chair for the day. He had no intention of letting the prisoner out of his sight until Dallas took over the responsibility.

From the barred window, he could see the drift of the curious villagers past the jail. It was not long before the window of the famous prisoner was located, and after that there was rarely a time when at least half a dozen boys and a few grown ups were not gathered to stare. But no visitors were admitted inside the jail.

The day turned very hot and still in the middle of the afternoon. Lancaster lay flat on his back on the cot in the cell with sweat running visibly on his face. He was flat-chested. He had pulled off his outer shirt and his naked arms were white to the elbow, sun-blackened below, and covered with hair. Except for the hair, they looked like the lank, powerless arms of a boy. Ripley looked at him with disgust, and with a certain pity. The sweat kept on running. Now and then the flat chest heaved for a greater breath, but there were no complaints.

The Negro, Josh, tapped on the door and pushed it open. He left a telegram for Ripley and a small package labeled: FOR JACK RIPLEY. PERSONAL.

The telegram from Dallas said: CONGRATULATIONS WILL ARRIVE DALTON TOMORROW EVENING GREAT WORK.

When he opened the package he found a thick sheaf of bills, compacted by heavy pressure until they lay as snug as the pages of a book. Lancaster sat up and watched the patient counting of the money.

"Ten thousand," said Ripley, looking at his prisoner.

"That's a good slice," commented Lancaster.

Ripley wrapped the package carefully again. From the door he shouted for Josh and when the gray-headed Negro came running he said: "You know the look of the fellow who brought this package?"

"He's kind of tall and loose-jointed and—"

"Throw this at his head, will you?" asked Ripley, and gave up the treasure.

Then he went back to his chair and rolled a smoke. The sweat had begun to drip rapidly down his own face; water beaded the backs of his hands.

"I forgot something," he said to Lancaster. "This belongs to you."

He pulled out the fold of bills which the

smuggler had given him that morning and tossed it through the bars. Lancaster picked it up and flicked it with the edge of his finger.

"Ten thousand—and this—a nice little start in the world," said Lancaster.

Ripley smoked in silence until his lungs began to burn and he found that the cigarette had turned into an inch-long coal of red-hot tobacco. He dropped it to the floor and put his heel on it.

"Kind of excited?" asked Lancaster, still sitting on the edge of his cot.

Ripley said nothing.

"You don't have to fix me up with a set of keys," went on the prisoner. "Just turn your back on me for a while. Just walk into another room and stay there for a bit this evening. That's all you need to do to earn your money."

It was hard for Ripley to meet Lancaster's eyes. He fought until he could do it, and they stared at one another for half a minute.

"Just a poor, damn fool!" concluded Lancaster, and stretched himself again on the cot.

The night was the worst time. The westering sun threw a square of gold on the wall of the room, and the golden square crawled upward, stained the ceiling, disappeared.

More people had gathered in the street. There were no women, no children, only men. Drifts of lamplight from across the way fingered them dimly as they shifted slowly from cluster to cluster. Lancaster, his face pressed close against the bars of his cell, peered out the window fixedly at those shadowy forms.

Deputy sheriff Haley came in and talked in a whisper.

"There's a hundred men in the street and half of 'em don't belong to Dalton," he said. "There's gunna be hell. They're getting together!"

"Say it out loud," urged Ripley.

"They're getting ready," said the whisper.

The man was a ghost, with his gray face and his mist of colorless hair that matched his soundless voice. "They're gunna tackle this window and smash through the front of the jail at the same minute—"

A noise from many throats broke out in front of the jail like the boom and crash of a wave against hollow rocks. A reverberating tremor ran back through the old frame building.

"They're coming!" gasped Haley. "Oh God, they're coming now!"

He ran at the door, banged it open, and was gone. A shaft of light moved over the threshold, pale as moonshine, from the electric bulb which hung from the ceiling in the next empty room. Ripley stepped in and smashed the globe with a tap from his revolver. It made a loud pop; the minute fragments of glass clattered against the floor. Some of them crunched under his foot as he stepped back into the darkness of Lancaster's cell.

That darkness was not complete for light entered from the street by the window and painted thin highlights up and down the bars

of the cell. Lancaster was vaguely seen as he
sat on his cot again. Beyond the window,
Ripley saw two dense clusters of men grouped
about the trunks of a pair of massive cottonwoods.

"Listen, kid," said Lancaster, so quietly
that the words entered Ripley's mind as easily
as thought, "they're going to pry me out of
this, anyway. But it's not too late for you. If
you pull out of here you still get the ten
grand."

Fear skyrocketed from Ripley's bowels into
his brain. Another loud shout roared at the
front of the jail; a heavy weight crashed
against the outer door; and all the fear
drained away with electric tinglings through
Ripley's arms and fingers. He held the riot
gun under his elbow.

"I can see you, Jim," he said, "and I'm
going to save the second barrel for you. Salt
that idea down in your head for the cold
weather; you may be able to use it."

Lancaster said nothing. But he came to the
bars of his cell and gripped them with his
hands, and waited.

That front door, Ripley remembered, was
reinforced with bands of iron; it ought to hold;
but the battering went on steadily and into the
boom of the strokes came a brittle splintering.
The next yell of the crowd began in the distance but finished suddenly inside the jail.
The door was down!

And feet were trampling thunder out of the

wooden floor; someone was yelling: "This way!"

Ripley looked back through the window. One group remained close to the shelter of its cottonwood; the other cluster was advancing cautiously. So he pulled his Colt and drove a bullet just over their heads.

They dived backward for safety. He had time to see that, and how the first group had disappeared behind the other cottonwood. Then the racket of the intruders exploded into the next room.

Someone was shouting: "Get the light! Where's the light? What's wrong?"

Through the open door, Ripley fired one barrel of the shotgun, high. The big slugs ripped and crashed across the ceiling. A redness remained across his mind—the long, crimson flash of the explosion.

"Close in on him!" they were shouting.

Then Lancaster screeched: "Keep back! He's got the second barrel ready—he'll blow you to hell, you fools!"

The crowd that was lost in the blackness paused. They groaned as a heavy wagon groans when its brakes take hold, down hill. Ripley broke the gun and slipped in a new cartridge.

"Ripley," called the unmistakable snarl of Missouri Slim. "If you walk out of there with your hands stuck up, we ain't gunna hurt you. But you stick in there, we're gunna go in and tear you to pieces."

"Boys," said Ripley, "it's a good bluff but it won't work. I put that first charge into the ceiling. The next one is for you. I've got a riot gun, here, and riot guns can see in the dark. I'm going to count to five, slow, and then you can have it."

He shouted in a louder voice: "One—two—three—"

The darkness must have helped him, the breathless dark that brings the fear of death close to the face of any man. He had hardly called the third count before the wave began to roar again, but this time it was a clattering diminuendo.

True to his word, he fired on the fifth beat. The shot rattled through wooden partitions. A whoop of anxious fear answered him from the last of the fugitives. And then the sounds began to issue from the echoing rooms of the jail and rise, small and harmless in the outer air of the night.

He looked out the window. From the cottonwoods men were breaking away down the street at full speed.

"Thanks, Jim," said Ripley. "Thanks for putting in that good word at the right time."

"I was talking for myself, brother," said Lancaster.

After a moment he added: "Dogs are wonderful, Ripley. I've been a fool all my life. I've never put in enough time with dogs. Snakes are pretty good, too; and rats. But men are a lousy lot."

CHAPTER XVIII

For a time noises went up and down the town of Dalton. It seemed that the long night silence would never begin; just as perfect peace gathered, a single rider would bolt his horse up the main street. But finally the quiet was complete. Lancaster began to snore softly. Through the western window, Ripley looked so long and earnestly that he saw the stars falling towards the horizon. For his own part, he kept telling himself that the wait would not be long. Dallas had promised to come by the evening of the next day and in what new way could his strength be tempted? They had tried bribery—they had tried the rush of a mob—and yet there remained in him a tenseness and tremor of mounting expectation which he could not argue away.

He was not asleep, hours later, but it was from a semi-coma that Lancaster roused him.

The voice was husky, panting; it reminded Ripley of something which he could not place exactly in his mind, though his heart was sickened.

"Ripley—Jack—where are you?"

"Here," said Ripley.

"Get a light, will you? For God's sake, turn on a light!"

"I can't show a light in here. You know that."

"Why can't you? They're not even watching. They've given up. They'll never lift a hand for me, now. Turn on the light—any kind of a light. I can't breathe! The damn darkness is choking me like steam."

Even if it had been safe to illuminate the room, Ripley would not have wanted to see Lancaster's face because he had recognized at last the midnight terror.

He pulled his chair closer to the bars. "Take it easy, Jim," he advised. "I'll talk to you. You're all right. You'll forget all about this when the morning comes."

"The morning's gunna be the start of the day that brings Dallas here. After he gets his paws on me, I'm finished. As soon as he lands me, the jury reports me guilty, the judge puts on the black cap, the deathhouse is opened up, and the hangman begins to knot his rope. D'you hear me?"

"I hear you, Jim. Steady it up, will you?"

"Listen to me; talk to me, will you?"

"I'm right here, talking."

"You never seen what I seen. You never

seen a man hang. Did you?"

"No, I never did. Forget it, Jim."

The sickness increased in his heart.

"How could I forget it? When I stood down there in the little crowd, there was a bird chewing gum and making it crack on his back teeth; there was a reporter taking down notes; there was a coupla fellows telling smutty stories. They were all taking it easy, but I looked up and saw the platform and felt as if my own ghost was about to walk out there. After a while they did march a man out. And he—"

"Quit, it, Jim, will you? This won't do you any good."

"Lemme talk it out. I've got the words in my throat and if they stick there, they'll choke me. This hombre was only a kid. A good-looking kid with a towhead. He was white, but around the mouth he was green-white, like the belly of a lizard. There wasn't anything in his eyes. Nothing you'd ever seen in the eyes of anybody. Just emptiness. They had a minister along with him. The minister talked to him in a sing-song voice, and his glance wandered a good bit. You could see that he didn't give a damn about the business. He was making his bread and butter, I guess. It was an old story. The poor kid kept nodding and answering, and the minister droned along like a September afternoon."

"You'd better lay off this talk, Jim," said Ripley. "You'll empty out all the sand in your craw, if you keep on like this."

"Listen to me!" Lancaster insisted. "I looked around, and the hombre with the gum was still chewing it, and the reporter was making little sketches of the dead man—that's what he was—I wanted to say—I wanted to yell out—'Damn you, get down on your knees —he's a dead man!'"

Lancaster's voice screamed out suddenly, flaring like a strong light through the darkness, and Ripley's soul shrank to nothing. The unexpected yell jumped him out of his chair. He thrust a hand through the bars and caught Lancaster by the shoulder.

"They'll never get you to the rope, Jim," he said. "You've got too many friends and too much money. You're going to beat this rap."

Lancaster caught Ripley's hand in both of his.

"They put a black hood over the kid's face," he whispered. "Ever have an ether cone choking you? Two seconds of that is bad enough, but it's nothing compared with the black cap—the standing there—mind you— standing, and waiting—and God, they took forever before they dropped him. How could I stand the waiting? I'd begin to screech like a woman. Listen to me, Ripley—"

"I'm listening, all right. Remember, you're way out here in Dalton in a jail that's more full of holes than a Swiss cheese. Nothing has happened to you, yet."

"I'm going to give you the inside steer," said Lancaster. "This job I've had has been worth thirty grand a year, steady. And here's what'll make you laugh. I've been taking a fifty-fifty split. Me heading up everything and doing all the work, and still paying out a fifty-fifty split. Why? Because the other bird started the show and asked me into it. But I'm ready to grab the business all for myself, now. If you get me out of this hell-hole, I declare you in. Listen, Jack. You're a straight-shooter. You're the squarest kid in the world. I declare you in, for life. Not one year. Every year. Thirty thousand a year, for always. No matter what I clear, you get that. You can't say no to me. Not a white man like you—you wouldn't send me up to stand there with the damned black cap over my head—and—"

Ripley put his other hand through the bars and gripped the lean shoulder of Lancaster. He shook him. "You're talking yellow. That's all you are. You're a yellow coyote. Take this!"

He drew his hand back and flicked the flat of it across the face of Lancaster. Then he stepped back from the bars. His knees were water under him.

But there was no more hysteria from Lancaster; there were only the gasp and wheeze of his breathing.

After a time he said: "You're right, Ripley. The rope isn't going to get me. Not till I've had one try at you. There's a kind of God somewhere, and I'll get one whack at you, brother!"

The silence was better than the screaming or whispering voice of the hysteria, even when Lancaster began to walk up and down behind the bars, his footfall padding softly. The dawn came. It showed old Dalton's vacant house stuck up on the central hill like a black fist raised against the morning. It showed the glimmering of the windows of the town, and then Lancaster's eyes as he slouched up and down behind the bars. Afterward, slowly, the day poured across Dalton and the western wind began to come with a regular and warm pulsation through the window. Lancaster lay down and slept.

Old Josh brought two breakfasts of bacon and eggs and slabs of cornbread and huge mugs of coffee and cream.

"My Lord, boss," he said to Ripley, "you sure tore things up. There was fifty of them. This fella counted fifty of 'em, all rashin' and dashin'. But Mr. Ripley, he kicked 'em out faster than what they all run in! Ain't Mr. Lancaster gunna wake up for his breakfast?"

"Mr. Lancaster's all tuckered out," said Ripley, softly. "You take his tray off and bring it back hot when I tell you to. Mr. Lancaster needs a powerful lot of sleeping just now."

A committee of three angry and eminent citizens appeared later in the morning, with Deputy Sheriff Haley accompanying them. He was more than albino pale. Ripley stood in

the open doorway of the cell-room and hushed
the loud voices of the three.

"Lancaster is all in. He needs his sleep,"
said Ripley.

"I'm Tug O'Brien, of the General Merchandise Store," said a big block of a man.
"Speakin' of sleep, where was this here brave
deputy sheriff sleepin' when the gang of
roughs busted into his jail last night? The rest
of us in town put on a rotten show. But it was
hard for us to get together—and there was a
lot of those hombres hollering around. But
what we want to know is, where was our hired
man, all that time? Why didn't he keep 'em
away from the outside door of the jail the
same as you kept 'em away from *this* door?"

Ripley looked at the deputy sheriff and
found him still and cold, submissive to the
stroke that was to fall, empty of eye as that
towheaded lad Lancaster had described. No
black cap had been dropped over the head of
Haley at the moment when his reputation was
to be put to death.

"What did Haley care about the outside
rooms of an empty jail?" asked Ripley. "He
let the rest go and came back here with me."

"Hold on!" said Tug O'Brien. "Is that
straight? Nobody heard a yip out of him, if he
was in there with you."

"The best kind of fighting dogs don't bark,"
answered Ripley.

"We've been and made fools of ourselves,"
declared Tug O'Brien to his companions.

"Haley, if you'll shake hands with me, I'd be obliged."

Haley shook hands, but his vacant eyes took little notice of what was happening. There was nothing in them save dim bewilderment as he studied Ripley's face.

Mr. O'Brien concluded his mission to the jail with a brief and effective speech. "Ripley," he said, "they tell me you told that gang that a riot gun could see in the dark. I'm here for the whole damn town to tell you that blind men could see the sort of stuff that you're made of. When the jail of a town gets cracked open, all the thugs that are on the loose go for it to make headquarters in a soft spot, but you changed all that last night. We won't be forgetting you!"

He marshaled his two companions and they left at once, while the deputy sheriff still stared at Ripley.

"What I wanta know," said he, "is why you did it—after I run out on you like that."

"Well," said Ripley, "even champions are no good after they've been licked—and counted out. You haven't been counted out, Haley. Nobody even saw you take it on the chin. So what the hell? Forget it and pull yourself together for next time."

"That's right," sighed Haley. "There's another time to come. Will you shake on it?"

"Sure," agreed Ripley.

Haley leaned a good deal of weight on the proffered hand; then he stepped back and added: "A fellow like you, Ripley—a fellow like you—"

He finished off the sentence with a gesture as vague as his look; but he had managed to include universes in that wave of his hand.

CHAPTER XIX

The morning grew old, with a relaxing warmth that spread content through Ripley. Outside the window there was a steady attendance of boys, big and small, and wide-eyed little girls who stared as though the steel bars discoursed enchanting music for their ears.

There was no sense of pride in Ripley, or only a meager one; but chiefly he felt an enlarging relief as the day grew older, tending towards the evening which would bring Tom Dallas and an end of anxiety. To stay in the same room with the wolfish eyes of Lancaster was hard enough; and still there remained an uneasy expectation of things to come. Those on the outside who had made two such efforts to secure the release of the prisoner would try at least one time more.

It was after noon, and after lunch, when Josh brought in a neatly wrapped package addressed, like the first one, to "Jack Ripley," with the PERSONAL in printed capital letters.

"Take it back," exclaimed Ripley, without opening the thing. "Take it back and chuck it right in his face, Josh."

"That first fellow—I hit him with it, all right," chuckled Josh, and withdrew.

He returned with an air of apology a moment later. The bringer of the package had disappeared, so Ripley received it with unwilling hands.

He sat down and weighed the parcel. Of course the wise thing was to leave it unopened, but he trusted that Lancaster's sneering face would reinforce his virtue. And it was a larger, a much larger and heavier package than the first one.

He lighted a cigarette. "We'll take a look and see how much they want you, Jim," he said.

"Yeah, you'll take a look, all right," said Lancaster. It was the first time he had spoken since that midnight horror.

There were the same compressed stacks of bills, but far more of them. He divided the mass in quarters and counted one. Twelve thousand dollars. Four times that . . .

"Fifty thousand, Jimmy," said he. He tried to laugh. The laughter split to pieces and crackled in his throat. He was agape, thirsty, and what he held between his hands could assuage that thirst forever, he felt.

Sin is a comparative thing. For a big sin

there should be a big man. He, Jack Ripley, was big, was he not?

But his fingers, against his will, persisted in rewrapping the bundle, tying the strings tight. Then they tossed it through the bars to Lancaster.

"Damn you!" snarled Lancaster. "Why do you pass it up to me? Do you think *that* can hang with me?"

And he kicked it back so that it skidded to the feet of Ripley.

A panic broke out in him. He strode to the door and shouted for Haley. The deputy came on the run.

"Take this damned thing!" said Ripley, and threw the package. It missed Haley's hands, struck his chest and, rebounding, rolled back again to Ripley's feet.

"Sorry I missed it," apologized the deputy sheriff. "What is it?"

There was a fate in the way that money had returned to Ripley's feet; and who can resist the urge of his destiny? Ripley picked up the parcel.

"It's nothing. Don't bother about it," he explained. "Just—a sort of joke—that's all. Nothing that matters."

The thick, close heat of the mid-afternoon came over the jail before Lancaster broke out: "You've got the stuff. What are you going to do about it?"

"Give it back to the hombres that sent it.

Who are they?" asked Ripley.

"So you can pass the word to Dallas and rope them in?" said Lancaster, and the fire burned up in the dark hollows of his eyes. "Listen, Ripley—every minute is getting closer to the time when Dallas ought to show up. Do you think you can work the double-cross? You fool, if you try to keep me *and* the money, you'll be bumped off in the street by some gent you never seen before. That mean anything in your crooked life?"

Ripley made a cigarette. The smoke had no taste; it only burned his lungs. He felt helpless. There was fate in this thing and what could he do but abandon himself to a blind guidance?

Time no longer went slowly. It shot away like water down a flume, carrying him towards the hour when Tom Dallas would walk into the jail at Dalton to take over an offender against federal law.

It was in the golden hour of the afternoon that a letter came to Ripley addressed in a small, rapid hand like that of a man; but the letters were a little too rounded and smooth.

It said:

DEAR JACK,

I have to see you. I have only half an hour in town. No one must guess that I'm here, so I've hidden in the tower of the old Dalton house on the hill. And I'm praying to see you. Will you come, Jack?

Now you can see me—if you look up the hill from the jail.

CHING.

P.S. No one was ever so brave. But then, everyone knew about Jack Ripley. But I *must* see you, Jack—even for ten minutes. Will you come? Oh, will you come?

He folded the letter in quarters, unfolded it, read it again, looked up the hill. And there he saw the girl sitting in the square of a window that had been shuttered, the day before. The distance was great but no man could have made a miniature so delicate, laid against black velvet.

Lancaster, flat on the couch, pretended to be asleep—but that was sheer pretense indeed. He was watching from beneath the lashes of his eyes.

Ripley called to Josh and said: "Go saddle that gray mare of mine, will you, Josh? And send Haley in here."

When Haley came, he said to the deputy: "I may be out for half an hour. Here's the riot gun. And you'll give me your word that you won't leave this room?"

"Why, Ripley," said the deputy, "this is my second chance. I wouldn't leave that, would I?"

That was why Ripley got out of the jail into the warm, soft air of the late afternoon and looked about him as one who at last has escaped from a sickroom and for the first time in weeks sees the indescribable blue which curves around and holds our earth, instead of the flat, bald, white ceiling.

Beautiful Hickory Dickory was nosing him and calling him impatient names until he mounted. A running group of boys from school made a confused halt to watch his start. They kept repeating his name and that of the mare to reassure one another. They had the look of profound believers who are prepared with faith for any miracle. Ripley gave them a wave of his hand and sent Hickory like a jackrabbit up the hill. Halfway up, he took the parcel of money from under his coat and dropped it into the mouth of a saddlebag. Mentally, he had dropped it far into the past, a thing to be forgotten.

CHAPTER XX

The cypress hedge which marked out the Dalton block on the top of the hill had grown into ragged young trees, and behind the hedge a bit of wilderness had taken root in soil that had once been softened and moistened for the garden flowers. One panel of the entrance gate had fallen; the other hung drunkenly from a single hinge and let Ripley through onto a driveway overgrown with weeds and young brush. In the middle of the road a ten-year-old lodge-pole pine was pushing its roots of wire through gravel and stone and lifting its head higher every year.

The grounds were not large enough, really, to warrant a driveway, and this had been engineered by making it double, snakelike, back upon itself. A statue of Walter A. Dalton had once stood on a massive pedestal, the figured corners of which represented Hope, Faith,

Charity, and Texas; but now the old-fashioned boots of the great man were adrift above the varnished leaves of an impromptu growth of mesquite. Walter A. Dalton's coat still flowed down to faultless tails, his right hand was still thrust into his bosom after the fashion of the dignified orators who had to keep their fingers warm for gesturing, and the tall silk hat was still lofty on his brow. But the statue was carved from a rather soft sandstone and time and thrown stones had been too much for the face of the great man. The nose and one cheek bone were gone; the chin was almost worn away and a deep fissure opening across the neck promised another headless masterpiece to the world before long.

But Ripley did not smile at this. He did not even pause to comment on people who allow statues of themselves to be erected in their front yards. All his gaze was reserved for the square central tower which rose above the house, but the tower window that looked to this side was still shuttered; it was a blind face to which he looked up.

He threw Hickory's reins as soon as he was near the front steps, dismounted, and started running up to the veranda. The crackling and groaning of the warped boards made him step more slowly, for he had a sudden feeling of midnight desolation in the full daylight. The front door was locked. Through its light he looked into the pompous setting of the hall. Even the mirror was dim with dust. The carved head of the newel post at the bottom of the stairway lay on the boards, cracked in two; but that was the only sign of damage or of decay.

He went around to the side door, tiptoeing along the crackling veranda, and made an easy entrance; there was only the faint shudder of a groan from the rusted old hinges. He closed the door behind him with a very odd sense of apprehension. At the foot of the main hall a door remained open to let the fear of something that listened follow him up the stairs. He was very grateful that these boards did not complain under his weight; but when he stepped past an open bedroom of the second story, he saw a striding figure inside. A startled pulse struck him, like a handclap on the brain. He stepped back; his own image moved with him in the big mirror on the bedroom wall.

As he went on up the steps toward the tower, he took satisfaction because he had not drawn a revolver. It was not actual fear that had been in him, perhaps, but merely the melancholy, the unreality which are its forerunners.

The stairway turned, paused at a small landing in front of the tower door. Doubt, with a shadowy wing-beat, troubled his mind. She would not be there. . . .

He thrust the door suddenly open. The hinges howled. And then he saw Ching turning in sudden fear toward him from the window, with one hand raised in that gesture which is between defense and appeal. After the watery thinness of the China silk, the swagger of this tan riding outfit seemed out of place. He paid no attention to it, confining himself to her head and her brown throat which he could see against the sky. The hills and the lifting mountains of the distance reached no higher than her cheeks. It was not the window which looked on the jail. Those shutters had been closed and now the view was to the north.

"They said you would never leave him; but I hoped," she told Ripley.

He shook her hand and saw the golden snake which clasped her arm. Its eyes were bright green jewels. "Who told you that I wouldn't come to you, Ching?"

"Sam Li. But for this once, he was wrong, and I am happy!"

This she said without smiling, but a brightness of faith invested her. "Sam Li said that you would never leave Jim Lancaster until he was dead; and where would poor Dong be then? But I remembered your promise that you would help until he was found."

"I'll keep the promise," he said. "But will you talk to me, Ching?"

"Oh, yes. As much as you will listen. Are you angry?"

"I'm a thousand miles from angry. Why? Because I'm frowning? It's the strangeness that upsets me, Ching. It's the mystery that points a gun at my head. Will you answer questions?"

"Yes. Every one!"

He took a long, deep breath.

"Then I'll be through with my worst troubles in five minutes," he told her. "I haven't more than that. There are people who would pay their blood to get Lancaster out of the jail. I must hurry back."

At this, she held out her hands to him and smiled, saying in that gesture that all that was in her would be his for the asking. He had to look past her into the sky, squinting hard, before he could recover the trend of his thoughts.

"Lancaster," he said. "I want to know about him, first."

"Jim Lancaster? Every Chinaman that comes over the river—Jim knows about them all."

"It was because of Dong, then?"

"Dong? Poor, poor Dong!" said the girl.

"I mean to say, you've been nice to Lancaster because you felt that he'd help you to reach Dong. Isn't that the story?"

"Yes," she agreed, thoughtfully. "Yes."

"And what else?"

"Also, I like him."

He digested the bitterness of this for a moment.

"I've seen him act as though you belong to him. Had he a right to do that?"

She looked away from him. In her face there was the pain of a child trying to understand.

"Ching, don't you know what I mean?" begged Ripley.

Sorrow and trouble increased in her. "You

are angry again," she said.

"Not angry. God knows I'm not angry. I'm only trying to get at the truth. Don't you see what a darkness I stand in? You—you in Chinese clothes in the house of a Chinaman—the scarfaced fellow, Dong—"

"Poor, poor Dong!" she murmured.

"Don't interrupt me, please," said he.

"I'm sorry. So sorry."

"Ching, don't look every moment as though I were beating you."

"I won't look that way," said the girl. Her eyes became enormous. She drew back a few frightened inches.

"I can't tell how to go on," groaned Ripley. "Nothing I say will fit—everything is wrong—"

He turned in a nervous despair and strode across the tower floor. A voice of gentle lament followed him. "Are you going away? Are you leaving me?"

"No!" cried Ripley. He turned with a great gesture that made her shrink, as though he had shaken a fist at her! He thrust his hands into his pockets. He controlled his voice. It rang like the shivering of steel.

"I'm not going away. I'm going to see this thing through, if only I can get the mystery straightened out a little. Try it from another angle. What is Sam Li to you?"

"He's very wise and calm. I never knew such a wise, strong man, I think."

"Yes, but to you—what's he to you?"

"He gives me a place to stay in his house.

He gives me good advice, too."

The despair came over Ripley again. He could not win from her a single answer that definitely dismissed a doubt or made or killed a hope.

"I'll try Dong," he said, slowly. "There I surely can get at the facts. Tell me, Ching—"

"Yes, yes, anything!"

"Well, you want to find Dong, don't you?"

"Yes, of course!"

"Is there anything else you want more?"

"Nothing in the world."

"Now, then, why do you try so hard to find him?"

"Because I love poor Dong."

"I know. But what happened to him? Why was he heading for the United States and slavery?"

"He was trying to come to me, of course."

"Ah, that's something, at last. Dong was trying to come to you?"

"Yes." She smiled and nodded, anxiously pleased because Ripley was showing his first satisfaction.

"Where did Dong start from?" he went on.

"If I knew that!"

"You don't know where he started?"

"How I wish I did."

"Persia, Brazil, Alaska—you don't know the country he came from?"

"Yes. China is the country."

"Were you ever in China?"

"Yes."

"And you knew Dong, there?"

"Yes."

"What was he in your life over there?"

"He was very big. I have always loved Dong."

"That's good. What was he?"

"He was always the same—kind, gentle, faithful, true, and he could always sing wonderful songs."

"I'm glad of that," said Ripley. "I've heard a couple of them, and they're wonderful, all right. But tackling it in another way, I'd like to know what he was in China—business man?"

She laughed for the first time. Pleasure invaded him deeply.

"Poor Dong!" she said. "What a business man he is!"

"Ching—listen to me!" he groaned. "I'm trying to find out things about you and Lancaster and Sam Li and Dong—and I'm going out of my head because I don't learn any facts —will you please, please, please try to answer me, now? In short words?"

"Yes!" she whispered.

"Will you stop being afraid?"

"Yes," said the breathless voice.

"Great God, Ching, do you think I'm an enemy or a friend?"

"Oh, be my friend!" said the girl.

"I am—look—with both hands—with all my might—I *am* your friend. Listen to me— damn everything else, but let me try to make this clear—from the minute I saw you with the canaries—I wanted to be your friend. I never saw anything so beautiful. I was going out of my head about you—I was dizzy."

"I am sorry," said the girl. She put out deprecating hands. "Ah, I am so sorry," she said.

Ripley stepped back from her and drew in a breath. "My God," he said, "if I could only talk Chinese to you!"

"Do you wish to learn?" asked the girl, brightening from her anxiety. "Let me try to teach you. It is not very hard—and if—"

"Forget it!" exclaimed Ripley. "You're what—American?"

"Yes. Of course, yes."

"Yeah. It's as clear as midnight and a fog," said Ripley. "But you're an American, then, and you can speak English. Look me in the eye."

"Yes," said Ching.

"If you understand English, what do I mean when I say that I love you?"

"I understand," said the girl. "I say it to my canaries, and to poor Dong."

"It isn't a question of 'poor.' There's no pity in it. It's my heart shouting."

"No pity? Your heart?" said the girl, bewilderment enlarging her eyes again. "Poor man, have you a pain there?"

He groaned loudly.

"How sorry I am!" she said.

He stood at a balance, trying to turn his mind back to a new beginning. But how could words be plainer? Would he have to smile and mope and make faces and sigh and use gestures, as if to a foreigner?

A clamor of voices drifted up from the street and then, like the spatting of fists inside the tower room, he heard guns.

He jumped to the eastern window and wrenched the shutters open. A dust-cloud was wheeling up into the air from the street in front of the jail, and men were running toward the front door of the old house. But it was through the window on the nearest side of the jail that two men clambered, and two more behind them.

Horses waited near the cottonwoods. He recognized the lofty, meager body of Missouri Slim holding a horse which Jim Lancaster was mounting. And a yell came out of Ripley's throat and rang in his ears until they ached.

He had his answer. Jim Lancaster, sweeping off his sombrero, waved it toward the Dalton house on the hill, and then the gallop of his horse snatched him from view.

Ripley, turning, found himself alone. She had fled, soundlessly.

He rushed to the door. It was locked from the outside.

That, surely, was sufficient proof that she had drawn him as bait draws a fish; and with exquisite self-control she had pretended her bewilderment. Insane rage pressed weights against his temples.

He smashed the lock with a bullet, tore the door open, and leaped down the stairs to the upper hall. Wild echoes rang all about him through the house. It was his own voice calling for Ching.

CHAPTER XXI

To hunt for Ching, he felt, would be like hunting for a weasel in a rabbit warren. Besides, what would he do when he caught her? He got out to Hickory Dickory and flew the mare through the ragged shrubbery of the driveway and down the street to the jail. People were ebbing in and out through the open doorway.

"There's the man that would of kept Lancaster!" someone shouted. But he jumped from the saddle and strode up the steps.

One glance into the west showed him the sun reddening on the edge of the sky; then he walked forward into the enclosed warmth of the jail. His footsteps had secondary echoes that called out to him, announcing the emptiness of the place that once had held so much of his freedom and his honor.

In Jim Lancaster's cell he found the deputy

sheriff. He lay flat. A doctor was laying out a medical kit, producing bandages. Half a dozen other people gestured vaguely toward helpfulness. They had stripped the wounded man to the waist. A driblet of blood kept running from the bullet hole high on the chest, toward the shoulder.

"Lungs or shoulder?" asked Ripley of the doctor.

"Get out of my way and let me work," said the doctor.

"This is Ripley, doc," said one of the bystanders.

"It's the shoulder," said the doctor, and he looked at Ripley with a sudden lift of his head.

"Hey, Jack," murmured Haley.

Ripley kneeled beside him. A trembling hand pulled him down close to the face where pain was alternately pinching and widening the nostrils.

"Listen, Jack," whispered Haley, "they came on the run. I saw I was a goner but I opened up. I got some lead into one of them. Once the guns began, I wasn't scared. I'll never be scared again. That's what *you* done for me."

His hand slipped from Ripley's shoulder and fumbled. Ripley took it in a hard grip. Then he stood up and left the cell-room. One of the idlers said in a low, confidential voice: "Too damn bad, old timer. All your work gone out the window!"

Ripley made no answer. He went on to the door of the jail and paused there for a moment. The sun was down, leaving hot flares in the west, and the night would be settling in very soon; a similar darkness was closing on his mind. But out there in the street, the jail delivery already forgotten, half a dozen boys were sprinting through the dust in a game of tag. One of them was screaming: "That ain't fair. That ain't fair!"

He went down to Hickory and tossed the reins over the pommel of the saddle. She followed him down the street, through the alley beside the hotel, into the stable at the rear. "I'll take care of her, boss," said the Negro in charge. He spoke gently, as if in a sickroom. "Too doggone bad! I'll bet you get him again, though. Lemme take Hickory. She knows me pretty good." So he gave the mare to the Negro. She whinnied dolefully after him as he left the barn, but her grief was no pleasure to him. It was only an added pain.

When he got to the hotel desk he found that the clerk had already been to the jail and was panting from his run. He kept gasping out comments as he showed Ripley up the stairs to a room. "Right on the corner where you can have a look up both streets, if you lean out the window." The clerk opened the window and waved to the color of the sunset, as though it were specially provided for honored guests.

"If you'd been back there in the jail," he said before he left, "nothing would of happened. They wouldn't of dared. Everybody knows that, Mr. Ripley."

Then he was gone, and Ripley could throw

himself on the bed. There was pain of weariness in his knees, in the deep pulse in his throat, in the ache across the base of his skull; but more than that was the nausea of grief and shame. Sometimes he could push the thought of Ching into a dim corner of his mind, but again her voice had physical compass and weight in his ears.

He could not fight her away, so he closed his eyes and let the thought grow as it would. Of all actresses, she was the greatest; of all fools he was the most profound; and before long she would be sitting with Lancaster and narrating in detail her interview with Jack Ripley. Her mimicry would be worth hearing as she repeated how he had talked about the shouting of his heart!

She would be bringing cold beer to Lancaster, filling his glass with careful slowness so that the head would not be too deep. Now she was lighting his cigarette. Now she was sitting on his knees with one arm around his throat and her head against his shoulder.

There would be no good way of killing Lancaster except under her eyes. No, that would not do, because her mourning for the dead would break any man's heart.

A hand tapped at the door of the room. Ripley looked up into the dark of the night through the window and saw a star slinking sleepily through the horizon mist.

"Hello!" he called.

"Can I come in?" asked Marshal Dallas' voice.

"Yeah, come on in," said Ripley, and he relaxed on the bed again.

The door opened.

"Got a light in here?" asked Dallas.

"Yeah. Somewhere."

There was fumbling up and down; then a light snapped on. It hung from the center of the ceiling, casting intolerable brilliance.

Ripley swung his legs over the edge of the bed and sat up.

"They ought to have shades on these damn lights," he said.

"Maybe they ought to. I never thought," said the marshal. He sat down in a squeaking chair beside the little deal table in the middle of the room. The light gleamed on his sun-whitened eyebrows and made his red nose glisten. Big, ragged shadows hung over most of his face. "I found this in your saddlebag," he went on. "Maybe you better keep good care of it."

He pointed to the package wrapped in brown paper. Ripley looked at the door and then at the window. He stood up.

"What about it?" he asked.

"You know what about it more'n I do," answered Dallas.

"Have you opened it?" asked Ripley.

The marshal picked it up, weighed it in his hand, laid it down again. "No," he said. "I haven't opened it."

"What you mean, going through my saddlebags?" asked Ripley. This was not Lancaster that he had before him but it was a fighting man. Beggars can't be choosers. "I want to know what in hell you mean going through my saddlebags?"

"I put my horse right next to yours, Jack," said the marshal's deep, husky voice. "When I hung up the saddle I bumped my hand into your saddlebag, and there was something in it. I didn't think you'd want to leave things out over night in a saddlebag; there's plenty of thieves around. So I brought it in. Shouldn't I of done that?"

"Now you've brought it," said Ripley, "you know what you can do next? You can get the hell out of here."

"I'm sorry you're so riled up," said the marshal. He stood up. "I'll be seeing you," he added, and went toward the door.

"Wait a minute!" called Ripley.

"What's the matter?" asked Dallas, turning.

"Take this along with you."

He threw the deputy's badge on the table. It bounced off and rolled on the floor. The marshal stooped with pain and picked it up.

"I wouldn't like to take this, Jack," he said. "You've done a lot of honor to it."

"I'm through with your dirty work," answered Ripley. "We'll start where we left off— me on the way to jail—you trying to put me there. Let me see your first move, Dallas."

"Lancaster is my dirty work," said the marshal. "And you'll never be through with him, after what happened today. Not till one of you is dead."

"You fool," cried Ripley, "don't you guess what's in that parcel?"

"That's your business," said the marshal.

"Money—that's what's inside, and you damn well know it."

"Kind of careless, usin' brown paper for a purse, ain't you?"

"There's fifty thousand dollars in that."

"Fifty thousand is a pile of money," answered Dallas. "I'd sure retire on fifty thousand!"

"Why don't you talk out, free and open, the way I'm talking?" demanded Ripley. "Why don't you say what you think of me?"

"I think you're terrible excited—and terrible young," said the marshal. "But you're a good boy, Jack."

"You lie!" said Ripley. "If you had the drop on me, you'd herd me for jail right now."

"I guess you don't think that," murmured Dallas. "I'll be seeing you in the morning, Jack. But here—keep this." He extended the bright little badge in the open palm of his hand. "You'll take better care of it than I will," he said.

A great stroke of joy clove through the brain and through the heart of Ripley. "Are you meaning this?" he asked.

"Here! Here!" snapped Dallas. "What's all this fool hemming and hawing about? You come down and have a drink with me, son."

Ripley took the badge, turned it in his hand, slipped it back into a pocket. "Wait a minute," he said. "I need talk more than a drink. Sit down."

The marshal sat down. Ripley dragged another chair to the table and dropped into it. He put his elbows on the edge of the table and rested his face on his fists. "What'll I talk about, Jack?" the marshal was asking.

"Don't talk," said Ripley. "Just sit there a while."

It was only a moment later that Ripley looked up and saw the marshal with one hand hanging toward the floor and his head lopped over on a shoulder, asleep, with pain and weariness in his face. Ripley's watch said that it was one o'clock. So he got up and patted the shoulder of Dallas.

"Doggone me," said the marshal, starting. "I must of dropped off for a snooze. What were you saying?"

"I was saying to take this stuff and see that it gets back to Lancaster," said Ripley.

"It wouldn't be legal," protested Dallas, "sending money to an hombre that the government wants in jail."

"Take this and see it gets back to him," insisted Ripley.

"I gotta do what you say," answered the marshal.

"Go to bed, now," said Ripley, but at the door he halted Dallas again.

"Someday you might need the whole innards of a man," remarked Ripley.

"Yeah. Most likely I will," agreed Dallas.

"When the time comes, ask me for mine, will you?" demanded Ripley.

"Why, Jack, who else would I ask?" said Tom Dallas.

CHAPTER XXII

The marshal and Jack Ripley sat, the next morning, under a small tree behind the barn while the gray mare, already saddled, wandered close at hand, nibbling at the grass or wantonly stripping leaves from the shrubbery. Ripley, telling his story in detail from the first, walked up and down or else sat cross-legged, his back against the tree trunk. Dallas had perched himself on a big outcropping root like a twist of a petrified boa-constrictor. He whittled at a stick with a knife so sharp and a touch so delicate that the shavings were thinner and more translucent than fine linen paper. Now and again the marshal sighted down his stick, almost in an agony to keep it straight, and perfectly round. When the story ended, Ripley summed up:

"I'm back where I started. Who is Ching? I don't know! Who is Lancaster—head of the smuggling game, but you told me that in the beginning. Who is Dong? A coolie that Ching wants to see. That's all I know about him. Who is the higher-up that Tolliver is working for—the fellow who's willing to throw Lancaster out and give me that job? I don't know that, either. In fact, I know practically nothing!"

"You left out one thing," said the marshal. "Who is Sam Li?"

"Oh, he has nothing to do with this game," said Ripley.

"He's in the picture a good part of the time, anyway," said Dallas.

"Well, I'll tell you," declared Ripley, with deliberation. "I've never met a white man or a yellow man that was any better than Sam Li. I never met a bigger, kinder-hearted fellow than Sam Li. I never met a calmer, stronger man than Li."

"Why would a white girl go and stay in his house as though he was an uncle or something?" asked the marshal.

"Because she wants his help and knows that she can trust him."

"How does he happen to know Lancaster so well?"

"Simply because Lancaster won't stay away from Ching."

"Whatever it is, it ain't simple," answered Dallas. "If I was you, I'd look out for Sam Li."

"Tell me why?"

"It's this way," explained Dallas. "The girl

wants to see Dong; Dong wants to get to the girl; Lancaster is in love with the girl and he also wants to hog the whole smuggling business. There's a motive behind everyone of 'em in the whole show. All except Sam Li. And when I run up agin a case like that, I always do a lot of watching of the gent that ain't got any reason to be around."

"Maybe—maybe—" muttered Ripley, impatiently. "But to go back to another point— who could have stolen Dong away from the house of Sam Li?"

"The man who's higher up, maybe?" suggested the marshal.

"The man that Tolliver works for? Then Dong is dead by this time."

"Likely," agreed Dallas.

"He can't be!" exclaimed Ripley.

"Why not?"

"Poor old Dong!" murmured Ripley. "I tell you what, Dallas—I'm going to try to get on his trail. The rest of the job can wait; it's Dong that I'm going to work for now."

"Sure, and that's a good idea," answered Dallas. "If you get one of them, you'll get them all. But what about Ching? Ain't you tempted to take after her first?"

Ripley looked away across the hills, across the mountains. The brilliance of the sun was painful to his eyes. "I never expect to see her again," he said at last.

When Ripley came over the hills in the middle of the day he made a pause at the top

of the divide and looked down at Los Altos by
the river. It had always seemed a pretty little
town to him but now it looked like a white and
crowded graveyard. He found himself straining his eyes toward that innermost curve of
buildings which bordered the river, for there
was the house of Sam Li, and that was where
Ching might now be whistling to the bright
golden cloud of canaries.

To ride down from the height was to de-
scend into unhappiness. He could not help
looking away to the north where a great land
waited to receive him and cover him from the
past; but all the love of new trails seemed to
have left him and presently he was riding
down the slope.

He cut into the river road that brought him
before long to the house of Jose Oñate. They
were all in the truck garden, Jose and Maria
swaying short-handled hoes whose blades
were polished by infinite toil and the children
working the pump which raised water from
the river and filled a ditch with creeping
brightness.

Young Juan saw him first, and came leaping; the whole family clamored up behind
him. The youngsters took the mare to the
shed. Maria and Jose escorted the guest into
the adobe house and there she set to work in a
flurry to prepare food, while Oñate began to
grin and nod his head.

"We have heard all about it," said Jose.
"They know a little more about you now, do
they? All the great men and their guns, they

know you a little better, now. The first day, we all drank red wine when we heard. I beat the mules with the whip all the way home and shouted the news. We all shouted. We laughed. That Señor Lancaster in prison, he would not be so fierce and great. Then the other news came down the road—that he was escaped. But what thick gloves he will wear before he touches you again!"

"There's another thing, Jose," said Ripley, "that means more to me than Lancaster, just now. You remember the scarfaced Chinaman that I talked to you about?"

Jose pulled at his jowls with both hands as he shook his head.

"I've seen nothing," he said, "but I've heard a Chinaman singing back there in the hills."

"How did it sound?"

"Like a wind on a March day."

"Well, you might say that it sounds like that, too. But how could you have heard without seeing?"

"I was coming back from a place I know on a creek; I had a great load of watercress behind the saddle and, because I was in a hurry, I left the trail and went across the hills. Part of the way was very good, but then I came to sand. You know the sand dunes that keep walking?"

"They're worse than mud to go through," agreed Ripley.

"They are worse than anything," answered Oñate, "because how should the earth come to life like water and move in waves? But I came to a swale with a little shack in the bottom of it. The sand had covered almost one side of the house. Dead tree tops stuck up. But on the other side of the house there was still some honest ground and a good, big, living tree to pour a cool shadow in the middle of the day. That was when I heard the singing, señor."

"And you went to see who it was?" asked Ripley.

The Mexican was troubled.

"Señor," said Oñate, "I thought of you and started to ride down into the hollow, but then I heard blows striking flesh; and the singing stopped."

"Beating him! Beating poor Dong?" groaned Ripley. "What did you do, Jose? If you ran a knife into a couple of the devils, I'll take the blame for it."

"It was the end of the day," said Oñate, miserably. "There was still enough light to see by up where I was, but it was pretty dark down there in the swale. And the sound of the blows made me a little sick. Señor, I am not a fighting man, and besides, I thought that just hearing a Chinaman sing might be enough. In fact, I turned my horse around and rode away as I had come, and hurried home, and came late, and the cursed watercress was too withered to sell the next day."

"When was it?" asked Ripley.

"It was just last evening."

"Take me now to the place."

"Before you have eaten? Before the mare

has tasted the oats?"

"I don't want to eat," said Ripley, "but I have to sleep. Let me stretch out over here. I'm dead for sleep, Jose."

"Ah, señor, to be dead for sleep is better than to be dead with bullets. Lie down and I'll keep you cool."

He sat on his heels beside the bed on which Ripley stretched himself, and with the ragged half of a fan he raised a current of air that blew Ripley quickly into profound slumber.

Three hours of exhausted sleep, and then Ripley wakened. Little Juan, like a tiger unleashed, was off the floor at once and at him with a flood of questions about that night when the crowd smashed its way into the jail —and ran out again. How many had the señor killed with his gun? How many with his knife? How many with his empty hands?

Ripley ate some hot frijoles, scooping them up with tortillas. "Those fellows ran away because they were in a gang," he said. "Gangs mostly run the wrong way. You keep out of 'em, Juan, and keep your hands free for your own fights."

On the earth floor of the house, Jose Oñate drew a map of the country to show the way to the sand dunes and the swale in which the house lay. Then he followed with the family to the horse shed, where Hickory was quickly mounted. Jose tied a small silver image into the mane of gray.

"What is that?" asked Ripley.

"My own St. Christopher," answered Jose
Oñate.

"Take it back," urged Ripley. "I don't want
to steal your luck, Jose."

"No, no," insisted Oñate, "he is the patron
of travelers. I am stopped still for the rest of
my life. But you were born with a spur in your
flank!"

CHAPTER XXIII

It was one of those impromptu shacks which can be found in the West, part frame, part logs, part flimsy wattle work of tough mesquite. Ripley, stretched in the soft of the sand on a dune which overlooked the hollow, studied the place with great care.

The whole building leaned from the pressure of an encroaching dune which eventually would flatten it and roll over its site. The wind-wrinkles on the head of the sandhill were like the marks which indicate hair on an archaic statue, and the whole effect was that of a prone monster thrusting itself up through the earth. But more compelling than the dune and the falling house, to Ripley, was the sight of Dan Tolliver seated in the shade of a tree near the front door and playing solitaire on a little wooden table with a bottle of whisky to keep him company.

For an hour, with the sun roasting his back, Ripley peered down through a screen of long-bladed grass. He might dispose of Tolliver, but there were apt to be other men in the shack; and it was quite possible that if Dong had ever been in the place he had been removed before this, or he was dead. All combined to make Ripley use the true hunting patience.

Dan Tolliver, rising suddenly, flung the pack of cards on the ground and took another jolt of whisky. After that he rounded the house and appeared again jogging a pinto slowly down the hollow. Toward the foot of it, the depth of the soft sand stopped the mustang to a walk but Tolliver, with a howl of rage, roweled the poor little beast into a frantic effort. Up to its knees at every jump, it flung forward over the rise and disappeared; the dust-cloud continued to rise and bloom in the golden light of the afternoon.

Now Ripley got to his feet. It might be that Tolliver merely wanted a brief change of scene, and that he would be back in a few moments; the cards still waited for him on the ground and the whisky on the table. But this was an invitation to explore that Ripley could not resist. He looked back to the shaded spot where Hickory lay close to the ground like a well-schooled faun, and then he went down the slope.

The nearest window had a sack for a curtain, flopping back and forth in the breeze. He peered through into a kitchen. The old stove

sagged to the side; the stovepipe wavered like
a rubber hose toward the ceiling. On a shelf
appeared cans with bright labels; empties had
been flung into a corner; a bloodstained length
of brown paper wavered on the table.

He crossed to the window on the farther
side of the house and through it saw no more
than one roll of blankets stretched on the
floor.

That was all there was to the house, apparently, and it was empty. Tolliver had been
the only occupant and he, perhaps, was not
out here as the guard posted over Dong but as
a refugee crouching away from Lancaster's
anger.

Ripley went inside. There was a thin, stale
scent of cookery. Bare rafters stretched above
the rooms and no attic floor had been laid. But
the boards over which he walked gave out a
hollow sound that suggested a cellar beneath.

In a corner he found a trap door that
opened up a flight of steps, and these he descended unwillingly. For Tolliver might return at any moment and notice, where Ripley
had approached, dimples in the sand which
the wind had not yet rubbed out. Besides,
there could be nothing in the cellar.

He looked at the foot of the stairs and
looked helplessly around him. For light, he
had one brilliant shaft that struck through a
hole under the foundation of the shack; the
brightness of that round arm of sunshine left
the rest of the cellar room doubly black.

He turned back to the stairs when some-

thing that was not wind sighed in the
darkness. He dropped to one knee and stared
from behind his Colt. Then he saw the thing in
the corner. It looked like a crude frame, of
some sort, not like a human being. But it was
in fact a man lashed by his hands and ankles
to opposite cornerposts and drawn taut by a
low sawbuck which had been worked in under
his hips.

Ripley passed a hand across his eyes, but
the horrible image was still before him. This
agony had continued while Tolliver played
solitaire in front of the house and freshened
his leisure with swigs out of the whisky bottle.

He went closer. In that dimness he could
not have made out most faces clearly, but the
silver glint of the scar helped him to recognize
Dong.

No white man could have endured this, but
the Chinaman had not even fainted. His
bright eyes looked steadily up at Ripley; and
then from his throat came a cry as thin as a
whistle.

"Ching!" he was saying. "Ching! Ching!
Ching!"

Ripley slashed the ropes. The released body
dropped like a wet cloth on either side of the
hurdle. He picked up the helpless thing beneath the armpits, changed his hold, and carried him up the stairs to the light. There he
laid Dong down on the floor and as he lowered
the body, the head and legs of the Chinaman
crumpled weakly down—the very bone of his
back seemed to be gone.

The face—a durable mask—was not much altered except that the skin had a curiously dry, stiff look, as though it had been covered by a hard, brittle, non-luminous varnish. Dust seemed to fill the wrinkles about the eyes and the mouth; the lips were a trifle swollen and cracked to the red.

The face was not much altered; the body had been tormented until it was an abomination. The thin garment let the size of the weals and bumps show through, clearly. Some of the wounds, particularly where the hurdle had sawed into the flesh, were still bleeding; big Jack Ripley's hands were encrimsoned. But nothing was horrible in comparison with the way the ropes about the wrists had pulled the skin and muscles to the glimmer of tendons and the white of bone. These immense furrows had been engraved for so long that they were dry; the ridged flesh showed no tendency to soften and close over the wound.

Yet it was plain from Dong's expression that he had not been blowing the strength of his spirit away in screams and lamentations. There was only a peculiar deadness, a flatness, of the eyes as though the living soul had been poured forth.

From the throat of this monster—because the pain he had endured made him terrible—singing had issued within twenty-four hours of that moment! In fact, at this moment sounds of apology passed Dong's lips. As Ripley extended his hands to lift the body once more, the Chinaman put down his elbows and strove to lift himself, but his utmost agony of effort barely sufficed to raise his shoulders inches from the floor.

Ripley watched that effort to the full, to the end.

He needed to see the perfection of pain, so that his soul might be tempered and annealed in fire against the day when he should have the joy of laying his hands on Dan Tolliver and the super-devil who existed behind that brutal figure, the unknown rival of Lancaster. Then Ripley caught up a blanket from the floor, swathed Dong stiffly in the folds, and raised him again in his arms. On the floor beneath remained a pattern sketched in strokes of red, some bold and others faint, but making a picture curiously exact.

It was a heavy weight to carry from the house, but under the tree in front, Ripley braced the limp body on his knee and with one arm poured a swallow of whisky between Dong's teeth. The Chinaman coughed and choked. Tears of pain stung his eyes. He gasped. But when the bottle was offered again he parted his lips with a sigh of submission to receive the liquid fire again.

Afterward, Ripley carried the burden up the deep, slippery hill of sand, making only inches with every stride, the subtle grains poured so fluidly about his feet. He reached the top; and there was no sight of Dan Tolliver coming up the lower valley.

Just over the crest, he had to sink down on a knee, his exhausted breath coming in a rapid panting. Dong began to struggle faintly to be free, to make his own way forward. One of his arms lifted uncertainly in a gesture of protest that only served to show Ripley the dry, monstrous gash across the wrist.

He stood up and made the place where the mare lay at his next effort. When he bestraddled her, she lurched suddenly to her feet. His hands were employed supporting the loose give of Dong's body, but he guided the mare with his knees and with his voice.

The depth of the sand, the double burden, kept her lurching, struggling, but she put her head down and went earnestly on with her work.

In a few moments they had passed the dunes and came over a flinty slope into a ravine of rocks. The walls of it held the small voice of a rivulet which kept a dancing echo among the rocks. And down this canyon, as down a road, the way led straight towards Los Altos.

Here, as he made sure that he had almost succeeded in his task, Dong's head slipped to the side; the weak body turned to water. He had fainted.

The mare kneeled at command. Ripley, stepping from the saddle, carried the inert form into a nest of brush. He laid it on the ground and put his ear over Dong's heart. Only by degrees could he hear first a flutter and then the resolving beat, very weak, very distant in sound.

He brought water from the creek and

bathed the Chinaman's face, and bared and bathed his throat as well. And as Dong roused slowly, he gave him a drink from the canteen which was always tied to his saddle. The taste of water cast a lust like madness into Dong's eyes. Twice he emptied the canteen and then lay with wet lips parted, eyes closed, breathing deeply.

They had tormented him by thirst, too, it seemed. And Ripley patted Dong's shoulder with lingering touches until the Chinaman opened his eyes. There was more light in them now, or suffering more completely mastered.

Ripley, standing up, showed with gestures that he would leave now and return later. He would surely return. He would come again and lift Dong and place him in an easy conveyance and so they would depart together.

And Dong made another futile struggle to lift himself on his elbow so that the nodding of his head would be more like a bow.

Ripley pressed him back against the ground.

And as Dong lay impassive, unresisting at last, the Chinaman asked faintly: "Ching? Ching?"

"Yes," nodded Ripley. "Ching!"

Whatever she was, actress, deceiver, decoy, poor Dong wanted her, and it was no time for Ripley to make decisions about her. He would bring her if he could.

CHAPTER XXIV

Gray Hickory went into Los Altos at a racing gait. Ripley turned her through the open double doors of the livery stable and skidded her to a halt on the wet planking. A fat man, with one suspender holding up his trousers and a cigar in his mouth, came limping from a glassed-in office. He talked without removing the cigar from his mouth. Splatterings of ash dribbled over his shirt.

"Hey, Mr. Ripley! Glad to see you! What's the news of the big fight?"

"Have you got two quiet horses?" asked Ripley. "And can you rig two poles to make a horse-stretcher with a hammock or something fastened between the poles?"

"I got the whole outfit ready for you," declared the livery man.

"How soon will you have it turned out on the street?"

"Five minutes—ten minutes."

"Make it five minutes."

"I'll do it, Mr. Ripley. Hey, Willie—Tom! Hey, Willie! One of these days I'd like to hear about the jail raid there in Dalton. Think of a whole damn town sitting down on its heels and letting—"

"Where's there a good doctor?"

"What's up?" asked the other.

"God knows what will be up unless I get a doctor."

"There's only one doctor in town. When he's right, he can't be beat. Come here to the door. You see down there around the second corner? Third house on the right-hand side. Doc Merriman. You get Doc Merriman and he'll fix things for you. But who's laid up?"

"Friend of mine—get that horse litter ready, will you?"

And Ripley sent Hickory Dickory headlong through the dust. As he swerved her around the corner, he saw the white flag which she had raised still unfurling behind them, drenching the street as though with a fog. Then he was pulling up in front of the third house on the right.

The face of the house was like a back turned. There was one small window beside the door. He beat on this, then threw it open. A tall, pale man walked out of an inner room toward him.

"Are you Doc Merriman?" he asked.

"I am the doctor, sir," said the other.

"I've got a case for you. Take it on the run,

will you? Right out Third Street—right out to
the end and up the ravine there. Keep straight
up. You can't miss it. You'll find a man
stretched out there in a patch of brush. You
can't miss the brush. It's the only patch in the
whole length of the canyon. A Chinaman inside—"

"Third Street—Chinaman—ravine—brush
—?" echoed Doctor Merriman.

"Throw a saddle on your horse. I'll be back
for you," said Ripley. "Be ready to move in
three minutes. Have some bandages. For open
wounds. And a stimulant of some sort—he's
almost dead—"

He flung the last words over his shoulder
and plunged from the door at Hickory.

There was danger in the next move, for
Lancaster or Lancaster's men might be in
Sam Li's house. But when he entered the door
of the little shop it was Ching alone whom he
found there, folding a great length of shimmering silk with meticulous care. She looked
up at him with the professional smile of a
shopkeeper. Then her smile went out; her
hand flashed toward a tasseled bell-pull that
hung beside the inner door.

"Leave that alone," directed Ripley.

Her hand came away again, slowly, and as
he advanced toward her she looked from side
to side, then helplessly at Ripley.

"Shrinking today, or standing and taking
it?" asked Ripley.

She swallowed. She put her hand to her
throat as though she were in pain there. Trou-

ble was in her large eyes. As he drew nearer
they continued lifting. Only the breadth of the
counter was between them. He leaned over it a
trifle.

"How did Lancaster like the story?" he
asked.

She said nothing. Her eyes shifted on his
face as though across a line of print.

"He had a good laugh, eh?" suggested
Ripley. "But for a little job like that, I don't
suppose that he even raises your pay. Is that
straight?"

She laid one hand against her cheek and
waited. The fingernails were pink, and they
shone. The baby red and the baby curves had
never gone out of her lips, entirely. The sheen
of the China silk was trembling a little over
her breast; at the base of her throat a pulse
beat under a delicate vein of blue.

He knew that what he was seeing would be
with him forever. It would waken him in the
middle of the night and the black, empty rolling of the darkness would be his only reward.
In the cold and dread of the morning he would
try to take comfort out of the unforgotten
image again.

The iron in him struck like a harsh chime
into his next words.

"Don't stand there babying me with your
eyes. Do you think you can make a fool of the
same man twice in the same way?"

She took a quick, deep breath.

"Answer me!" exclaimed Ripley.

Her lips seemed to be struggling to make

words. Pity went through him, a deep thrust of pain. He looked down and saw red stains on his hands.

"I'm not coming here willingly," said Ripley. "Poor old Dong is one who doesn't see through you. He's sent me for you."

"Dong?" she cried. "Dong? You haven't found him!"

"Do you mean to say that *you* knew where he was?" demanded Ripley. Then the horror receded in him a little; for whatever was in her, she could not have had a part in Dong's tormenting. And however well she could act, she could not call into her voice the tremor, or bring the happiness into her eyes as she repeated: "Dong? Have you found him, really?"

Watching her fixedly, he lifted a hand.

"That's his blood," said Ripley. And then as the blow struck her, he was sick with shame.

"He'll be all right," he assured her. "I've started the doctor to get ready. Have you got a horse here under the saddle?"

"Yes," she whispered. "Yes, yes!"

It was the exact voice that he had heard from her in the tower room of the old Dalton place. But once more he could not doubt her. Old tales, legends overwhelmed him. Samson was the kind of fool who could not see the truth in woman.

He pointed away. "Out Third Street," he explained. "And straight up the ravine to the first big patch of brush. You'll find him there. Go fast, Ching. The sight of you will be better

than medicine for him. I have a horse litter
waiting at the livery stable."

She went past him in a flash and through
the inner door, running like a boy.

And he went slowly back to the street. For
one breath the faintly sweet and Oriental
pungency of the air in the shop remained in
his nostrils. Then he flung himself into the
saddle and raced back to Doc Merriman's
house.

"Are you ready, doc?" he called, as he hit
the ground in front of the place. "Hey, Doc
Merriman!"

But there might be the preparation of a
medical kit, of course, and therefore he followed his own voice to the front door and flung
it open.

The doctor's tall, pale form advanced from
the inner room. A sombrero was on his head
now.

"Are you ready?" shouted Ripley.

"Ready?" said the doctor.

"Ready to start. My God, haven't you even
saddled a horse by this time? Where's your
kit? What have you been doing?"

The violence of his words seemed to thrust
the doctor back. Merriman checked himself
with a hand against the jamb of the inner
door. His hat toppled awry over his forehead.

That last touch of strangeness made Ripley
stride to him. Through the door he had a
glimpse of a loose leather kit spread out on a
table—and then the doctor's breath reached
him, reeking with whisky fumes.

He looked again into the pale face. The eyes were fixed.

"Ravine—Chinaman—brush—Third Street—" the doctor mumbled, in a voice of quiet concentration.

And a rising wind howled softly in mockery past the corner of the house.

Ripley brushed the tall figure aside and entering the room rolled the kit hastily, and snapped the fastening catch. When he turned, Doctor Merriman was leaning to pick up his sombrero, which evaded his reach. So the doctor laid his other hand on the floor and stretched again with poised, clawlike fingers, ready to pounce.

Ripley crashed the front door open with his shoulder, left it swinging, and jumped into the saddle. He sent Hickory flashing to the livery stable and into it—but the horses for the litter were not in sight.

He shouted and received no answer. But footfalls were moving on the floor above him, and he bolted up the ladder into the loft. There he found the fat proprietor cutting open a bale of hay, sweating at his work.

"The horse litter!" exclaimed Ripley.

"Yeah—and what's wrong with it?" asked the fat man.

"Wrong with it? Where is it?"

"The Chinaman took it. He said you sent him. Why, damn his hide if you didn't—"

"What Chinaman?"

"Sam Li, and the Chinese gal along with him—they came pelting. Never knew there was a hoss big enough to pack a bundle like that Sam Li, but he sure had a whale under him. Hey—wait a minute—was it wrong?"

"It's right," answered Ripley. "Right as can be."

He climbed down the ladder more slowly, because there was no need for haste, now that Sam Li had appeared on the scene. A sense of the big Chinaman's wisdom and sufficiency released all the tension in Ripley's brain, and at a quiet canter he sent Hickory up the ravine, at length. The medical kit would be needed, of course; but even without it, Sam Li would accomplish some magic by the touch of his hands.

A bend of the ravine showed Ripley the patch of brush. But there was no horse litter beside it. Sam Li's bulk loomed nowhere in sight. The canyon lay totally empty, half golden with afternoon sunlight, half black with the shadow.

CHAPTER XXV

There was some possibility that Sam Li and the horse litter had gone astray by turning from the straight way of the ravine into one of the numerous little side gullies which opened off the main gulch. Then Dong would be found lying still in the patch of shrubbery. But even as Ripley sent Hickory forward again he was sure that Dong would not be there.

And he was right. He found the spot where Dong had been and one thin streak of red on the leaves of a bush; but the shadow from the western wall, as he looked, crossed the shrub as though anxious to wipe out even this evidence.

A dizzy sense of ghostly unreality took possession of Ripley. At the most, he could hardly have been more than four or five minutes behind the horse litter; and what

earthly reason had Sam Li for rushing the
wounded man away before Ripley appeared
on the scene with medical help? Wherever the
litter was, it could not be far away.

There was a craggy little eminence not far
away. Up the side of that Hickory ran like a
goat and stopped at the top, panting, while her
master looked over the landscape. It was cut
with ravines as lines divide a human face. In
any one of twenty of the nearest draws, Sam
Li and the girl and Dong might be traveling,
the hoofs of the animals muffled by the sand
which had blown into the gullies. To begin the
search would be to lose it at once.

A sort of madness came on Ripley, the
frenzy of a child that beats its fists against a
solid wall or throws itself down on the ground
to kick and scream. From the moment when
he was commissioned by Tom Dallas in this
work, he had met with nothing but strange
failures. The success for which he reached was
squeezed out of his grasp almost as though by
the strength of his own hand. At this moment
of triumph the stakes disappeared. And now,
by a stroke of singular legerdemain, the prize
was snatched away from him at the very moment when the sun was nearing the horizon
and the night would soon cover hills and
mountains.

Then he heard two sounds in quick suc-
cession. They might have been made by the
slapping of hands in the ravine to his right.
No, that was empty. The noises must have

come from beyond the round heads of the sand dunes in the direction of the little shack where Dong had been tormented. Was it not possible that Sam Li had known of the house and had turned towards it to get Dong to shelter, never guessing that he would be putting his head into the lion's mouth?

As fast as Hickory Dickory could step through the sand and over the rocks, Ripley hurried toward the place; but when his head rose to a view of the shack, he saw only Dan Tolliver seated again at the little table in front of the house with the whisky bottle at his right hand. And Tolliver, lifting his head, looked steadily toward Ripley—and then resumed his game of solitaire!

Nevertheless, it was with gun in hand that Ripley went down the slope. He only ventured a few glances at the face of the ground and made sure that there was no running of the sand into little pools such as he would have found if other riders had been this way before him. It seemed clear that Sam Li and the horse litter had not come by this way; and yet he could not be sure. Dong and the others might at this moment be inside the house.

Tolliver's bland indifference was the most amazing thing, and it was also odd that, although the afternoon was very close and warm, Tolliver had wrapped his coat around the middle of his body. Strangest of all, Tolliver did not even glance up again as Ripley dismounted before him.

"Tolliver," he said, "do you think you can bluff your way through this? No, old son, you're going to talk for once in your life. Where's Dong gone?"

"To hell, I hope," said Tolliver, gathering the cards with slow hands.

Ripley laid the muzzle of the Colt on the edge of the table.

"Have you seen Sam Li and Ching pass near here?" he asked.

"Sam Li?" asked Tolliver, and he looked up in a flash of surprise. "What would the Chinaman be doing out here?"

There was only one more question that had to be asked and Ripley put it at once, for he was losing much valuable time. Already the sun was puffing its red cheeks in the horizon mist.

"I want to know the name of the higher-up," he said. "The one who would have hired me."

"Like to have the job, now?" asked Tolliver, laying out the cards in four precise rows.

"His name is what I'm asking for, not the job."

Tolliver lifted the whisky bottle and took a good swallow. He put down the bottle and rested his hand on the neck of it for a moment, breathing hard. Then he said: "Why ask me? I'll never tell you."

"You don't understand," said Ripley. "I saw Dong in the cellar. I saw what you'd been doing to him. I'll do the same to you, Tolliver, until I've burned what I want out of you!"

"It's a funny thing what a fool you are," said Tolliver, looking casually up at the other. "I did those things to Dong, did I?"

"Who else?" asked Ripley.

"The big boss—the gent higher up. Not that I gave a damn, but I wouldn't have ideas that good," answered Tolliver. "Now what about it?"

"His name—that's what about it!"

"Yeah, if you had that, you'd be on the inside, wouldn't you?" sneered Tolliver. "You'd know all you want, and you could raise hell. But you won't find it out through me."

"Won't I?" asked Ripley, savagely.

"Beat it, will you?" asked Tolliver.

"By God," said Ripley, lifting his gun, "why don't I let you have it now—through the middle of the face?"

Tolliver grinned. His lips parted. His mouth sprawled wide and he spoke thickly. "Yeah, and why not?" he asked.

"Are you drunk?" asked Ripley, staring.

"Better'n that," said Tolliver.

And then Ripley, stepping back in bewilderment from a man to whom guns had ceased to have a meaning, saw a little pool of red forming around the left foot of Tolliver. A grisly suspicion made him reach out and pull the coat away from the body of Tolliver. It was red and sopping with blood. With golden teeth, Tolliver continued grinning. The blood pumped slowly from a spot in the middle of the breast—no, it was below the lungs.

"You're a dead one," said Ripley.

"You're telling me, are you?" asked Tolliver, and he dragged the whisky bottle toward him again.

It fell from his nerveless fingers. A quantity of the brown liquid spurted out and covered the playing cards. Ripley retrieved the bottle and held it to Tolliver's lips who drank deep.

"Putting in whisky and taking out blood, that oughta be a fair exchange," said Tolliver. "Sit down and have a drink with me, kid."

"I don't want it. Keep it for yourself," said Ripley.

"You're a thoughtful bastard, ain't you?" asked Tolliver. "Gimme another slug of it, will you?"

Ripley obeyed. There was a coldness about his mouth, a shudder in his knees.

"Who did this?" he asked.

"Who you think? Lancaster, with that long-drawn-out drink of water, Missouri Slim, standing behind him. It nearly killed Missouri to see Jim have the shooting all to himself."

He grinned as he remembered Slim's disappointment. His head leaned a little to the side. It did not straighten, but kept on leaning. He commenced to seem a trifle sleepy.

"You ain't a bad kid," said Tolliver. "I'll tell you something. Haul yourself out of all this. Head that way—"

He jerked his thumb toward the setting sun.

"Head that way and keep going, a coupla

thousand miles. Lancaster, he can't be stopped now."

"Why not, Dan?"

"Because he knows everything now. He's on the inside. He promised that he'd let me clean off if I told him everything, and I told him. And he drilled me when I finished. Missouri wanted to finish me on the spot, but Lancaster took a good look at where the bullet went in and come out and he says what's the good of letting me have at one swaller what I can keep tasting a long time."

"Tolliver," begged Ripley, "what did you tell Lancaster? Let me stretch you out—you'll last—I've got bandages and stuff, ready for you."

"Hell, no! Leave me sit up. I want it over with and I drain a lot faster sitting up."

"Will you let me know what you told Lancaster?"

"Quit teasing me," growled Tolliver. "I've told you what to do. Get out! The whole game's in Lancaster's hands now. He's gotta win, with what I've told him."

"You're passing out, Dan!" exclaimed Ripley, looking closely into the misting eyes. "Forget Lancaster and all the rest. Tell me what I can do for you."

"It's a funny thing," muttered Tolliver. "There ain't hardly any pain. Straighten my head up."

Ripley took the bulldog head between his hands and raised it.

"Ask me for anything I can do," said Ripley.

"You're a good kid," said Tolliver, faintly. "Pull the watch out of the top pocket of my trousers, in front."

Ripley found and drew out a thin gold watch.

"Crack the back of it open," ordered Tolliver.

That was done, and Ripley saw a tiny photograph of a broad-faced woman of middle age, a heavy, sullen, fat face.

"What you think of her?" asked Tolliver. "She's a sweetheart, ain't she?"

"She's beautiful," said Ripley.

"Lemme see her," gasped Tolliver. "Closer —turn on a light, will you?—that's better. She's a beauty, ain't she? But she left me last year. Damn her heart! For a Chinaman is what she left me for. She was sure a—"

A gargling sound in his throat closed over the last words.

"Keep my head up, you clumsy fool!" whispered Tolliver.

Ripley raised the head again; the dull eyes stared at nothingness.

"Suppose the fool talk you hear as a kid had anything in it?" asked Tolliver. "It'd be hell on me—it'd be hell *for* me in another minute."

"What's the use supposing?" asked Ripley. "You'll be all right. You'll be all comfortable in another minute, Dan."

"Sure—" murmured Tolliver. "Just like sleeping—just like—"

A hand seemed to strike him, violently. After that electric shudder he was still, and the head became a looser weight in Ripley's hands.

CHAPTER XXVI

He went straight back to Los Altos, because it was more than possible that Sam Li, after finding Dong, had turned back toward the town—though why he should have used any way other than that by which he went out was a mystery. But when the giant Chinaman found Dong so close to death, many impulses beyond Ripley's understanding might have swayed him. And there would be the girl's mournful voice, urging speed.

That was what Ripley kept telling himself all the way back to Los Altos—not that it was time for him to leave the country, as Dan Tolliver had said—not that the whole game was now in Lancaster's powerful hands—but simply that there must be some good in the girl, for surely she loved old Dong. And those who love one thing surely have the gift of loving all. She was a trickster, an actress, a decoy, a mistress of infinite deceit, perhaps, but evil may be taught and learned and afterward forgotten.

Who had taught her? Who had prepared her for her roles? That mysterious man whose hand had appeared, dimly, in Dan Tolliver's brutal actions: it might be he who pulled the strings and controlled Ching's motions.

The melancholy beauty of the sunset and the oncoming of the night entered Ripley's soul, and he had a sense that he had embarked on the last stage of a journey. If he took Tolliver's advice and rode out of the country, east or west, he would be safe; but if he continued on this trail it might be the last one. He could not leave the trail, he knew, and therefore he was embarked in darkness. Strangely enough, it was not Lancaster and the strength of his hand-built machine that he feared so much as that unknown, that shadowy rival who, it appeared, had been overthrown by the betrayal of Tolliver.

The stars were white in the sky and the lights were yellow in the town when he rode into Los Altos. The evening choir of children's voices, barking dogs, men laughing at the end of the day's work, women calling home their truants, came gently to Ripley's ears. The fear and the uncertainty began to fall away from him. And when he reached the familiar little curved street where Sam Li's house stood behind its shop sign, he was ready to laugh at the depression of his heart.

Lights showed in faint streaks through the

shuttered upper windows of Sam Li's house. And nothing was wrong except that one Mexican in his high-peaked straw sombrero was halted in the middle of the street, staring at the place.

"What is wrong, brother?" asked Ripley.

"Who knows that?" answered the Mexican. "Not even God."

This philosophical Mexican walked on, while Ripley threw the reins of the mare and tapped lightly on the front door of the house.

He heard no answer. Only his ear could detect a considerable bustling far inside the place, and a murmuring of continually subdued voices.

He tried the doorknob, pushed the door open, and entered.

He stopped in amazement. Every roll or fold of cloth on Sam Li's shelves had been tumbled onto the counters and over the floor. The counters themselves had been ripped open here and there, at the top, and down the hall he saw the gleaming streak of a canary that darted into the front room and round and round it, the wings making a quivering translucence in the lamplight. The frightened bird perched in a corner, on top of the highest shelf. And now Lancaster's voice rolled dimly to Ripley's ears.

"Not an iron box, you bonehead. An ivory box about eight inches long. Ivory. Old, yaller ivory. With carvings on the lid that look like nothing at all. Find the ivory box and we know that he's coming back. If it's gone—*he's* gone.

And I'll have the heart out of the big Chinaman. If it takes me the rest of my life—"

Ripley drew softly back into the street. He walked Hickory past the house, mounted, and rode to the end of the lane.

Sam Li was not in his house. He was out yonder—out toward the north east. And full in the east itself, Ripley saw a moon rising like a golden fish through a purple sea. There would be light, not long after this sunset, and if only he had eyes and wits to use on the trail, he might still decipher the way by which Sam Li had made his retreat with Dong.

Then he remembered eyes that, for a trail, were far, far better than his would ever be. Straightway he headed the mare up the river road toward Oñate's house.

Ripley stood back in the shadow of the ravine, hardly breathing. His senses were too dim to give much assistance to the Mexican. A tenseness like that of prayer was in his throat and hands as he watched Jose Oñate, on hands and knees, crawling around through the brush where Dong had last been seen.

Now and then Oñate made a long pause. Sometimes he peered at the leaves, sometimes at the stems of the brush, sometimes he put his face close to the rock and the ground.

At last he stood up and said in Mexican, to himself: "This way they come. This way they go—"

He remained standing, pointing with the flat of his hand.

"Can you find the trail that way? It won't show on those rocks, will it?" asked Ripley.

The Mexican ran suddenly forward to a place where the rocks lay as flat as a table, a polished table. Here he dropped on his knees, again. Ripley, following at a distance, sat down on his heels and watched the operations, helplessly.

"Not here!" said Oñate.

He rose again and began to turn in a hopeless circle, agape, staring with wide eyes.

"There—there!" said Oñate, and pointed to the rough rocks that climbed the side of the ravine.

"Not that way, Jose," protested Ripley. "If the horse litter went up such a slope, it would have spilled Dong out on his face."

Oñate, waving a hand for silence, ran up to the top of the rise and dropped on his knees again. Almost instantly his voice was sounding with triumph.

"This is the way! This way, señor!"

Ripley took Oñate's mule on the lead and rode Hickory up the difficult way.

He came to the top of a rocky little eminence with scatterings of grass sprouted from crevices.

"Why would a man come this way, Oñate?" he asked.

"A man who doesn't want to do ordinary things," answered the Mexican. "Those who hunt for him will ride up the ravine or down the ravine and look into the mouth of every gulley to see which way he has gone. But this

is the way—right up the steep rocks—here is
the sign. Here are two horses stepping one
right behind the other. And those are the
horses that carry the litter. Now it goes this
way—the trail! Follow me!"

Oñate, pausing only now and then to peer at
something on the ground, ran back across the
stony little tableland, dipped through the narrows of a gulley, and climbed the farther side
onto rolling ground.

It was hard for the horse and the mule to
follow. Plainly the only way of transporting
Dong over such obstructions was to carry him,
and while the girl managed the animals, huge
Sam Li must have handled Dong.

Oñate kept to a steady run. After a time, he
mounted the mule and rode with his body,
most of the time, bent low, so that he could
scan the ground more easily. He made towards a gap between two hills.

"Here it was growing dark—it was quite
dark as they came to this place," said Oñate.

"How in the name of the Lord can you tell
that?" asked Ripley.

"See where the trail goes there? Can you
see? They would never ride so close under that
tree except that it surprised them in the
darkness."

"Then they were here a long time ago.
We're far behind them, Oñate. Go faster."

Oñate beat the ribs of his mule with his
heels, but the mule had only one gait and
stuck to it, merely shaking his head. But now

they were climbing the slope into the pass between the hills. Now they passed beneath the light of the rising moon into thick shadow, and came out into a ravine of hard, gleaming rock.

And Ripley groaned aloud, for he was sure that not even a bloodhound could follow a scent across such terrain as this, to say nothing of eyes discovering sign. Oñate, in fact, was soon on his hands and knees again until he reached a narrow stream that twisted back and forth among the boulders of the central valley.

Into that water he dived, throwing up a sheet of black and a spray of brilliant jewels. On the farther shore he was soon down on his hands and knees again, but after a moment he swam back to the near shore and went up the bank at a dogtrot, his head thrust out like a hunting hound's.

For a full hundred yards he continued in this manner, then paused with a shout.

Ripley, following, saw a bit of bright water that shone on the face of a hollowed rock.

"Here!" said Oñate. "The air has dried the rest of it, but here is where they came out of the water and dripped some to make this little pool. You see?"

He began to laugh, exultant, and clambered on the mule again. At a sharp trot they proceeded up the rocky ravine until it narrowed and became a small upland valley. In place of rocks there was soil underfoot at last, and here Oñate was perfectly at home, for the ground spread a printed story under his eyes and the climbing moon lighted the page clearly for him.

They crossed a rise. A broader valley extended before them with a grove of trees backed against the face of an opposite hill. Oñate lifted his hand and pointed.

"That is the place!" he said. "That is where you will find them!"

"They won't be so close," declared Ripley.

"Look!" said Oñate. "You see how this horse is dragging a hind foot? You see how he scuffs the ground with it? With a lame horse, they will not go very far tonight. Besides, they have left a hard trail to follow. No one could follow it, they are sure. That is because they do not know Jose Oñate!" He began to laugh.

But Ripley rode eagerly down the slope and across the valley to the trees. They were young pines, holding up their spear-shaped heads close to one another. And before Ripley had advanced far into the gloom, he saw the glimmering of a light before him, wavering among the tree trunks with the motion of the horse.

CHAPTER XXVII

In the thick of the trees, with the outline of the house just showing before them and the one light gleaming through a window, Ripley halted Oñate.

"Who lives here?" he asked.

"No one, señor."

"You've been up here before?"

"No one has lived here for ten years. There was a family here once but a plague hit all their cattle; afterward, the people went away."

"Hold the horses here, Jose," said Ripley, dismounting, and giving the reins of the mare to Oñate, he went forward alone.

There was only a brief clearing about the old ranch house. The moonlight painted the roof and one wall with silver; the other side was black, with the splintered rays of the lamplight striking through one window. To this light he went and through the open window looked into a kitchen that held the entire party he was pursuing. And such a weakness of relief came over Ripley that he leaned his elbows on the sill and stared like a child, smiling.

Ching was busy at the old stove, which was so rust-eaten that puffs and curlings of smoke continually poured out of it. They were drawn upward, however, and when he looked toward the ceiling, he saw that a great rent was broken through the roof and the entire ceiling sagged toward it. Through that rent he could see now the tip of the great crescent of the moon.

An old cot had been brought into the kitchen and on this lay Dong, with his hands crossed on his breast and big white bandages covering his wrists. He was stripped to the waist and the monstrous form of Sam Li bent over him, caring for the welts and the wounds that crossed his body.

They mattered—the vast Chinaman and Dong—but the eye of Ripley kept coming back to the girl. She poured something hot into a tin cup and going to the bed kneeled by it and lifted the ugly head of Dong in the crook of her arm. He watched the brightness and the beauty of her face grow tender, and grief passed suddenly through Ripley.

She was giving Dong a drink now, and the old Chinaman at every swallow lifted his eyes with a dimness of adoration in them to Ching's face.

If there was so much grace in her, how could there be hypocrisy and evil, also? She looked to Ripley like an angel of gentleness—and this to the battered hulk that was Dong!

"Sam Li!" called Ripley.

"Hai!" cried Ching, and leaped to her feet. What a pallor and tension of dread were in her face as she whirled to the window. But big Sam Li turned his head over his shoulder with a smile and murmured: "Ah, Mr. Ripley! At last you have come to us!"

Old Dong, holding out his muffled hands suddenly, uttered a strange cry that was not ended suddenly, but rose and fell on an eerie note. It might have been a lament, as far Ripley's understanding followed it, but that gesture of the hands told the story.

It made Ripley leave the window and round the corner of the house, calling out cheerfully to Oñate, who came in with the horse and the mule at once. They were unsaddled and put to graze in the clearing and after that Ripley led the way into the house.

Even in that short time, Sam Li had finished his ministrations to Dong, and he came in the great silken sweep of his robe with his hand held out to Ripley.

"So I told them," said Sam Li, "that with our care we would be able to leave our enemies behind us, but that you would find us, surely. A good man sheds a light that shows him his way."

He turned from Ripley and with perfect democracy gave his hand and the deep, distant thunder of his voice to Oñate. Ripley was leaning above Dong, who slowly waved his bandaged hands back and forth and muttered a rapid jargon. Then a light touch fell on Ripley's shoulder. Ching was there.

"Dong must be quiet," she said. She rattled a bit of sing-song and shook a finger at Dong. He smiled at her and then, as though in obedience, closed his eyes.

"You are a god to him," said the girl to Ripley. "You've given him his life twice—that's what he said to you just now—and his mother gave him his life only once. He has put you among his ancestors."

He looked at her quietly until a slight flush ran over her face.

She said: "You're despising me for a trickster, and all that. Oh, I'm bad enough. But there's a way of explaining, if you'll ever want to listen."

"Yes," said Ripley. "I want to listen."

Sam Li was booming conversation at Oñate, and Ripley followed the girl back to the stove. Leaning a bit over her he said: "I've been hating you, Ching. But I'm rubbing out everything I know about you except the first time—the canaries, and that. I'm a fool about you. But don't make me a mean fool again if you can help it."

She was scrambling a stew of rabbit's meat and odds and ends in a big, flat pan; and she looked suddenly up to him over her shoulder. There were no words, only the look, swift and wonder-stricken. But Ripley turned back to Sam Li with ease in his heart. For there *was*, perhaps, an explanation of everything she had done in the past.

"Trouble makes new friends old," Sam Li was saying. "We are happy to have you with us, Mr. Ripley."

"Tell me," said Ripley, "why you went out of the ravine without waiting for me?"

"Because we heard horses entering the gulley," said Sam Li. "If it had been one horse, we would have waited; but two riders— we knew it could not be our friend. I picked Dong out of the litter. Danger makes the legs strong. I was able to carry him up the steep rocks. The horses came after us. We went away quickly. We tried to cover our way of going, also. But always I trusted that *you* would be able to follow us."

"Sam Li, were you afraid of Lancaster?" asked Ripley.

The fat man smiled.

"I have made him angry by discovering how bad a man he is," said the Chinaman.

"But if Lancaster could not follow you, did you really think that I'd be able to work out your trail?" asked Ripley, with a quick, deep sting of suspicion.

"Yes. You had our hope to guide you," said Sam Li. "Speak to Dong. He is hungrier for you than for food."

"There is only one word we both understand," said Ripley.

"And that word is a name?" asked Sam Li. And he began to laugh, making a gentle thunder.

They sat or stood around the table and ate from the rust-worn, time-battered tins and irons which had been abandoned with the house. The whole place was decaying and the winter mold in the corners of the floor was brown now with the summer.

The moonlight, stronger than the lamp, struck out a white patch on the floor and the creeping edge of that spot told Ripley how time was moving. He ate a share of the stew and drank some strong coffee.

"How did you happen to bring food along with you?" he asked Sam Li.

"When the wolf sniffs at the front door, the fox prepares to leave his home," answered the Chinaman. "And I have had saddlebags of food and coffee ready for several days."

"You mean that you're leaving Los Altos for good?" asked Ripley, amazed.

"Ching has need of me," declared Sam Li, speaking with that deep softness of voice which always charmed Ripley. "I leave a shop stored with silks and tea because I had rather be with a friend stored with love. That is an exchange which makes my soul rich."

"And your purse poor!" exclaimed the girl. "Sam Li, Sam Li, you have thrown everything away because of Ching!"

She threw out her hands to the Chinaman;

and Ripley, looking into her eyes, saw the tears there.

Well, if there were trickery and cunning in her, better her dishonesty than all the truth that could be found in ordinary people. She had heart. God save him from cold virtue which lives in the head only.

"Why do you grieve because of what I have done?" asked Sam Li. "I am happy, Ching, and no happy man is poor."

Something swelled hot and big in the soul of Ripley. Never again would he think or speak lightly of a Chinaman.

"But now for the next step," he suggested. "What should we do now? Do you think that Lancaster will trail you?"

"Look!" said Sam Li, gesturing with both hands to the girl. "Will a thirsty man hunt for water, or a starving man for food?"

"Has Lancaster any reason to think you might come here?" went on Ripley.

"No. None," answered Sam Li.

"Then you've shaken him off. Nobody but my friend Oñate could have worked out this trail, I think."

"We have shaken him off, but perhaps we have not shaken off a greater danger than Jim Lancaster," said Sam Li. "Something that can see farther than a buzzard and follow a scent through water and air."

"What do you mean?" asked the girl.

"I mean Death!" said Sam Li. And he pointed toward Dong. "Half of his breath has been stolen from him. One touch and he may go from us."

Dong lay with heaving breast, his eyes closed, the yellow-green of his face shining with perspiration. Now and then his thick, horrible lips gaped open to drag in an audible breath.

"He must have a doctor!" said Sam Li. "I know a few herbs and simples, but Dong should have a good doctor to prescribe for him."

"The drunken fool in Los Altos—that's the man I should have had along," groaned Ripley. "I'll go back for him, now. If he isn't sober, I'll tie him on a horse and jolt his wits back into him. Oñate will go with me."

"Good!" said Sam Li, smiling his pleasure. "Now you know how to find us. We stay here till you return. We take the chance that Jim Lancaster cannot find us. Go quickly, my friends!"

Oñate, who had sat with shining eyes to watch all of this scene, now at a word from Ripley went out of the house to saddle the horse and the mule. But when Ripley moved to follow, a crying of groaning protest from Dong made him pause.

The sick man was making gestures of pitiful entreaty. Sweat now ran fast down his face as he begged Ripley to remain.

The girl, in a rapid voice, translated:

"Stay with me, father. There is very much darkness. The heart dies when there are only strangers about it."

"Think of that!" said the girl. "Even I am

only a stranger to Dong, compared with you!"

"Poor Dong! Poor Dong!" said Sam Li.

He leaned over Dong and spoke to him in a murmur which was almost inaudible. Dong, staring up at the fat face of Sam Li, listened with eyes of agony; but he broke out again in a sudden clamor.

"Let him stay and I shall not be afraid!" translated the girl. "If I breathe, I must talk. If he goes, I shall have to keep talking."

Sam Li turned slowly from Dong's cot.

"We must be patient," said Sam Li, but there was a visible cloud on his face.

"I don't understand that last bit," said Ching. "If Jack Ripley goes, Dong must keep on talking. Now, what can that mean?"

"The brain needs blood as well as the body," said Sam Li, "and Dong is very weak. This is the trouble. If we send Señor Oñate only, will he be able to bring back the doctor? Is it wise to send a child to do the work that is meant for a man?"

Ching put her hand on Ripley's arm and shook her head as she looked at Dong.

"He must stay here," she said, "or Dong will go mad with fear. As long as Jack is here, Dong feels that he cannot die. That feeling is worth almost more than blood, it seems to me." She added something in the rapid, up and down, sing-song of the Chinese language. Dong promptly uttered a great sigh and closed his eyes.

"I've promised him that Jack will stay. And now you see?" said the girl.

Sam Li murmured something indistinct. His face was calm, but there was a darkness on his brow that Ripley had not seen there before. He went out to see Oñate away. The Mexican had the saddle already on the mule. Before he mounted, he spoke seriously to Ripley. His concern was so great that he took off his peaked sombrero and addressed Ripley with the hat in his hand.

"All of these people," he said, "mean trouble. A sick man, a fat man, and a pretty girl. Who can cook a dish like that and make it fit for eating? Come away with me, Señor. My father had the second sight; and there is an old scar in my left thumb that aches when trouble is coming towards me. Once I was riding on a trail from—"

"Jose, ride that mule hard," said Ripley. "Get the doctor. Tell him that if he won't come with you, men will take him at the end of a rope. Go quickly."

"Ah, well," groaned Oñate, "what is in the heart can only be changed by the Father in heaven. Farewell!"

He mounted at once, kicked his mule to a trot, and went jouncing off among the trees with his head far fallen on his breast. Not once did he look back.

CHAPTER XXVIII

Ripley, turning back toward the house, ran a melancholy eye over the broken roof-line. One of the barns was quite gone, lying in a heap of splintered ruins. Another was sagging from the north; one more good blow might send it crashing. Just past the standing barn, Sam Li's hobbled horses and those of the others were grazing; gray Hickory had come from among them at a trot to join her master, and as he rubbed his hand over the sleek of her neck, he had a sudden panic desire to saddle her and fly. It was not only the superstitious mind of Oñate that worked in him but a definite foreboding that he must meet Lancaster again; and if the meeting were on this night, it would be the end of Ripley.

He took comfort in remembering the intricacies of the trail which only the skill of Oñate had untangled. No white man attains the animal skill of a Mexican or an Indian on the trail; and perhaps not one of Lancaster's followers would be able to uncover the way of Sam Li's retreat. Yet it was very dangerous for them to remain so long in one spot.

Sam Li's voice sounded in deep, quiet laughter, inside the house, and the thought of the big Chinaman suddenly scattered Ripley's doubts. He went back into the kitchen and found Ching finishing the last of the dishes.

"A good woman is never weary," said Sam Li, who sat puffing at a long, thick-stemmed pipe. "And virtue does not need to sleep. Hai —but you are tired, Ching! Eh?"

"Talk to Jack," said the girl, turning from the wreckage of the sink where she was working. "Ask him how he could forgive me. Ask him if he *has* forgiven me?"

"Blame cannot stick to a smooth face," said Sam Li. "But harsh words catch in the wrinkles of a woman. Be always young, Ching, and you can never be wrong."

She looked somberly at Sam Li.

"Very well," she said. "I shall always be young."

Ripley went over to Dong. The coolie had a better color; his eyes were wide open and he smiled his horrible smile at Ripley; he turned his eyes toward the girl as he rattled off something in Chinese, which she translated: "We are a great trouble. But the heart of a father is always patient."

"And now he wants me, also," said Ching.

She came over to the cot and sat down on a three-legged stool which had once been a four-legged chair. She leaned close to Dong, smiling at him, and the coolie worshiped her silently for a moment. At last Dong shook his head and sighed. His next few phrases the girl translated with a gasp:

"I will tell you of your father." She turned her head. "Sam Li! Do you hear? He is going to tell me of father!"

"Is that wise?" asked Sam Li. "Well, perhaps talking will not take all of his strength. So let him begin. It is only a wise mind that must empty itself with labor. The speech of simple people flows fast because it flows downhill. Let him speak, Ching."

He himself rose, pulled his chair closer, and sat down again. The vastness of his weight brought a shrill squeak of complaint from the chair.

Dong began to talk, making a good many pauses, scattering his thoughts and his words freely, without much effort to gather them into coherent and narrative form.

"We leave the home.—Our boat leans in the river, there is such a wind.—Sometimes I see myself in the mirror of the water. With its speed, it makes a rain that blows coldly against me.—It would be a good thing to be blown on wings. The wind does not get tired, but my legs get very tired.—Now they are tired, Ching!—Now we are walking through mud. It makes popping noises under my feet.

The load on my back drives my heels down like anchors. Your father tries to take the load and carry it himself a while.—Ah hai! He has taken it away from me. I run after him and weep. He will not give it back to me.—At last he divides it into two parts. We each carry one part. Your father, Ching, carrying a burden like a four-legged beast!"

The girl, with her hands hard against her breast, drank in the story, but lifted her eyes once to Ripley; and tenderness at a stroke stupefied him and made his body sway. He barely understood the next words.

"Every day of journeying lays an extra pound on the pack. The knees begin to shiver before noon. But not the knees of the father of Ching. He sings songs which are not good to my ears but that show he is happy.—We are among strange men. They are Chinese but I cannot understand what they say. Not very easily. It is like listening to someone who shouts against the wind in the distance. I only know what is said but not the words which say it.—The nights are cold. There is not much wood for building the fire.—On a cold night, who can tell which is sleep and which is dreaming?—The father of Ching begins to tap the rocks. We are always climbing up and down. We are looking at a river, or at the sky. And the nights are always cold. Your father holds a piece of rock in his hands, Ching. He throws up one hand at the sky and laughs. It is never like the sound of Chinese laughter, but I laugh, also. I begin to dance. Now we are to go home. Yes, we are going toward home. The miles are shorter, that way. Our knees are stronger, taking steps towards home."

Here Dong closed his eyes and shook his head a little.

The girl, frozen with excitement, pale, and wide-eyed, could hardly translate the words that followed.

"We are near the home again. I know the rocks and the trees like faces. I want to call out to them and tell them who we are. We are near the house—"

"Ah, Dong! Dong!" murmured the girl, clasping her hands together.

He made a gesture for silence, looking mournfully at her, and she continued the translation:

"Here are people following us. They are going before us, also. There are people I know and I talk to them. I ask them why they have such strange faces. They tell me that there is war in the land. Everything is changed. It is a turning upside-down."

"Revolution!" added the girl, breathlessly, staring up at Ripley.

A cold touch of foreknowledge made him wish that he had been back there in the far land with Ching's father, who had carried his share of the burdens and who sang when the going was the hardest.

"We come at last to the house. But it not there. The forehead of the house does not stand up above the trees. There is only empty sky above the tips of the trees. We go closer. Through the trees we see heaps of black. The garden is burned away, also. The wind carries away ashes like puffs of black smoke.—That is all that is left of the house. And the father of Ching cries out her name: 'Ching! Ching! Ching!'"

At that, Ripley was sure that the girl would burst into tears. But instead, it was merely her breathing that was audible, and her head swayed a little from side to side.

"We are back beside the river. We will take a boat and go down to the city, down to the sea.—But men come on us with cries and howlings. They come like growling dogs. My brain is knocked into a darkness. I am on my knees. Through that darkness I see the father fall, still striking. And the people go away, howling against foreigners.—Why? They are men, like Chinamen! They eat food and breathe air like Chinamen. They are not bad!"

Ching, on her knees, held one of Dong's bandaged hands.

"They had killed him, Dong? They had killed him?"

"There was red on his face," Dong went on —and still she translated in a whisper, as though she were thinking aloud. "He is only asleep. He wakes up when I pour water over him. But I know that he must go to sleep again. He holds out his hand, and in it there is the little rock which he has carried all that way. He says: 'Ching! Ching!'—That is all—that is all—that is the end—"

Dong laid his white-wrapped hands crosswise over his face and made a moaning sound.

And the girl? She was not sobbing, even now. Her hand soothed the grief of Dong. Tears ran on her face, but slowly.

She spoke to Dong, and in a broken voice he went on—she still translating: "I go down to the sea. Far away there is Ching in her country, in her other home.—In San Francisco—yes.—There is a way to cross the sea. Men tell me about it. So I sell myself for a few years to go on a ship that will take me to another land, and out of that land I walk north to find Ching —and then many things happen. I am twice to die. But always he comes!"

Dong held out his hand to Ripley.

It was quite clear, now. Far up in the interior of China, among the mountains, Dong had accompanied the girl's father on a prospecting trip which had yielded, at last, a specimen of ore rich enough to make it seem that great fortune was there. And on the return to some river city of the land where the home of Ching stood, they had found that revolution was running through the country. They found the black ruins of the house; and before they could sail down the river to hunt for the lost family, Ching's father had been murdered and had given the specimen of ore to Dong, who was to carry it somewhere to the girl.

Sam Li's deep voice muttered something.

The girl urgently spoke to Dong, but he turned up his eyes towards the ceiling and made an erasing gesture with both hands.

"Where is the specimen of ore?" asked Ripley.

"That's what Sam Li wanted to know. That's what I've asked him. But he says that he lost it!"

"Ask him if he can describe the place where the ore was found," urged Ripley.

She nodded and asked the question. But again Dong closed his eyes and shook his head. He indicated with his hands a mist, a great mist into which it was impossible for him to look.

"There—that is all!" said Ching.

She added something more in Chinese to Dong. Such gentleness, thought Ripley, never had flowed before from the human throat. The quiet voice went on, making almost inaudible music. And Dong moved his head from side to side and uttered a mournful, dreary monotone of complaint against life.

It was her father who had died. But only the slow running of her tears showed her grief. And her voice and her hand were busy comforting this old servant of the family, this faithful friend.

Ripley drew back from her. He made a smoke and lighted it. And he saw Sam Li puffing at the thick-stemmed pipe with pursed lips, and his eyes staring fixedly at the ceiling. The eyes were as dark and dead as a stone. Ripley never had seen another thing in his life like the opaqueness of those eyes.

CHAPTER XXIX

Afterward, Dong lay with his eyes closed, motionless, and the girl crossed the room softly to Ripley.

"You must go to bed. You and Sam Li. There are plenty of blankets," she whispered. "I'll stay in here, close to Dong. He's sleeping now. And you and Sam Li will need your sleep, too. Because if Oñate comes back with the doctor before morning, perhaps we'll be able to start on again. And we have to hurry, hurry! Jim Lancaster *may* be coming over the hills and sighting this house in the trees. He may be coming this minute!"

"No," said Sam Li. He made his great voice hardly audible. It was a whisper, but there was resonance in it, like the dying strokes of a mighty bell that make a trembling through the air. "No. I must stay with Dong. You know that I can even sleep in a chair, Ching. And the hours make no difference to me. Take the lamp. Show Mr. Ripley that old bed in the next room; and you take the room on the right."

Ripley started to protest, but the lifting of Sam Li's great hand and the quiet assurance of his smile stopped all speech.

"We must do as Sam Li says," said the girl. "It's true that he can go with three hours' sleep in a day. And he'll know how to take care of Dong."

She went back to the coolie and leaned over him for a moment. Sam Li, rising from his chair, had gone to the window and was looking out on the trees and the moon-whitened hills beyond them.

Now he came back as the girl lifted the lamp from the table. The top of the chimney was broken to rags; the bowl was cracked, and in it floated a pint of rust-reddened kerosene which had been drained out of the dregs of a five-gallon can. It was the color of blood.

Sam Li went with them into the hall. An open doorway to the left admitted them into a bedroom with the floor sagging in one corner and broken through in another. The wallpaper, covered with faded birds and foliage, hung in strips from the wall. The ceiling sagged like a discolored belly. And in one corner was a single bed on the rusted springs of which Ripley rolled down his blanket.

Sam Li stood again at the window, looking out on the hills.

"I've been thinking of those hilltops all evening," said the girl. "Would fire signals show in moonlight like this, Sam Li?"

"Like little red eyes," answered Sam Li, gently. "They would not be seen so far, but they might be seen far enough."

"What signals?" asked Ripley.

"Oh, but you know about Jim Lancaster's signaling?" said the girl. "You know about his ways or you surely wouldn't have come trailing him, Jack!"

"I came into this job in a blind smother," admitted Ripley. "I came into it like a fool. You mean that Lancaster has a regular way of telegraphing his news?"

"There are good brains in that head," said Sam Li. "It is narrow, but the head of a wolf is narrow, also. And a wolf is always thinking. It catches rabbits with its thoughts, not with its speed. And I have been wondering when a red light might begin to blink up there on one of the hills, calling the men of Lancaster, telling him that three people he wants badly are down here among the trees!"

He turned to the girl.

"Can you read his code?" he asked.

"No," she answered.

"I'll teach you that tomorrow," said Sam Li. "Good night. If you are nervous, Ching, close your eyes as hard as you can. Your eye-

lids will grow tired, after a while, and then you
will be asleep."

"You'll need the lamp for Dong!" she exclaimed, as he turned away.

"I have enough of the moonlight," answered
Sam Li. "Take the lamp, Ching. Good night
again!"

He passed from the room. The girl shaded
her face from the light, to stare after him. The
shadow of her hand floated big on the wall behind her.

"Was there ever a man so kind, or so gentle,
or so wise, or so good?" she asked.

He nodded.

And she added: "Poor Dong would say that
there were two other men. And one of them is
you, Jack."

The second? Well, the second was the man
the mob had killed in China, of course. She
was looking up at him. The light slid between
her fingers and passed over her forehead, over
her hair. And her eyes were glistening.

"Tell me, honestly—" said Ripley.

"Yes. Anything now. Ask me anything!"

"Only this. Are you sick with fear?"

"No," she said. "If any two other men in
the world were with me, I'd be dying of fear.
But now—no, it isn't fear!"

She waited while he looked blankly down at
her.

"What next do you want to know?" she
asked.

"I don't want to know anything," said

Ripley. "I think I know everything. About you, and Sam Li, and where Lancaster came into the game—about those things I know nothing. But I know about you, Ching."

"You know that I'm deceitful—and bad?" she asked.

"Why do you lift your eyebrows and purse your mouth and look the pathetic baby?" he demanded, angrily.

She rubbed the back of her hand across her forehead.

"I won't do it any more," she declared.

"Thanks," said Ripley. "I only wanted to say that after I watched you with Dong, I knew enough. There's a heart in you, Ching. There's a great heart in you and—"

She waited. He had been on tiptoe with the swelling emotion. Now he checked himself hard.

"Yes?" she asked.

"You'll always be acting a part," sighed Ripley. "Making yourself eager, bright, frank, and open—hanging on my words as though what I said mattered."

Her head drooped.

"Why don't you laugh in my face?" snapped Ripley. "I'd rather have you do that. Look at me, Ching, will you?"

She looked up. Her face was blank. Her eyes were blank.

"That's better," said Ripley. "There's the old Orient for me to puzzle over, and I know that's the truth about you. But what I want to

tell you may be important. I want to say that
I've chucked pride over my shoulder. You've
made a fool of me before and I suppose that
you'll make a fool of me again."

"Don't!" said the girl. And her voice had a
flat, weary ring.

"I've got to say it. The point is that what
you do with me doesn't matter. You can
blindfold me and ride me over a cliff. I don't
care. I'd rather—I'd rather look at your hand,
Ching, than at the face of the most beautiful
woman in the world. Look at me now, will
you?"

"Yes," said the girl.

"Smile, Ching!"

The smile flashed suddenly. He took her
softly by the shoulders. The heat of the lamp
beat into his face. He saw everything. He saw
even the up-struck pattern of the eyelashes
across the lids of her eyes.

"Why, you're wonderful, Ching," he said,
sadly. "By God, you're simply wonderful. I'd
rather have your smile—I'd rather have your
damned, lying smile—than a song and dance
from all the beauties of the world."

The smile went out.

"You're tired, eh?" said Ripley.

"Not if you want to talk some more," said
the girl.

"On the same night when you've heard—
Dong's story—on that same night to talk to
you the way I've talked—that's rotten. I know
it's rotten. But somehow I had to tell you

where I stand. Before you went to sleep I had to tell you that nothing matters to me except being on your side."

She swallowed. Then: "Thank you," she said.

"Only," he ended, "try to be a little more open with me. I've told you that the truth won't matter. Use me for three days and throw me away forever. That won't matter. Only—no more baby-stuff—no more of this damned kindergarten baby face, eh?"

"No," said the girl. "No more of that."

"Good night, Ching," said he.

She went to the door. She crossed the hall to another open threshold beyond which a door sagged crazily. There she paused.

He went after her at once. "Is there anything wrong, Ching?" he asked.

He took the lamp and looked rapidly over the room. It was in better repair than his. A bookshelf had been built out from the wall and an old magazine lay molding on the board. A blanket roll already had been made down on the big bed.

"It's all right, isn't it?" he asked.

He put the lamp down on the table but when he turned he saw that she was still waiting at the door with a downward head.

"Well?" he asked.

"Back there," said Ching, pointing a finger behind her, "back there across the hall—years ago—thousands of miles away—back there in your room, Jack—"

"Yes?" said Ripley, frowning.

Thought kept her head bowed.

"Back there among all your words that were so sharp—they *were* cruel words, weren't they?"

He scowled more blackly at her. This quietly insistent voice entered his mind more and more deeply, like an unfolding theme of music.

"But there was another meaning in what you said," went on the girl. "Tell me if I am wrong. I thought you were also saying that you loved me—" her head jerked up—"not very much, but a little?"

He got in one big breath and leaned a hand against the wall.

"All right," he said. "I was saying that, too."

"And it was true?"

"Yes,—damn it!—true!"

"Then will you do one thing for me before I go to bed?"

"I will."

"Kiss me, then," said the girl, and lifted her face.

Ripley, leaning over her, ground out his words.

"Why do you do it, Ching? By God, it's rotten of you! I've told you that you have me. I've told you that you've got me in the palm of your hand—but why do you want to smash me to pieces?"

He drew himself back and slipped sideways

through the door and back into his own room.
When he looked across his shoulder toward
her, she was still standing like that, with her
face raised.

CHAPTER XXX

Ripley slept like a weary man in a saddle, dipping into oblivion and starting out of it again. He had undressed by pulling off his boots; his revolver was under his hand; and he had his face toward the sheen of moonlight which, like a thin silver curtain, only partially screened away the faces of the stars.

Perhaps he was deeper in sleep than he would have admitted when something crossed his threshold with a very light dragging sound, and the sound of muffled breathing. He came off his bed with a leap and saw a crawling creature coming through the door toward his bed. And then the face of a man looked up through the darkness and Dong's unmistakable accent said, plaintively: "Ching? Ching?"

Ripley leaned over him. "What's the matter?" he asked.

"Ching! Ching!" whispered the Chinaman.

There was Sam Li to be consulted before Ching, no doubt, but Ripley could not deny anything to this poor wounded man who had dragged himself on knees and elbows this far. Now Dong lay flat on his face, collapsed along the floor, and breathing hard.

Ripley crossed the hall, and reaching inside the door—it was lodged so that it could not be closed—he tapped lightly. He had an answer that was a musical babbling of Chinese, a rustling of silks.

"It's I," he said. "Come along. Dong wants you."

She was with him almost at once. He let her slide past and lead the way across the hall. Inside his threshold, she dropped to her knees beside Dong. Ripley followed her, muttering: "Find out what's the matter, Ching. Why didn't he ask Sam Li for whatever he wants?"

"Hush," said the girl. "Dong says to be still —or we'll all die! Everyone will die if there's a sound!"

Ripley looked back over his shoulder at the dark yawning of the doorway. He stared again out the window at the silvered tips of the trees, and the peace of the windless night.

Dong was murmuring, and the girl in a whisper translating. She kept her face close to that of Ripley and without turning to him she put the Chinese into the English tongue.

"Sam Li has gone outside—Sam Li has given me up tonight to kill me tomorrow—"

Ching said something as abrupt as it was

quietly uttered. Then she went on with the translation of Dong's answer.

"I tell you, Sam Li will kill me—he'll kill you all—only he wants to know where your father found the stone that has gold in it."

And again the breath was struck out of Ripley's body as though he had been plunged to the throat in cold water.

"It isn't true—it's a dream," the girl murmured to Ripley.

But again she was translating the murmur of Dong: "It was Sam Li that came every day when I lay in the ropes. Sam Li made the ropes tight. He pushed the hurdle under me. When my body was pulled tight, he beat me. He gave me salt meat and then no water. And the ropes chewed at my flesh and worked against my bones."

He stopped, panting from effort and excitement.

And Ripley beat the soft of his hand against his head, bewildered. Sam Li the torturer? Gentle Sam Li?

No wonder he had not wanted Ching to stay with the coolie that night!

Dong's murmur and the translating whisper began again.

"When I come to see Ching in the house of Sam Li—when I am taken away—there are men ready to kill Dong, but first they search him until one man finds inside the knot of my belt a piece of the stone that Ching's father had taken from the mountains. They looked at the stone. Maybe they saw the gold in it.

There *is* gold in it, like little fires. They held me, and afterward Sam Li comes down into the cellar and looks at the stone, and then looks at me. He says he will kill me if I don't say where the stone was found. I say I cannot remember—and then I am taken away to that little house where my father found me and saved me—"

He had to stop again to take breath.

"Not Sam Li!" murmured the girl. "Any other person in the world, but not Sam Li. He has been like a kind brother. Not Sam Li! Not Sam Li!"

"Now, because I may die quickly—" she was translating Dong again, and the voice of Dong had lifted into a great effort, "I tell you where to find the place where Ching's father discovered the stone."

His voice ran on. The girl stopped him.

Then, more slowly, she was repeating: "In Tibet—in Changtan. Near the birthplace of the Hwang-ho, but south of that. South of the Hwang-ho and north of where the Yang-tsze-kiang jumps out of the ground—in the mountains—there are three peaks as one comes up the valley of the Yang-tsze-kiang. They are higher than the others and they are close as three fingers on one hand. Go for the central peak—on the way, at the foot of the mountain, there is a ravine cut across the belly of the mountain like a sword gash. There is a small run of water in the bottom of it. And to the left, one old tree, a rotten stump with a new, young, slender tree climbing up from the side of it—but among the roots of the rotten old tree-stump—among those roots there is a ledge of rock, and in the ledge there are the little eyes of golden fire—"

Dong paused, panting. He murmured something in a weary voice, and the name of Sam Li came out of him once more. And Ching translated.

"He is ready to die, now that he has told me where the gold can be found. You are to go back with me, Jack. You are to find the gold in the rock. You are to marry me. We shall have many children. Twelve sons. And no girls at all. That is Chinese heaven, Jack—but ah, Sam Li! Sam Li!"

Ripley stood up.

"Wait quietly here with Dong," he said. "I'll go get Sam Li, and then we'll hear the damned, smooth-faced hypocrite talk."

"Dong says that he went outside. He trusted that Dong could not walk—and he was right—poor Dong could only crawl. But—ah, Sam Li! Sam Li!"

She began to sob, soundlessly. There was only a pulsation in the air, and that was all. But every throb of the weeping struck on Ripley's heart and drove a strange panic through him.

"I'll step into the kitchen," said Ripley. "Only one moment, in case the beast is in there now."

He moved down the hall, following the wall with his left hand. When he pushed the kitchen door slowly open, a red eye stared at him, but that was the last coal of the fire looking through the broken side of the stove.

He sat down on his heels and swept the room with his eyes. There was only a narrow patch of moonlight from the window; the silver spot that lay under the torn place in the roof had traveled half across the room; and nowhere was there a sign or a token of Sam Li.

Ripley went back to his own room. The girl, cross-legged beside Dong, his head in her lap, whispered: "Dong wants us to go quickly. He says that Sam Li is preparing now to murder us all—"

"What do you think?" asked Ripley.

"If he is what Dong says—and he must be that—then there is no other devil. There is only Sam Li in the world. But why did he leave Dong alone?"

"To take a walk in the moonlight and think up a new way of making Dong talk. Do you remember, how he wanted Dong to tell where the stone was found—and still poor Dong said that he could not describe it?"

"Sam Li would never walk a step, if he could help it. He's too fat and heavy. Ah—listen!"

Ripley, touched with dread, crouched a little, to make himself ready against attack.

"Sam Li," whispered the girl, "let Dong go because he knew that poor Dong would come to us when he dared. All day long, Dong could not talk while Sam Li was listening. But at night, Dong would try to come to us, and Sam

Li let him go, and followed, and heard what Dong has said!"

"He—he was not in the hall!" muttered Ripley.

"Outside the window, then?" suggested the girl.

Ripley went to the window, stalking carefully, his revolver at the ready before him. Cautiously he peered outside—and found nothing! But when he looked down to the clean sand at the base of the wall beside the window he saw—clear in the moonlight and shadow as ink tracery on white paper—the imprints of enormous feet.

He turned back to the girl with a groan.

"He was here, Ching. But could he have heard?"

"Yes. Because Dong spoke that part more loudly. Sam Li knows about it, now. And he has gone. What does he care about a thing in the world except that ledge of gold-bearing rock? He has gone, and perhaps he has taken the horses with him!"

Ripley's whistle rang shrill across the moonlit night; and the gray mare, bright as snow, came instantly around the corner of the barn and approached with her flaunting gallop, her head lifted to look this way and that. One call from Ripley brought her to the window.

"He hasn't taken the horses. Not Hickory Dickory, at least," said Ripley. "But he's gone —and thank God for that! If there's danger in

him, Ching, there's more of it than in any other man in the world. Lancaster—he's a baby
compared—"

And then intuition ran a thread of fire
through his brain.

Tolliver had worked for Sam Li. Tolliver it
was, also, who knew that man "higher up"
than Lancaster. Tolliver it was who had offered Lancaster's place to another man. And
the whole matter became clear, in Ripley's
mind. It was Sam Li who was the power behind the throne in the smuggling of the Chinese—he and his innocent silk and tea shop,
he with his gentle maxims, his cultured voice.
It was not Lancaster that Tom Dallas would
really want. A thousand Lancasters could
come and go, if a single Sam Li remained.

But the girl's voice cut suddenly through
these flooding thoughts.

"Look up to the hill top!" she was calling,
with a gasp in her voice. "Do you see?"

He stared over the ridges, smoothly flowing
as the crests of waves when no wind is blowing, and at last he saw, to the left, a small eye
of red which was shining, winking, shining,
winking. . . .

"It's a signal," said Ripley. "What does it
say, Ching?"

"I don't know. I didn't see enough—there!
—it's stopped. It must be a message to Lancaster. Does it say: 'Nothing in this direction'?
Or does it say: 'Come, quickly!'"

"We'd better move," answered Ripley.

"Get Dong ready. I'll go out and saddle the horses."

"Go by yourself, Jack," she urged. "We can't move Dong easily. Get yourself free, and then if danger comes, you can strike back to help us." She broke off to say a few words to Dong, and he rattled an eager answer.

"He says for you to go," she translated. "He says that a broken thing is not worth money; and only children waste time over old toys."

Ripley looked silently from the girl to Dong's horrible face and back at Ching again. Then he laughed a little, softly, and left the house.

CHAPTER XXXI

It seemed as though the intensity of the moonlight prevented all sound. He went past the tall trees, and their deep, quiet shadows, into the pasture ground and caught up first the pair of hired mustangs for the horse litter. The litter itself and the saddles for these horses he had left in the barn, and he was leading the pair toward it when he first heard the thudding of hoofs.

He threw himself on the back of one of the mustangs and drove his heels into it. The brute lowered its head, braced its legs, and stood fast. And then Ripley saw four riders issue from the trees on his right.

Vainly he thumped the ribs of the horse. It stood like a wall, humping its back and ready to buck. And one side glance showed him the leading figure of the riders—the gaunt body of Jim Lancaster!

"Ripley!" he heard Lancaster shout.

A great yell whooped from the throats of the others. Ripley slid down between the two horses and leveled a revolver across the withers of one. But before him the riders had fanned out, circling rapidly as Lancaster called orders. Swung low along the sides of their mounts, they offered only slight targets to Ripley's gun.

And while he delayed to fire, groaning with helplessness, he saw them halt, each at a corner of a square of which he was the center. They were out of the saddles, now, their long-barreled rifles balanced and ready as Lancaster shouted: "Ripley, do you hear me? Four rifles to a Colt. Is your game finished?"

Ay, it was finished, and he knew it. One volley and they would have his sheltering mustangs flat on the ground. To finish him would need only another moment. He was done—unless he could bargain with them a little.

Dong and Ching in the ruined old house— they must have heard the yelling. What wild terror was in them now?

"You've got me, Lancaster," he said, "but you'll pay something before you snag me."

"I'll pay my right hand for you," said Lancaster. "Will you give up and take your chance, or do we simply blow you to hell?"

"Chief," said one of the three followers, quietly, "he'll take one or two of us along with him, if the fight starts."

"Are you afraid?" demanded Lancaster.

"I was just telling you, was all," said the other.

"Will you make a bargain and keep it, Jim?" asked Ripley.

"I'm going to have the heart out of you. Is that in the bargain?" asked Lancaster.

"That's in the bargain," agreed Ripley. "But the girl and Dong—you leave them alone to go where they please. Will you agree to that?"

"Ching? And the scarface?" Lancaster laughed. "Where would they *want* to go except where I'd have them. But I'll make that bargain. Does that suit you?"

"Hold up your right hand and swear," said Ripley.

"There's the right hand. I'm swearing it," said Lancaster. He laughed again.

"All right," answered Ripley. "I'll walk out with my hands in the air—and Ching and the Chinaman are free to go where they please?"

"Of course they are!"

That supreme confidence on the part of Lancaster shook all Ripley's nerves, but he felt that he had bargained as well as he could.

So he walked out from between the mustangs as he had agreed, with his hands high in the air. Lancaster with a leveled gun came straight up to him. He thrust the muzzle of the gun into Ripley's stomach and pushed his face close.

"By God," said Lancaster, in a quivering

voice, "this is the best minute in my life. It won't be a quick exit for you, Jack. We're gunna give you time to get the taste of your finish clear down on the roots of your tongue."

He kept the gun in the midriff of Ripley while he waved his left hand.

"Missouri!" he called. "Come here and take care of this."

Missouri Slim was pulling twine out of his pocket as he closed on Ripley.

"Like something out of a book," he said. "Like something that I read when I was a kid. I kind of knew this was gunna happen the first time I laid eyes on you, Jack."

"Maybe your mama told you, Slim," said Ripley. "Be easy with that twine. I've got some sore places."

This jest worked home in the mind of Missouri only gradually. And then an immoderate laughter broke with a yell from his throat. He had to repeat the joke to his companions; he was doubled with mirth as he wound and rewound the twine to bind Ripley's wrists firmly behind his back.

More hoofbeats came toward them now through the trees and three riders appeared, with the huge form of Sam Li overflowing the saddle on the central horse, his silken robe lifting and fluttering in the wind.

Jim Lancaster threw up both hands and then shouted with amazement and joy.

"Hai, boys!" he yelled, "Is *this* what you got off the top of the hill? Is *this* what was sending the signal to fetch us to the house, here? Was Sam Li up there?"

One of the pair answered: "We got around behind the hill. When he saw us coming, he didn't try to run even. He simply kept on working his blanket up and down before the fire, spelling out his words faster than ever."

"Did he? Bring him here! Get him off that horse!"

Sam Li dismounted—stepped down, to be more accurate—and stood vast and calm before Lancaster.

"Now, you double-crossing, yellow-faced baboon, you," cried Lancaster. "Have I got you, or ain't I?"

"Of course you have me!" said Sam Li.

"Are you a double-crossing rat, or ain't you?"

"You know, Jim," said Sam Li, "that I've always been cursed with a brain that's too restless. It is hard for an ample mind to follow a straight, narrow line."

"It ain't hard for a narrow knife to cut a fat throat, though," said Lancaster. "Hey, Barry —Jump-up—a couple of you get into the old house, back there, and bring out whatever you find there. You'll find Ching and the scarface, according to the message off the top of the hill. Treat Ching dead easy, will you, boys?"

The messengers hurried away out of sight around the corner of the barn, and Lancaster turned back to Sam Li.

"My God, Sam," said Lancaster, "I was

never happier to see anybody than I am to see you. Only one other—and that's Ripley, here. Think of it—the two of you in one haul! Oh, wasn't I the bright gent to send a pair of the boys up there to the top of the hill!"

"The strong spirits must love you, Jim," said Sam Li. "For see how kind they are to you! They fill your hand. You can close your fingers and destroy the two men you hate the most."

"You wanted to throw Ripley to the dogs— to me, eh? And you got caught in the trap that should of nipped him, only!"

Sam Li's hands were tied behind his back, so that he could not indulge in those big, flowing gestures of which he was so fond, but nevertheless he had a way of nodding his head and moving his shoulders that fairly took the place of the missing freedom.

His booming voice rolled through the night. "Have you come to blame the old sinner, Jim? But see how easily I have been caught! A little evil will cover a long road; a great evil is the bog that catches us. So I have been caught, my friends."

Missouri said: "Lemme slam him in the mug with the heel of my Colt, will you, Chief? Just lemme slam him once. I won't hurt him much. I won't spoil him very bad. I just wanta slam him once in the middle of his fat mug."

Jim Lancaster laughed. "Leave him alone," he said. "Let him be, Missouri. When I wind up with him, it'll be something worth watching."

"No, Jim," said Sam Li. "Your anger will begin to soften in you before long."

"Soften?" said Lancaster. "Say that again for me, will you? Do you hear him, boys? Of all the damned crooks and sneaks and traitors and hypocrites in the world, this here Sam Li is the worst, I'll tell a man. And now he says that I'm gunna soften my anger for him!"

"Because you are right, Jim," said Sam Li. "There are a great many evil people in the world, but I suppose that there is none as great a wrong-doer as I am. And for that very reason you'll see that I cannot help being as I am."

"Listen to him," said Lancaster. "Damn my heart, but it's sort of good to hear him oiling up and turning out the talk, ain't it, Missouri."

"Just lemme slam him once, will you, Chief?" begged Missouri, in a whining voice.

"I want to hear him. I like to hear him," answered Lancaster, as they traveled on together. "I want to hear him tell me why and how I'm gunna let him off."

"No, Jim, not let me off," said Sam Li. "But see what a perfect harvest of revenge you have! You are rich with it. And the man who has killed a whole flock of ducks gives one away to the needy."

"By my way of thinking," said Lancaster, "if you were tied to a pole and the sun let to fry you out, and the lard on you rendered till you were down to normal size—if you were kept starving on bread and water till your ribs

showed through the four fingers of your fat,
that might be a starting point."

"Do that, Jim," said the Chinaman, in his
melodious voice. "Yes, do that. It will be a bitter thing. For think how much pains I've been
at to build up this gross body of mine? How
many flocks of young lambs have passed into
me, and the droves of fat, grunting swine, and
the soft-eyed beefs, with shambling feet; how
many fish have turned brown in the pan for
me; how much golden acres of wheat have
turned into soft bread for Sam Li; how many
groves of bright oranges have been stripped
for me; how many orchards of apples have
shaken their fruit down my throat; what a
river of liquor has flowed through me. And to
tie poor old Sam Li to a pole, like a bear and
watch him dwindle day by day, while all those
droves and groves and rivers oozed out of him
—that would be punishment enough, I should
say."

Lancaster began to laugh.

"He does me good, damn him," said he. "I
like to hear his lingo. I always liked to hear it.
Listen to me, you fat pig!"

"Yes, Jim—I listen," said the cheerful Sam
Li.

"Do you know that I did for Tolliver?"

"You did for him?" echoed Sam Li. "I want
to tell you about him, Jim. There was the
vainest man in the world. And he was my
slave for life because I gave him enough money to let him put golden teeth in place of the

bad ones in the front of his mouth. After that day, he practiced smiling!"

They laughed together, at this, and Sam Li looked at Ripley as though inviting him to join in the mirth.

Lancaster cut the laughter short, snarling: "Before I did him in, I got the truth out of him. He told me everything. He told me how you'd directed him to kill the scarface, here, rather than let him come north and see the girl. Now, you fat devil, tell me any reason you could have for that—except *pure* devilishness."

"Not devilishness," said Sam Li. "No, no! Not devilishness, Jim. Only a stroke of practical business, you see."

"Business?" said Lancaster. "I'm listening. You explain, if you can, how that murder could have been good business for you."

"Ah, but that's simple. For several months, Jim, you had been growing restless. It was I who invited you into the smuggling game. It was poor Sam Li who showed you the way to become rich. It was Sam Li who put all the cards in your hand, and made you the Number One boy. But then you grew restless. You seemed to everyone the head of affairs, and you didn't see why you shouldn't be the head in fact—and throw me out."

"Well, what of it? I'm the head now, Sam Li. And be damned to you."

"Yes, yes. But for a time I held you. Only with a silken string, but I held you. That dear girl, the lovely Ching, when she came down from San Francisco with her story—in her I saw my chance. When she brought me the letter from her friend the San Francisco merchant, and told me that she had traced an old, scarfaced family servant as far as the boat on which he had left China for Mexico—when she told me that, of course I promised to help her. I promised to have every drove of the coolies searched before they came over the border so that her man would be found for her. In the meantime, since she would have to be close to us, day and night, it was better for her to live the part of a Chinese girl in my house. Then, at any moment, we might have the good news for her. And then, also, I could show her to you as a daughter to a friend, so to speak. Do you see, Jim?"

"You pouch-faced old rat!" said Lancaster. "Was Ching the rope that held me? Ay, and she was."

"Let me go on, Jim. We hear at last that the scarface has appeared. What am I to do? When he reaches Ching and tells her what she wants to know about her father, that is the end. Then she leaves me, and when she is gone, what hold have I over you to keep you from throwing me over and becoming the sole head of the business I had started? No, but with the scarface gone, I keep Ching waiting, hoping—perhaps for months—and every day or so, Jim Lancaster comes to see her and is grateful to me for keeping her on the border.

An endless chain of services rendered and gratitude given—a chain that would be broken by the arrival of Dong. You see?"

"When you listen to him," said Lancaster, his mouth snarling, "it sounds almost like a good man talking, doesn't it? But after you got hold of Dong for yourself, why didn't you cut his throat and throw him into the river, if you wanted Ching still to stay for a while? Why did you have to beat hell out of him, that way, and torture the poor feller?"

"Because of this, Jim," said Sam Li, and he nodded. "Open the saddle bag on the left, here."

It was done, and Lancaster drew out a carved, ivory box.

"What the devil!" said Lancaster. "This is where you keep the sacred relic, eh? What had that to do with Dong?"

"Look inside, Jim, and see what it holds now."

Lancaster opened the ivory box and took from it a long, narrow shard of dark stone.

"Light a match and try to look through the stone at the flame," said Sam Li.

The match was struck.

"Do you see the little gold fish?" asked Sam Li.

"It's ore!" cried Lancaster. "It's the richest piece of stuff that I ever looked at in my life! It's *loaded*! What has this to do with Dong?"

"Why, this is the ore sample that Ching's father brought down from the mountains of

Tibet. And then the mob of revolutionaries rubbed him out, as you say. And it was I who found this little treasure in the knot of Dong's belt. He brings to Ching the unhappy word of her father's death; he also brings to her the fortune that her father had found. A pretty story of faith and truth, Jim. I knew that you would like it a great deal. You see how my position was changed at once? The moment I saw that piece of stone with the pretty little golden fish in it, I could forget all about smuggling on the border. There were swift wings that carried me to a far land. But just where was I to go? That I must learn from Dong."

He sighed, and the sigh was almost a groan. "I did what I could. Perhaps I would have won in a little while. But then came our stupid friend who never steps where he is wanted. Then came this Ripley, and snatched Dong away. Ah hai! It was a rapid moment, yesterday, when the poor, silly man came to tell Ching that Dong had been found! I almost shook myself free from Ripley—but his Mexican held him on the trail—and so you see that from the first, Jim, I've only been working as a good business man should do."

"Ay, listen to him!" murmured Lancaster. Then a new thought struck a chime of anger into his voice. "And when I was still in the game with you, you wanted to put Ripley into my job. Tolliver told me that!"

"With a stupid, good man like Ripley, I could have gone on for a long time," said Sam

Li, "and when he hanged, he would have hanged alone. I love company, Jim, but not hanging on the end of a rope."

And again Lancaster laughed, his mirth bursting out heartily and ringing freely through the night.

CHAPTER XXXII

Ripley had been amazed by the perfect frankness with which Sam Li exposed his hand to Lancaster; yet he could see a reason. Sam Li was playing for his life, and against that stake even the possession of the most fabulous mines of gold could not be counted important.

"What were you doing with your fire-signals, Sam?" asked Lancaster. "Why did you keep on flashing something after my boys were ready to grab you?"

"I was calling for you, Jim," said Sam Li. "I thought that some of your men might be pretty rough with me. But the master is always kinder than the servant. I knew I could appeal to your reason. A man who thinks twice forgets hatred."

"I'll tell you how well I forget it," said Lancaster. "You see Ripley, here? You know what I'll do to him?"

"I know that he seems to be living, but he is really dead," answered Sam Li.

"And so are you!" exclaimed Lancaster. "Damn you and the mines you talk about in China. Ripley fought me fair; you played friend and double-crossed me. Why, you fatfaced hunk of blubber, you think you've been oiling me down with your talk, do you? I've been laughing to see how you've wasted your time."

"Ah, have you, Jim?" asked Sam Li, in the gentlest of his booming voices.

"If there's a hell I can send Ripley to," declared Lancaster, "I'll find two hells for you!"

"Will you, Jim?" said Sam Li. "No, I think I can trust the happy old days more than that!"

"Happy old days?" shouted Lancaster. "Damn you, do you dare to talk to me to my face about 'em? Happy old days? And all the time you were ready to cut my heart out! Ready to double-cross!"

"No, Jim, no!" said Sam Li, and Ripley looked with singular admiration on the vast, fat, beneficent face of the Chinaman; he listened to the rich unction of that voice as to a blessing. And the Chinese liar and philosopher said: "In all those days I looked on you as a brother, Jim. A younger brother. But finally a great temptation came. Virtue is ice but there is always a sun which can melt it. It took a great, shining sun to make me bad to you, but even when I was evil I thought kindly of you, Jim, and—"

Lancaster's bony fist cracked suddenly home against Sam Li's face.

"That ought to shut your mouth for you," said Lancaster.

Sam Li was still. A dark dribbling ran down from his mouth. He had not flinched from the brutal blow.

"Well," said Lancaster, "wipe his mouth for him, Slim."

There was a slight trace of compunction in his voice.

A moment later Ching's voice was crying out, merrily: "Jim! Oh, Jim!" and she came around the corner of the barn, with old Dong carried behind her by Lancaster's men.

She ran forward, with her hands outstretched; Lancaster went striding to meet her. "Now—at last you've come!" cried the girl. And she fairly threw herself into Lancaster's arms to kiss him.

Ripley, sickened, stared at the ground. But their voices still came to him.

"They dragged you a long ways from me, Ching," Lancaster was saying. "I've been telling myself that I'd lost the most important trick in the game. But the fellow that stays to the finish sometimes changes his luck. Lord God, how glad I am to see you! You look all made new in the moonlight, Ching. But tell me what I'll do with this hound of a Ripley?"

"Why should I care?" she asked.

"You don't care a bit?"

"Well, he's so stupid that I'm a little sorry for him," she said.

Vaguely, Ripley tried to fit the parts of the picture together. Had she not been fleeing willingly—trying to leave Lancaster behind her? Had it been sheer compulsion on the part of Sam Li? He was staggered. And more than he was staggered, he was sickened.

"Yeah? Stupid, is he?" remarked Lancaster. "You must be a lightning calculator, honey, because one more of his stupid days and I'd of had my neck stretched by a rope, by my way of figuring. Slim, what'll we do with him?"

Missouri Slim took in a relishing breath before he said: "Go right ahead back to the valley, all of you. The Chinamen are ready to raise hell there and you need to be on deck. Just leave Ripley behind with me."

"How does that sound to you?" snapped Lancaster, beside the girl.

"Why, Missouri seems to want him—and why not?" asked the girl.

"You don't care?" asked Lancaster.

"Care?" she demanded. "Why should I care?"

"It does me good to hear you," said Lancaster. "There was a while when I thought his handsome mug might of made a difference with you. Missouri, I'd sure like to let you have your hand with him, but he knows some things that I could use—about Dallas. We'll take him back to the valley with us. Hurry it up, some of you. Chuck Warren, where are you?"

"Here!" called Chuck.

His twisted face came looming through the dust and the moonshine.

"Take the lead and pelt back there to the valley as fast as you can hop. There's only two men back yonder, and there's doggone near two hundred mad Chinamen boiling up. Make it fast!"

"It ain't luck," Missouri was assuring Ripley. "It ain't even a chance for luck. It only means that me and Jim are gunna have more time to think things out. It's better this way, for us. I wouldn't wanta get rid of you too soon. I wouldn't wanta have it all over with!"

"Wait till I look at the Chinaman," Lancaster was saying. "This is him, is it? This is the scarface? Doggone me, he ain't a pretty sight, Ching. Is he dead or alive?"

Lancaster turned suddenly, and lifted a hand.

"Wait a minute!" he exclaimed. "Hold on, Chuck. Steady, boys. Don't you hear hoofbeats? Who could be riding this way, this time of night?"

Ripley and all the rest could hear now. For a number of riders suddenly crashed through the underbrush of the woods.

"What in hell fire is this?" demanded Lancaster. "Sam Li, you fat-faced snake, do you know what this means?"

"How can I tell who will be riding to enjoy the moonlight, Jim?" asked Sam Li's voice, gentle as always.

Six riders burst out from the shadows of the trees.

"It's Klein—and Rudy Wallace—and Skinny—all our boys," said Chuck Warren, lowering the muzzle of the rifle which he had raised.

"But what the devil are they doing up here?" asked Lancaster, putting down his own gun.

The six newcomers drew up close, dismounting.

Lancaster bawled out: "Who gave you orders to come up here?"

"Chuck—Rudy—my boys—cover the rest of 'em!" cried Sam Li. And now his voice rang out like a mighty gong that sent metallic vibrations through Ripley's body and very soul.

He saw the flash of many guns.

"Lancaster! Cover Lancaster!" roared Sam Li. "Steady, my lads, and no shooting."

They stood in agonized suspense. Every face that the moonlight showed to Ripley was contorted in agony. Lancaster and his men, more scattered and some of them surprised before they had a chance to draw, would nevertheless be a bitter morsel for the others to swallow. Lancaster himself had a gun in either hand, ready to begin.

But Sam Li's deep, rich voice continued

again: "You see, Jim, there are two sides to the game!"

Lancaster shouted: "Klein—Rudy—all of you—what in hell do you mean? Who's been paying you hard cash? Who's your boss here?"

The tallest and the thinnest of the six answered: "Hello, Jim. We been getting plenty of dough from you, but we been getting a lot more from the Chinaman, yonder. He's the one we call boss in this outfit."

He side-stepped to Sam Li and cut the cords that tied his hands.

"Let us be peaceful, Jim," said Sam Li, pouring oil on those troubled waters. "If we examine everything, we see that we are about equal. When you were planning to throw me out of my position—when you were going to take over all the work for yourself, and open a new mouth in Sam Li's throat so that he could drink plenty of dirty Rio Grande water, was it strange that Sam Li should make a few friends among the boys—like poor Tolliver— and these?"

"All the Chinese in the world—I wish they were in hell!" said Lancaster.

"That is angry talk, Jim," said Sam Li. "The truth is probably shining behind clouds. Let us brush the clouds away. Then what do you see, Jim? You see that while you and I were working together, everything went very smoothly. But when we tried to separate, when each of us tried to swallow all the profits, then we came to grief. Isn't it a lesson that we should go back to the old ways, my friend?"

"I dunno," groaned Lancaster. "I had the whole damn world in my hand—and now it's no better than an even break! I'm kind of sick! Sam Li, those last words that you spelled out on the hill—after you saw my two men— that was a message to your own men, to come fast!"

"Yes, yes. Of course," said the Chinaman. "And like good fellows they rode hard and fast."

"And you might of had him dead an hour ago," commented Missouri Slim.

"Damn you and what might of been!" snapped Lancaster.

He took a great, audible breath and then exclaimed: "Well, Sam Li—maybe you're right. Each of us tried to crook the other fellow. Each of us was wrong!"

"My right hand waits for you, to forgive everything and to welcome a new day," said Sam Li.

Several of the men spoke at once, urging the reconciliation.

The thin fellow who had been spokesman before now added: "You two gents got plenty of brains, plenty of cash, but you need one another. Shake hands with him, Jim, and get back into the old game all together."

"I kind of hate to do it," said Jim Lancaster. "But it's the best way. Ching, give me

a woman's hunch. Is this the right thing for
me to do?"

"You know, Jim," said the girl, "that living
is better than dying, for everyone."

At this, he laughed.

"We got an even chance each way," he said.
"But before the shooting was over, one thing is
sure. You and *me* would be dead, Sam, no
matter what happened to the other. Give me
your fat paw. Now, you damned old liar, we're
shaking; we're quits; and we start on the old
basis, level. Is that right?"

A good, hearty shout from the men who had
been teetering on the verge of battle as on the
edge of a cliff gave the answer in the place of
Sam Li's voice. The handshake completed the
bargain. And a last, final hope dwindled and
disappeared from Ripley's mind. Out of the
fight there might have come a dim chance of
liberty to him.

But that did not matter so much. Whatever
happened, the girl was a traitor a thousand
times over. And that knowledge struck him
like a bullet through the brain.

He had a dreamlike knowledge, too, that
there was a bustle of people about him, and
that he was being put on Hickory's back
again. He saw the horse litter rigged and Dong
laid in it. He knew they were heading back for
a valley where, Lancaster had said, there were
two hundred Chinese on the verge of revolt.
But all of this was like happenings in sleep.

Only one thing was clear—the picture of the girl, riding beside Lancaster, laughing and chattering with him.

Chuck Warren's twisted face appeared beside Ripley.

"And here you are, Jack, eh?" he said. "Well, none of us thought that we'd ever have you except dead! Of all the tough hombres that we've ever ridden after, you were the hardest!"

Ripley looked blankly at him.

He was thinking of that bargain which he had made with Lancaster—that bargain that the girl could go free—she who had run with extended arms to meet the gunman and kiss him—she who now rode at Lancaster's side— she who did not care what became of Ripley— because he was so stupid.

Chuck Warren went on: "We get a good split out of the chief because you're cornered and caught. But tell me something, Jack. Why did you want to give yourself up just for the sake of the girl? Did you figger that she gave a damn about you? Was that what you were thinking about?"

"I wasn't thinking," declared Ripley. "I was only being a damn fool."

"Yeah?" said Chuck Warren.

He sighed and shook his head.

"The same way with me," he said. "The females can sure stop the clock for me—yeah, and turn the hands back, too! But what's gunna happen to you now, Ripley?"

Ripley made no answer. He could see an answer to that question far better than he could speak it in words.

CHAPTER XXXIII

They came to hills which lifted rocky knees and great, gleaming heads and shoulders out of the sands. A narrow pass opened through the cordon and they were still in the middle of this way when Ripley began to hear a rapid, excited babbling of distant voices.

"The Chinamen are warmin' themselves up," said Missouri Slim. "They was warmin' themselves up for a coupla days. I dunno why for except that rat that tried to get away, and I shot him on the wing. It seemed to bother 'em, some."

"You never should of plugged that Chinaman," said Lancaster. "On this side of the river, it's murder, is what it is."

"You gunna call that murder?" asked Missouri, with a good deal of indignant passion. "I give him a fair run for his money, too. I

297

wouldn't make it easy. I took him left-handed
and only got him the second shot. If that ain't
sporting, I wanta know what is!"

"Leave it be," soothed Lancaster. "Only,
there's a lot of gents that wouldn't understand
your idea of good sport. The next time, let the
Chinaman run, and catch him up with a rope.
Hear me?"

"Yeah. But it's hell," said Missouri. "It's
hell. There ain't any more education in those
Chinamen than there is in a pack of cards. It
kind of boils me up, is what it does, when I see
them treated so fancy."

Racing hoofbeats ran at them; a horseman
shot out into view and waved his hand at
them. He began shouting before he reined in
his horse.

"Hurry it up, Lancaster, will you? The Chinamen are gettin' pretty high. Move it along
will you?"

"What's the matter with you dummies?"
demanded Lancaster. "I told you boys to hold
that job down. I didn't tell you to come
hollerin' for help to papa! Get back there on
the job, will you? And get fast! What's the
matter with you?"

The messenger jerked his mustang around.
A whirl of dust fanned up from around him.

"Knives! That's what's the matter. The
damn Chinamen have got knives—and if they
try to jump us—we're gunna sow a lot of meat
in the ground. That's what!"

He was off again, his mustang grunting as

the spur went into its flanks like a knife.

"Take it easy, boys!" said Lancaster. "We'll be there in a minute, anyway, and if we start racing, the first thing you know, Mr. Jack Ripley is gunna be slidin' away from us on his gray mare. And maybe Sam Li is too fat to catch up. What's the matter with you Chinamen, anyway?" he demanded of Sam Li. "I give that gang of Chinese rice every day, three times, and a whole flock of rabbit meat, a couple of days back, too. And just because them rabbits was a little high, the whole doggone lot get sick on me and say they're poisoned or something. I never handled such a doggone, unreasonable bunch of Chinamen in all my life!"

Instead of waiting for an answer, he swung his horse over beside Ripley, and muttered: "I could pass you out cold, now, instead of bothering about you, Jack. But this leaves us at evens, now. Even-up for that night—that night back there in Dalton. That sock in the face you gave me, it done me a lot of good. But we're even-up for everything, and from now on you catch hell as fast as I can figger it out."

He pulled back from Ripley.

"It's all right, Ching," went on Lancaster. "I been held up on transportation. Sam Li used to work that all out for us, and now there's a little tie-up, is why the Chinamen are bunched in the ravine. I'll have 'em all cleared out in the morning. There's plenty of transportation showing up then! Hey, Jerry!"

"Ay?" said Jerry.

"Where would the Chinamen be picking up knives, anyway?"

"I dunno," said Jerry. "That fool of a cook, he *would* always carry an extra case of knives. I told him many's the time, but he would have to have 'em along. He thinks that he's still a trader in the South Seas. He's got a can of beads along, too. Where does he think we travel? Through a lot of wild Indian countries, or something like that?"

They turned the corner of the rocks and dipped sheer down a narrow trail toward the mouth of the box canyon. Across the entrance, a number of riders moved back and forth; and half in shadow, half in moonlight, the Chinese contraband were held in the throat of the canyon by the usual rope corral. They were not in their usual places for sleep, however, but moving here and there, and as they chattered, something brighter than the gesture of empty hands flashed now and then.

"Yeah, they're all heated up," agreed Jim Lancaster, "but we'll cool 'em down again!"

A ripple of voices and then a yell went up from the Chinese as they saw the new riders approaching.

That long and undulating cry was a song of despair. Ripley listened to it with a deep recognition. The whole scene was to him like something remembered, as if he had entered the place long ago, and in another age had lost his life here as he would lose it now. For one thing was certain—that Lancaster would not let him escape. He had learned too much; but beyond that, he had made a shameful stain on Lancaster's record.

He pulled back his horse beside Dong, and as the litter swayed painfully from side to side, as the horses shortened their steps down the grade, the coolie called softly up to him: "Ching? Ching?"

"Dong's calling for you," he said to Ching. She turned her horse back from Lancaster, at once; as Ripley drifted the gray mare rapidly ahead, he heard her voice making a gentle music over the coolie. Dong, at least, would never be able to see through her. Love would blind him, and that was as well. It seemed to Ripley that clear-seeing is no blessing, in this world of ours. Was it not far better to be equipped with a blind faith that refuses to question all that lies around us? If he could live in that manner he would face the rest of life.

He had been a fool. He had galloped merrily through the world, as though happiness were composed of the miles that a man covers! Now, if he had another chance, he would understand that the majority are right, those who bow their necks to a yoke and pull heavily to move a burden; for the burden is only the weight of true happiness. He had gone with empty hands. He had gone like a wind and a noise through life. Like a wind he would disappear and be forgotten.

They were down on the level now and drawing into the mouth of the valley as Sam Li said: "Let me offer you advice, Jim. You know that truth may be spoken even by fools and fat men."

"Fire away, brother," said Lancaster. "Nobody ever called you a fool. Not while I was listening. What can you offer to put that gang of Chinese to sleep?"

"Well, you have Dong," said Sam Li.

"Him? The poor dummy that you beat up so bad? What can he do except waste Ching's time?"

"He can sing to them, and make them answer," said Sam Li. "Put him where they can hear him well. And then I'll tell him to sing to them. You'll see what happens, Jim."

"Why, it's such a damn funny idea," said Lancaster, "that there may be something in it." Then he added: "But why shouldn't you talk to them, Sam? You do that. We'll ride right down close to the corral and you make 'em a speech, will you?"

"Yes. Gladly," said Sam Li. "But China is such a great country, brother, that we cannot understand what every man from China says. A great many of those men speak Cantonese, and that is a language of which I know only a few words. However, I'll talk to them and try to find out why they are unhappy."

"It's the spoiled rabbit meat," said Lancaster.

"No. Not the food. It must be something else. I shall try to draw it from them," said Sam Li.

They took a course, therefore, that led down

from the slope and straight past the face of the corral. A portion of it lay under the steep shadow cast by the moon from the nearest cliff. The rest of the crowd was almost as well illumined as though sunshine were falling.

Ripley, looking down into the faces of those people, thought that he had never seen so much brutal and ugly distortion of human features.

As they saw the riders coming toward them, they pressed in so close that the ropes of the corral bulged.

"Beat 'em back!" commanded Lancaster.

A pair of his men rode close to the rope fence, using their quirts right across the bare faces of the Chinamen. And to Ripley's bewilderment, the men hardly flinched from the blows. He literally saw the streaks and the welts left by the lashes, and still the men of the Orient remained steadfast, as though they were frozen in place.

A singular terror ran through Ripley's body. He had felt it once before when he watched a grown man hypnotized. So these Chinamen seemed to be held fast by an uncanny power.

Dong, raising his voice to a plaintive waver, called out a few short phrases in a monotone.

A groaning ripple of sound instantly passed through the mass of the prisoners.

And then a man stirred among the thickly packed throng. He followed Dong's litter right down the side of the fence. Now and then he beat at the people around him, and they in-

stantly pressed to the side and gave him way
through the jam. He seemed a privileged character.

He was not very big, but his face could be
selected at a glance from those around him. It
was very large across the skull and very narrow below—starved beneath the great
cheekbones, so much so that he seemed like a
famished man about to die.

Now and then he called out something in a
howling voice. Now and then Dong seemed to
make an answer, until Sam Li reined his horse
back and stretched out a huge, threatening
hand toward the helpless man in the litter.

He barked out a few rough words, and Dong
was still.

"What's the matter?" asked Lancaster.

"There are things that this fellow can tell to
the others—and I was afraid that he might be
telling them in his Cantonese. I could not be
sure."

"How about here?" asked Lancaster. "How
about talking to them now?"

"This is a good place," agreed Sam Li.

He halted his horse and held up both arms,
the loose silken sleeves flowing down like water about the great arms.

"Make it slow, will you, Sam?" asked Lan-
caster. "So's Ching can repeat it for me.
Ching, d'you know Cantonese as well as Sam
Li's dialect?"

"I know them both," she nodded.

"Tell me what Sam says," directed Lancaster. "It'll be something worth hearing, the damned oily old artist!"

Sam Li's great voice made music, pouring through the moonlight over that mob of wild Chinamen. In his impressive pauses, Ching's quick voice interpreted:

"All my fortunate brothers—now that you are entering into a free land—and now that you have left slavery behind you—now that you are beginning to be your own masters— why are you impatient?"

Ripley saw and heard the breathing of the many Chinese inside the ropes. They seemed to be breathing together; there seemed to be one heart in them. Their faces were upraised a little. Sweat polished the bronze skin, sweat and the moonlight that flowed over them. He saw above all the little man with the great skull and the starved face. His body was swaying from side to side so that his head seemed to be making a sign of negation.

"A long road is not covered in one step," Sam Li was saying. "The boy is not a man in one day—one mouthful does not fill the belly —and you must endure and be patient for a little time. All of these people on horseback want to be your friends. They cannot speak your tongue. Their ways are new to you. But you are also new to them—"

Here the man with the face of a skull cried out in a swift jabbering and the whole mob of those Chinese put back their heads and howled. The shrill, wailing sound stopped

Ripley's heart. It stopped Sam Li's speech as well.

"This is no damn good," said Lancaster. "What's the matter with you, Sam?"

"Well," said Sam Li, as the howl of his countrymen died down, "even if you put green spectacles on a donkey, it cannot get fat on wooden chips."

"What do you mean by that?" asked Lancaster.

"All of these," said Sam Li, with a sweeping gesture, "have been told about a green land of plenty. And they have sand in their throats and sand in their eyes."

Lancaster called: "Chuck, fetch me out that little Chinaman with the bald skull and the skinny face, will you?"

The rope instantly fled from the sure hand of Chuck Warren. The noose dropped over the shoulders of the Chinaman who had started the howling. Two pairs of hands dragged him out of the corral like a fish out of water.

CHAPTER XXXIV

When the man from the corral was put upright before him, Lancaster said: "Bring the other one down—bring the scarface. What he yipped in the first place was what boiled up this other Chinaman. And what Starvation Willie yelled was what started the whole gang hollering. Sam, ask Dong what he said, will you?"

Sam Li rattled words at Dong, and received a brief answer.

"He says," replied the giant Chinaman, "that when he came near the crowd he simply called out to them that he was their singer and that his heart was happy when he saw them again, because they were as brothers to him."

"D'you believe that's the truth?" asked Lancaster.

"It may be the truth," said Sam Li. "Dong is a simple man. You and I, Jim, think too quickly for our tongues to keep always on the one straight road."

"Speak for yourself, John Chinaman," answered Lancaster. "Go on, Sam. Talk to Starvation Willie and ask what's eating him."

Sam Li spoke. And as the little Chinaman answered it was the girl who made the translation.

"Oh my father, it is hard for a fat man to listen to one who has a thin belly. We are hungry. Rice is not enough to feed us. Our minds are hungry. We are going into a strange country. There is no green grass. The trees are dying. The mountains have strange faces. Kind ghosts cannot follow a man such a great distance. We shall never see happiness again! In the day, the ground burns under our feet; our masters beat us with whips; we are not happy; we are—"

The voice of the little Chinaman rose to a steady wailing; and a sort of vocal shudder ran groaning through the crowd as it took up his yell.

"Throw the fool back into the corral!" commanded Lancaster.

He added: "Hurry! This looks damned bad. I can see a lot of bare knives in that crowd!"

Ripley had seen them, too—quick, obscure flashings like the gleaming of bright eyes.

The little Chinaman was picked up by Warren and another and literally thrown back among his fellows, landing over the ropes sprawling on the heads and shoulders of his companions.

"Now, Sam Li, these are your people. Tell us how to ride herd on 'em. They're getting tough," said Lancaster. "They'll be making a break before long."

"There is Dong, who used to sing to them," said Sam Li.

"Can you trust him?" asked Lancaster. "Won't he tell then what's been happening to him?"

"I'll listen. Unless he sings the strangest Cantonese, I shall be able to understand. And here is Ching. She can make out every word he says."

"Good," said Lancaster. "Let's get back from the corral and then give Dong a chance to tune up."

They retreated a little distance to a white, smoothly rounded hummock of sand halfway between the corral and the mouth of the canyon. There they halted; Missouri Slim was constantly at Ripley's side, watching him as though he were sighting down a gun.

Lancaster commanded: "Tell the damn dummy there to open up and sing to those dogies, will you?"

They had taken Dong from the litter and made for him a sort of reclining chair in the sand. There he lay with his head back, and as Sam Li spoke sharply to him, he uttered a long, wavering note. His head began to sway a little from side to side as he continued the phrases of his song.

He paused. The Chinamen in the corral milled around as before, and the same broken chattering rattled through the moonlight and the blackness of the shadow from the west.

"It's no good," said Lancaster. "You can see that. No damn good at all. Ching, I'm going to get you out of here. Missouri, you can take care of these two—"

"I want to stay," said the girl.

She said something in Chinese to Dong.

The coolie nodded and began another chant, on a higher, thinner note.

This time, as he paused, a scattering of strange song came back to him from the corral.

"You hear?" said Sam Li. "Now they'll all be singing, soon. Men that sing cannot use knives for fighting, Jim."

"I always said you had a head on your shoulders," said Lancaster. "I always said it, and it's true. Listen to 'em now!"

The milling in the corral had stopped utterly. And from the contraband Chinese wailing answers were going up at the intervals of Dong's singing.

Finally he reached the end. Ripley could hear him panting.

"That'll hold 'em for a little while," said Lancaster. "Tell Dong to keep it up. I'm glad we brought him along. It'll be morning before long and then if the Chinks start anything the light'll be better for the guns."

He added: "Come here, Ching. Come here and sit with me. I gotta lot to tell you. You see that mob of Chinamen? I'm gunna make so much dough just out of that one gang that you and me could take a trip around the world on it, and hit the high spots all the way. But we've got to settle about Ripley first."

"Yes," said the girl, coming close to Lancaster and smiling up at him. "What shall we do with him?"

"As long as he's alive for the boys to see him or even to think about him," said Lancaster, "they'll be remembering the one man that came the nearest to putting me down. We've got to polish him off, Ching. You might as well know that!"

"I suppose so," said the girl, and the calmness of her voice was a cruel torture to Ripley. "But I know the best way."

"What's the best way, Ching? You tell me!"

"Put him on his horse and send him scooting up the valley. Put the whip on *his* back, and hear him yell as he runs his mare!" said the girl.

Lancaster laughed.

"You can be a mean little devil, Ching," he said. "That's from living with Sam Li, I guess. What do you think about this Ripley, though, if you wanta have me turn him loose?"

"He is very stupid, Jim. He is the most stupid man in the world."

"Yeah, and how stupid do you make him

out?" asked Lancaster.

"Come!" said the girl.

She led Lancaster straight to Ripley, where he sat in the sand, tied hand and foot, close to Dong. She snapped her fingers above Ripley's head.

"Look up and tell the truth!" she commanded. "At the very time when I was making a fool of you, did you not tell me that you loved me, Jack?"

Ripley rolled his head back on his shoulders and stared at her. The moonlight fell like a silver magic over her. And her smile and her eyes gleamed through the shadow.

"Ay," said Ripley, "I said it then. I say it now. Even if you had your teeth in my throat —I'd still say it!"

His own words surprised him. They had come suddenly out of his heart.

Lancaster made a great, bawling laughter.

"Doggone me if he ain't moonstruck by you, Ching," he said. "But you're wrong. He's a fool about you, but he ain't a fool about other things. He's made me worse trouble, bigger trouble than anybody I've ever hooked up against. But wait a minute. Maybe I could still do some kind of business with him. Listen, Jack. Would you work with me to rub out old Dallas?"

Ripley did not hesitate. He was so inured to the thought of death now that he hardly felt a shadow of temptation at the proposal.

"Dallas is a friend of mine," he answered.

"Damn you!" shouted Lancaster. "He's the friend of a dead man then. D'you know that? Ching, you're right. This here is a fool, but—"

"Jim!" called Sam Li's big, mellow voice.

"What part of this'll you have?" asked Lancaster.

"Do you think you are safe with that girl?" asked Sam Li.

"Safe with her? What you mean?"

"Brother," said Sam Li, "the thing that is nearest the heart is often the most deadly. You are sure of her, but suppose that she has been kind to you all this time tonight only because she hopes to make you kind to the other man?"

"What!" shouted Lancaster.

"Take her in your arms, brother!" chuckled Sam Li.

"Sam Li!" cried the girl.

"What's the matter, honey?" asked Lancaster. "What the devil does the Chinaman mean? Kiss me, Ching, and tell him he's crazy."

He held his arms half around her when she shrank away from him with a moan.

"Don't touch me!" she gasped.

"Hold on! Hold on!" exclaimed Lancaster. "What's this all about?"

"Keep your hands from me!" cried Ching.

She backed away from Lancaster and Ripley watched in utter amazement.

"What's the matter with my hands?" demanded Lancaster.

"There's blood on them!" said the girl.

"Lookat, Ching. Don't start being finicky," urged Lancaster.

"I thought I could stand it—for a little—but I can't—I can't stand it! Keep away from me. Don't follow me with your hands! Don't touch me!" shrilled Ching.

Old Dong began to struggle to rise from his chair of sand. Sam Li held him in place.

"Now, what in hell is this all about? Blood on my hands? Of all the damnedest things I ever heard!" said Lancaster. "Ching, what's busted loose in you?"

"I loathe you," said the girl. "I've always detested you. I've put up with you for the sake of finding Dong. Now I can't stand it. I'd rather die—I'd rather have a leper touch me!"

"She means it," said Lancaster. "Yeah, she sure means it. And I been the fool all the time!"

"Brother," said Sam Li, "you know that the mind of a girl is the mind of a child. It shines and darkens many times a day and—"

"Shut up!" thundered Lancaster.

"Lemme hear the rest of it," said he to the girl. "There never was a time when you gave a hang for me. You've had your head full of another man all the while, have you? Tell me who he is then, you crooked little rat."

"He's here!" said the girl.

She had been hurrying back from

Lancaster's advance, and now she paused at Ripley's side, and her hand reached out toward him, fumbling blindly.

CHAPTER XXXV

Ripley sat cross-legged in the sand, close to Dong, and the girl slipped down beside him. She clung to him. The shudder of her body ran through his flesh.

"I couldn't stand it!" she whispered. "I couldn't stand it!"

And a wind of darkness blew through Ripley's mind, and streaming fires burned in the gloom of it. He could not speak. There was Dong's sing-song chant filling the interval and then the roaring chorus of the Chinamen from the corral.

"I don't mind it so much," said Lancaster. "It's one in the eye for me. But I couldn't learn no younger. You—Ching—you—"

Here wrath stuffed a fist down his throat and he could not speak again for a moment.

"Lookat," said Missouri, "ain't it better this way? Lemme rub Ripley out—and that gives the gal a chance to watch him go—"

"No!" screamed Ching.

"You gotta brain, Slim," said Lancaster. "But I need to think for a spell."

He turned. "I'm kind of sorry that I socked you in the mug, back there, Sam Li," he said. "The kind of ideas you have, I could use one of 'em right now."

"We have become full partners, Jim," said Sam Li. "You see—I love Ching—and yet I've pulled the darkness away from your eyes so that you could see her. In all things we must work together. Even as far as the gold mine in China."

"Ay," said Lancaster, "I was a fool to try to get along without you. A plain fool. But back there in the town, when I thought that you'd slipped away from me—when I made sure that the ivory box that used to hold your god —or whatever you call it—was gone—well, I went sort of crazy. I wanted to bump you off."

"Will you kiss me now, Jack?" said the girl.

He kissed her.

"I want you to talk to me, Ching," he said. "I'm pretty staggered. I want you to talk to me."

"I love you," said Ching. "From the moment you came into Sam Li's house, I loved you. I sat up that night and held my face between my hands. I had to hold it—because otherwise I would have started laughing, or crying. I lay on the bed, face down. I kept saying: 'Jack Ripley! Jack Ripley! I love Jack Ripley!' And I didn't believe that it was love, either. I thought that love went step by step. But this was a pillar of fire. It carried me up so high that I could see the whole world. I could pick the world up in my hand and blow it away in dust. I had to keep from blowing the world away. Do you think I'm crazy, Jack?"

"Listen to 'em," said Lancaster. "It's pretty good, ain't it?"

"Women are like food," said Sam Li. "We cannot always be hungry. Music makes us think of women. Flowers and the breath of flowers makes us think of them. We are our own destroyers, Jim. Can't you see how that is true? It is love that we are in love with. White men and yellow men—all in love with love. But tomorrow rubs out today. And one woman rubs out another."

"Say that again," said Lancaster.

"A man in love is a child again," said Sam Li. "Then only one moment in the day is the beautiful moment; only one grape in the cluster is delicious. But tomorrow you will see things in a better way. He will be dead, Jim, and her face will be swollen; her face will be blotched. Grief makes a woman ugly, and grief will make you hate her, because the grief is not for you. I, Sam Li, tell you that within twenty-four hours you will be a free man!"

"You're never wrong, Sam Li," said Lancaster. "Only when you made the play agin me—then you were wrong. But all the other times you're right. Talk some more. It does me a lot of good, the hearing of you!"

"When I went up there to Dalton," said the girl, "I wanted to hold you until Jim Lancaster was set free because still I thought that he was the only man who could bring Dong to me. He owned the border and he would find Dong for me. But I wanted to hold you with my hands, Jack; and every silly word I said, when I lied and made confusions—every word I said, I was loving you more and more. Couldn't you feel that? I went away blind. I was blind with crying. I heard your voice calling me when I was on the first floor. I had to run and I didn't know where I was going. Do you believe me, Jack?"

"I've always believed you," said Ripley. "Even when I knew you were lying to me. Love is a way of believing, I suppose. I wish— God, how I wish that I had my hands free and my arms, to hold you. But that doesn't matter. Talk, Ching. I'd rather be blind than deaf, if I could hear you talking in the darkness."

"Dong has to know," said the girl. "He used to be my rickshaw man when I was too young to have a rickshaw. He used to make one and pull me around the garden. I used to hitch reins to drive him. He used to balk. Sometimes he ran away with me. Once when I was

very sick the only thing that made me go to
sleep was Dong's singing. He used to sing all
night for me when I was sick. So I have to tell
Dong."

She added: "First I'll tell him that you are
my man."

She spoke, and Dong, panting from his singing, answered briefly.

"He says: 'That is true. Who could you
have except the man that is my father?' Tell
me, Jack. Do you think Dong is very ugly?"

"I never thought so from the start," said
Ripley.

A hand gripped him by the hair and jerked
his head back. Missouri's lean, long, half-
witted face scowled down at him beyond the
vast length of arm.

"What keeps me from battin' you right
across the face?" asked Missouri, with the
heel of a Colt raised, ready to keep the threat.

"Leave them be!" commanded Lancaster.
"That ain't even good enough to be a start.
Sam Li is givin' me ideas about him."

Slowly Missouri relaxed his hold, and
stepped back.

"I dunno why it is," said Missouri, "but it
sort of gripes me when I see him with the gal
leanin' agin him, lovin' him with her eyes that
way. Look at her hand strokin' his hair
smooth agin. It makes me kind of wanta scalp
him!"

"You're going to have your innings with
him," said Lancaster. "Sam Li, tell that Dong

to start in singing some more, will you?"

"I'm going to die," said Ripley. "And I'm
not bothered about that."

"If you die, I'll follow you," said the girl.

"No," said Ripley. "There's no waste to a
thing like this. I've been riding all over the
world, trying to find happiness. And that was
wasted. But this isn't wasted, Ching. Poor
Lancaster, I pity him, and all the rest that are
going to keep on living. And you're going to
live with them, but in a different way.
Hickory!"

The mare came to him.

"There's the only other thing that ever
cared much about me," said Ripley. "Put up
your hand and rub her between the eyes.
She'll know you now. And listen to me carefully. The time is going to come when they'll
have their hands full. They'll be pretty busy—
with me or with something else. And that's the
time for you to swing into the saddle on
Hickory. And then race her."

"I'll never leave you," said the girl.

"You will," said Ripley. "There's no other
command that I can ever give you, but I give
you that one. Do you hear me, Ching? I want
to think, from now to the end, that you're
going to have a chance at life and remembering me. Nothing else will remember me except
you and Hickory."

She kept the palm of her hand against his
cheek. The fingers were cool. Her whole body

was cool. There was no warmth in her. There was only fragrance.

"Ching," said Ripley, "isn't it true that Dong has those Chinamen in the hollow of his hand? Then why shouldn't he use them for us?"

"How can he?" asked the girl.

"I've been thinking. If he could start them moving, they'd come up the canyon here in a flood. Could Dong make them strike where he wanted them to—and leave us safe?"

She stared at him.

"No wonder Jim Lancaster is afraid of you!" she said. "Now I understand—"

"He can sing them a Cantonese song—something that will wake them up—drive them crazy—start them charging—"

"And even Sam Li doesn't know enough Cantonese to understand what the song will be about!" said the girl. "Oh, Jack, it's the first taste of hope!"

She leaned and began to speak rapidly, close to Dong's ear.

"What's the matter with those Chinamen now?" asked Lancaster, suddenly. "What's happening down there in the corral all at once? Do you make it out?"

For, in fact, as Dong continued his chant, the answers that came to it from the corral were simply brutal grunts, in a vast, bestial chorus.

"I don't understand," said Sam Li.

"What's the song about?" asked Lancaster.

"It's Cantonese that Dong is singing, just now," said Sam Li, "and I don't know that tongue. Hardly a word of it."

The girl was translating the song, saying first: "Listen! He knows the right song for the trick! Do you hear them growl in the rope corral? This is what he is singing:

My voice is gone from my house.
    The strangers are in it.
My wife has gone away.
    Strangers have taken her.
My father lies buried.
    Strangers have made the grave.
But where is my son?
    Strangers have taken him—"

Here a deep, harsh cry broke out from the men of the corral.

"They have taken my son to a far land,"

the translation went on.

"Strangers have taken him.
They have fed him unclean food.
    Strangers have fed him.
His body is sore
    Strangers have beaten him—"

The answer from the rope corral was a wild

uproar. The ropes were slashed and broken all
across the front. A flood of humanity was
loosed suddenly down the valley.

CHAPTER XXXVI

It seemed to Ripley like a fantasy, one of those swiftly changing pictures that come into dreams. He could see the pigtails bobbing, or floating straight out from the heads of the Chinamen. He saw something else—and that was the flashing of the knives that jigged up and down in their hands as they ran.

"Call the rest up! Tell 'em to charge!" yelled Lancaster.

He ran forward, shouting: "Missouri—tell the rest of 'em to charge! If they once get outside of the valley, God knows where they'll scatter to—"

With two guns poised in his hands, Lancaster turned to watch the effect of Missouri's wild yell to the men at the mouth of the ravine.

Those horsemen of Lancaster's, from their higher position, must have had a clear view of the sweeping danger. Through the dust that boiled up around the heads of the Chinamen, the guards surely could see the glitter of the knives in the moonlight, and yet they charged straight in.

The nearest ones came in a good bit ahead of the rest. They whirled their horses along the face of the throng, shooting into the air, yelling like fiends to turn the human herd as though it had been composed of dumb, four-footed beasts. Some of them whirled their quirts. But they might as well have struck at the face of an avalanche.

Ripley saw a strange and frightful thing. A cowpuncher's quirt was caught at the lash end. Two hands of yellow iron clung to the whip, and since it was tied to the wrist of the rider, the Chinaman was yanked from his feet and dragged on his face. Nevertheless, he maintained that incredible grip. And the rider was dragged far back in the saddle, until a sidestep of his horse jerked him out of his stirrups. He was caught out of the air by a hundred Chinese hands.

At the same moment one of the Chinamen in a frenzy actually hurled himself with outspread arms at the forelegs of another galloping horse, and beast and rider went down with a crash. What happened to them no one could tell. The Chinese might have torn them to shreds—or simply cast them to one side and gone on, trampling over the bodies. Ripley could not say. But he saw the effect on the other guards. They hesitated, checked their rush.

"Shoot! Shoot to kill! Shoot to kill!" Lancaster was yelling in command.

But if they fired, it might bring disaster and death to the two fallen comrades. Indecision, confusion came over those cowpunchers. They were brave enough to take every chance in the world—but now they did not know what to do —and the yellow throng through the dust and the moonlight looked like a phantasm, a nightmare. Gradually the riders gave way— then, suddenly, they fled.

An arm of cloud had slid over the moon; suddenly its face was tarnished like dirty silver and by that light Ripley saw the paper-white flash of a small knife which Ching had spied in the sand and picked up. She slashed twice, and his hands and his feet were free.

Lancaster, with all the danger of the rush of the Chinamen before him, saw Ripley rising, and whirled to get at his chief enemy.

And there was the huge figure of Sam Li standing with raised, empty hands, thundering out in that gonglike voice words of great command.

To Lancaster, the truth must have come with terrible suddenness. One moment he had many men at his command; and a crowd of human wealth was roped into a corral for him. The next moment his men were scattered, the horses were swept away in a stampede. And his slaves had turned into a yellow river of vengeance, screeching as it rushed at him.

That thunderclap of astonishment probably accounted for his moment of delay. But

now he was turned, shouting out: "You'll go
one step before me, Ripley!"

And he fired.

Ripley had made no effort to dodge. But the
cords had stopped the blood in his feet and he
staggered crazily as he tried to run in and
close with big Jim Lancaster. His hands were
half numb, too, from the pressure of the cords
about the wrists.

It was the witlessness of his feet that made
him run, veering, like a snipe in the wind; and
Lancaster's bullets kissed the air about him
but did not strike home. The dimness of the
light must have accounted in large part for the
inaccurate shooting. That same dimness let
Missouri Slim almost take Ripley by surprise.

Missouri was not shooting. A gun was not
his chosen weapon at this moment. Instead,
he had pulled out a long hunting knife and he
came at Ripley from the side with the face of
a contorted devil.

Ripley flung his body sidelong through the
air at the knees of the tall figure. It was a swift
attack but not so swift as the knife hand of
Missouri. And as Ripley struck Slim's legs,
the latter's knife sliced through the flesh along
Ripley's left ribs, and the weight of Slim's
hand thumped heavily against his back.

They went down in a heap, a confusion.

"Cut his throat, damn him!" yelled Lancaster.

But Ripley had caught Missouri's knife-
arm inside the crook of his own elbow. He
made one twisting effort and heard the bone of

the arm crack and smash.

Then he was up with Slim's revolver in his grasp. Missouri himself, one arm dangling, got up more slowly, cursing in a voice as shrill as the scream of a woman.

Off there on the right, clouds of dust streamed upward toward the tarnished moon, and through the dust the Chinese were coming on them; but Lancaster had no thought for that rushing danger. He wanted one life before he gave up his own.

His sombrero was off. His long hair, caught by the wind, blew to the side, streaming across his shoulder. He had waited with poised gun to get in a well-sighted shot as the heap of Missouri and Ripley dissolved.

But Ripley was already shooting from the hip as he stumbled forward. He saw his first bullet strike into the sand and knock up a thin spray. His second jerked Lancaster sidewise.

Then a heavy impact knocked the gun out of Ripley's grasp and left him with an empty, bleeding hand.

It was only one stride more, however. He closed that distance with a shout, striking out for Lancaster's head. Their two bodies beat heavily together, fell. And, in falling, Ripley found his weight on top.

The feet of the charging Chinese were almost on them. That meant death to them both perhaps. But in falling he had wit enough to jerk his left elbow across and drive it into the face of Lancaster as they struck the ground.

The strength went instantly out of Lancaster's long, lean body. He lay still—not senseless but half stunned, his eyes wide and empty as they stared up toward the sky.

There was one glance for Ripley then, and only one. But the picture he saw was something that would never afterward leave his brain.

Missouri, a little on the left, had been struck by the advancing wave of the Chinamen. That wave tossed him up, as rushing water will toss a fragment of dry wood. Ripley could see the crazy, broken gesture of the smashed arm. Then the wave swallowed the flotsam—Missouri Slim disappeared and left in the air one ringing, echoing scream to curdle the blood.

In the same single glance, Ripley saw huge Sam Li attacked by a little figure of a man with a great, polished skull, with a snake of pigtail hanging down at the back, twisting, leaping as if of its own accord. That was "Starvation Willie," of course.

Whatever he had heard from Dong, it was enough to make him choose Sam Li as the great enemy. And a burning zeal had driven the little man far ahead of the others, to use his knife.

That knife Ripley saw gleam in the air and then the blade disappeared into Sam Li's breast.

There was one other picture to complete the scene.

Still at his post, leaning back, his head

raised, Dong was singing. And in his weak arms the poor fellow held the girl close to him, to save her from the dreadful flood.

It seemed a miracle to Ripley. He whose life had been shielded and who had finally been tortured almost to the verge of death was now the great master and, with his voice, ruled all the madness of this scene.

That single sweeping glance had showed Ripley the essentials of the wide picture before him. Then the uproar of beating feet overtook him. In the air there was that strange pungency which he had noted before. Hands gripped him with such force that his flesh was bruised and his clothes ripped away in great sections, but the strength of the Chinese was used merely to cast him aside.

Perhaps they had seen him fighting their battle against the great enemy, and that was why they spared him.

He, dizzy, staggered, reeled away a little to the rear and saw the flash of knives driving down toward the spot where Lancaster had been lying.

There would be no saving of that life.

But what of Ching?

The throng was already pouring past her. And old Dong could be seen dimly through the dust with his head tilted back, his horrible mouth gaped wide in the song that had meant death to so many strong men.

One figure remained standing. Like a tower stood the vastness of Sam Li, with men pouring over him.

Gradually that tower swayed, but it would not fall.

The little men were brushed away like ants by the giant. Ripley was striking forward. He heard Sam Li's mighty voice shouting out a battle cry.

A glory came out of the dying Chinaman and filled Ripley's astonished soul. He had not dreamed that one man could do so much with empty hands!

But the tower was leaning, it was falling, it was down; and the crowd of leaping, screeching Chinese poured over it.

They rushed down the valley in vain pursuit of the dust clouds which told how the men of Lancaster, giving up the cause when they saw their master fall, had now disappeared through the side ravines, each man now a fugitive from the vengeance of the law.

Another picture rushed over Ripley's mind. Old Dallas in his office, his worn, kind face lighting with the triumph which had crowned his life of service on the border.

His, after all, was the credit for the great victory—his, and Dong's!

CHAPTER XXXVII

Looking before him, Ripley saw Missouri lying so twisted, the shape of his body so frightfully deformed, that there was no need to step to him to see if he were dead.

He had been broken by a hundred hands.

Still further back, two other forms made small, dark spots on the ground—they were those chosen men of Lancaster's who had ridden in so gallantly, so brutally, to stop the Chinese charge. They would rise no more.

And Lancaster himself lay on his back with one arm thrown over his face, as though his last gesture had been to shut out the horror of the distorted faces that loomed above him.

His clothes were rent by the knife slashes. His body was wet with blood.

The peculiar, stifling, pungent odor still hung in the air. The dust was thick.

The dense mass of the Chinese still raced

toward the mouth of the canyon, and the jerking pigtails tossed above the rolling dust cloud.

Far up the ravine the noise of the charge traveled. It diminished as the running Chinese diverted into this canyon and into that. And presently even the dust clouds had lifted. There was only the silent beauty of the moon and the empty valley and the prostrate forms.

Ripley went stumbling forward. Pain from his wound bit into him. His side was a-drip with blood.

He saw old Dong lying exhausted in his sand-chair. Ching was leaning over the prostrate form of Sam Li. He was beginning to struggle into a sitting position. He kept his great left arm across his body.

"Get the kit of bandages!" Ching cried. "Do you hear, Jack? We can still save him!"

"Be still, Ching," replied Sam Li, in booming, muffled tones. "But get the canteen there. I am thirsty."

Ripley brought the canteen and held it up to Sam Li's lips as the giant drank. His face was unmarked except for Lancaster's blow, which had left a dark stain from the mouth to the chin. As for the injuries that lay under the cover of Sam Li's crosswise arm, his own voice spoke for them.

"Knife wounds always are painful; because even the sharpest knives will do a little tearing. However, I am glad that they struck deep enough. You know, Ching, it is better to taste the wine, and then to drain the glass. So with me—I shall be at rest soon."

She was on her knees. She looked like a small child before Sam Li's giant bulk, as he sat cross-legged.

"Let me help you, Sam Li," she pleaded. "Let me stop the bleeding."

"You cannot catch life, Ching," said Sam Li. "You can catch the wind more easily than you can catch life. Every breath empties something from near my heart, and something that will not return. But that is all right. Do you know how many years have passed behind me?"

He said something in Chinese, but instantly stopped himself and added: "I ask your pardon, Jack. I was telling Ching that nearly sixty years have gone behind me; only the fat makes my face seem young. And most of those years have been happy. So I am ready to die. I have always been a good accountant. My balance is not in the red. And what more can I ask?"

Ching began to sob.

"You cry like a white girl," said Sam Li. "There was a time when I almost hoped that I could make a pure Chinese of you, but you have always cried like a white girl, and that is a pity. But I am glad you can cry because of me, Ching."

"Even if your mind was bad, your heart was not always bad," said Ching.

"Not bad? Perhaps you're right," said Sam Li. "This thinking is what undoes us. We think our way, step by step, toward heaven;

but when the thinking ends, we have only prepared a great fall. So I have fallen, Ching. But
now stop crying."

"I *shall* stop," said the girl.

"Really stop," said Sam Li.

"Yes," she gasped.

"If I could see the canaries now whistling
their wings all around you," said the Chinaman, "I should be happier. Do you remember how I taught you to call them?"

"I remember," said the girl in a trembling
voice.

"Well, before long they came to you more
gladly than they came to me. And that day—
when they left me for you—that day I came
close to repenting. If you had only known,
Ching, with a touch of your hand you could
have led me. But how could you know such a
great liar as Sam Li?"

"You were not all pretending," said the girl.
"There were some happy days."

"Were they happy?" said Sam Li.

"You are changing," she told him. "Sam Li,
Sam Li, let me do something!"

"Ah, yes," said the Chinaman.

He made a gesture with one hand.

"Catch up the life and give it back to me,
Ching. You have such pretty hands that even
my life ought to come back into them, if you
try hard enough."

"Are you going to laugh even now?" she
asked.

"Tell me how you shall remember me,"
said Sam Li.

"The day when I sat in the corner and cried because my father was gone, and you talked to me until *I* was laughing," said Ching.

"Will you remember me that way?" asked Sam Li, dreamily.

"Yes," said the girl.

He bowed his head for a moment.

"Turn your head, Ching," said Sam Li.

"Yes," she said.

She stood up and turned away; and Sam Li made a gesture to Ripley. He came instantly to the big Chinaman, who held out a hand; and that hand Ripley gripped with both of his. A vast pressure threatened to snap his bones. Sam Li's head jerked down. The grinding of his teeth was like the breaking of bones.

"Sam Li!" cried Ching, suddenly.

"So!" said the Chinaman, and all his body relaxed and leaned backwards. Ripley lowered him to the ground. "Now, Ching," said Sam Li, faintly. "Now it is nearly over."

She was instantly beside him on the ground.

"Hush!" said Sam Li. "You are young and beautiful, Ching, but you are not Chinese. Ask Dong—because there is a good man—ask him to sing one chant for me!"

She spoke to Dong, and at once the weird, unmusical song broke from the coolie's lips.

A deep, bass murmur issued faintly from Sam Li's throat. His great head turned a little from side to side. Beside him a pool of darkness was spreading on the sand.

His voice ceased.

"Sam Li!" cried the girl.

With a last movement Sam Li's hand moved toward her and was still.

"Sam Li!" cried Ching. "Sam Li! Sam Li!"

CHAPTER XXXVIII

On the hottest day of the year Tom Dallas was sticking pins into another map, consulting a sheaf of telegrams as he put in one marker after another. Now and again he mopped his forehead with a bandana and again pored over his work; and again, on the flat of the map, his imagination raised the mountains and sank the valleys. Here it caused a muddy water hole to lift through the sand, and there it ran the double gleam of a railroad through the wilderness.

When the tap came at the door and the door was pushed open, he did not turn his head, but the high-pitched voice of his deputy struck in a jangle on his ears: "Marshal Dallas—here's Mr. Jack Ripley!"

The marshal got out of his chair, pulled off his glasses, and straightened by degrees. His back was not as strong as it should have been and sometimes it felt like old wire that had been bent so many times that it is ready to break.

The door was closing behind Ripley, and the white flare of the street was being shut away.

"Here," said the marshal, as he grabbed the hand of Ripley. "Here—sit down here—"

"That's your chair," answered Ripley.

"That's why I want you to take it," answered Dallas. "In my chair you can see my ideas better. Wait a minute. Telegrams. Telegrams from Washington. Telegrams from five sheriffs. Telegrams from the governor of the state. They mention a gent named Ripley, but they give the credit to Tom Dallas. That's the way it ought to be, because I had the brains to use you. Sit there. You see that map?"

"Yes," said Ripley.

"Counterfeiters!" said the marshal. "Damned, ornery, low-down counterfeiters, Jack. Fellers that don't work for their living, but they pass out one dollar bills so doggone good that I pretty nigh wish for a barrel of them myself. I could use a pocketful of those one dollar bills. Understand me?"

Ripley put his hand on the map, opened his fingers, and disclosed the bright, steel shield of a deputy marshal.

"Hello," said Dallas. "Want it raised to something? By the way, the price on Lancaster will be through in a coupla days—"

"Keep it, Tom," said Ripley.

The marshal came hastily to him and

leaned one hand and a great part of his weight on the shoulder of Ripley. And Ripley looked squarely up into his face.

"What's the matter?" asked Dallas.

"I can't use that kind of money," said Ripley. "I'd—I'd rather use counterfeit."

"All right—all right," murmured Dallas. He turned suddenly on his office deputy and shouted: "Get the hell out of here, will you?"

The deputy vanished.

"All right," said Dallas. "You look sort of quiet, but sort of happy. But what's the matter? There's a lot of money on Lancaster."

He added: "But a lot more glory."

Ripley said: "I've just been burying three men, Tom. Any one of the three was as good a man as I am. You keep the badge and the glory and the cash."

"Suppose the cash goes to charity," said Dallas. "But what's the matter with you, Jack?"

"There's another reason," said Ripley. "I'll show it to you pretty soon."

"Loosen up, old son," urged the marshal. "I expect some thanks before long for setting you on the new trail."

"I've got to settle down a bit before I can send you thanks," said Ripley.

"But what are you going to do, Jack?"

"I don't know. Go to China, perhaps, on a wild-goose chase."

"China? They're choppin' off people's heads out there now. You know that?"

"I know. Out here we shoot 'em."

"Ah, ha," nodded the marshal. "You don't like it. You don't like guns when you've got a right to use 'em. Is that it? I had a dog once that would never use a tooth or bark a bark in my yard. All the thieves in the world could of walked into my house and that dog would of licked their hands. But when I walked out onto the street that doggone dog would light into anything on four legs. Nigh to costing me a lot of money one day when it bit a mule, and the mule kicked it right through the front door of Molly Applethwaite, and into Molly's two-year-old baby; and Molly swore that dog had bit her baby. And doggone me, but I had a time. The same way with you, Jack. When you were outside the law a gun was a handy tool for you. Now you got a right to use a Colt you don't want it. It's the mean streak that's in most of us all right."

There was another tap at the door, which was then pushed open by a slender girl in black. The marshal jumped up and jerked the sombrero from his head.

"Yes, ma'am?" he said. "Anything I can do for you?"

"This is Tom Dallas," said Ripley. "My wife, Tom."

"Good God—I mean, good Lord!" said Dallas. "Come in, won't you?"

"Thank you," said the girl.

She walked to a chair in the corner.

"I'll wait here," she said. "If I'm not interrupting."

"Have you got the rig outside?" asked Ripley.

"Yes."

"I'll be out in a minute," said Ripley. "I have to say good-by to Tom."

Dallas went toward the door with her.

"Young lady," he said, sternly, "it ain't what you're taking away from me—it's what you're taking away from the border!"

She smiled up at him, and was gone.

A Chinaman helped the girl into the buckboard that waited close to the door. He was the ugliest Chinaman Dallas had ever seen, with a mouth hideously enlarged by huge smiles, but he helped the girl with an almost fatherly, possessive air, and when she was in the seat she smiled down at him with such tenderness that he might have been a father, indeed.

"And that's what's happened, is it?" said the marshal. "That's why you got the dizzy look? Well, I understand. You wouldn't be no good to me for a coupla years, I guess. But I don't understand the black she's wearing. Somebody in her family, or somebody in yours?"

"It was a Chinaman," said Ripley.